HUNTED

HUNTED

ANTONY DUNFORD

This edition published in Great Britain in 2021

by Hobeck Books Limited, Unit 14, Sugnall Business Centre, Sugnall, Stafford, Staffordshire, ST21 6NF

www.hobeck.net

ISBN 978-1-913-793-06-7 (pbk)

ISBN 978-1-913-793-07-4 (ebook)

Cover design by Jayne Mapp Design

Printed and bound in Great Britain

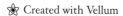 Created with Vellum

ARE YOU A THRILLER SEEKER?

Hobeck Books is an independent publisher of crime, thrillers and suspense fiction and we have one aim – to bring you the books you want to read.

For more details about our books, our authors and our plans, plus the chance to download free novellas, sign up for our newsletter at **www.hobeck.net**.

You can also find us on Twitter **@hobeckbooks** or on Facebook **www.facebook.com/hobeckbooks10**.

For Clare

CHAPTER ONE

THE OWLS HAD BEEN NESTING IN THE RHINO ENCLOSURE for over a month, and the chick was close to fledging.

Jane watched the female bird, invisible in the top corner of the roof unless you knew what to look for. The long ears and closed eyes made her look more like part of the structure than an owl, the greys and browns of her feathers textured like weathered bark. Camouflage. The nest was completely concealed, the male bird out of sight on another beam.

'That's it, my friend. That's it,' said Festo.

Festo was rubbing a sharp-smelling yellow ointment into Douglas's cracked skin. The season was uncommonly dry, with less mud for wallowing than the animal needed in the summer. Douglas didn't seem to mind. Just under two metres tall at the shoulder when standing, weighing a little shy of three tonnes, the massive animal lay peacefully in the shade as Festo worked in the last of the cream.

'All done. OK, I'll give you a little scratch, then how about some grass?' he said.

Festo walked across the straw to collect a stiff-bristled

broom from the corner of the stall. Douglas gave a snort, jerking his huge body twice as he got to his feet. Jane watched. Festo grinned as he strolled out of the enclosure into the paddock twirling the broom. Douglas lumbered after him.

Jane picked up her rifle and followed them.

It was shortly after noon and the sun was at its strongest. Out here on the Laikipia plateau it was pleasant. Not too hot, not too cool. The drought, into its second year, had changed the land. The greens were drying out, now limited to trees and bushes lining the valleys of the small rivers and streams that drained the surrounding hills. The yellows and browns were starting to dominate, the grass dry, the earth baked.

Festo walked steadily into the paddock swinging the broom. The bristles made a whooshing sound as they whipped through the air. Douglas followed him. When Festo reached the shade of a young acacia tree they both stopped.

Jane, her rifle over her shoulder, took up a position not too far away. Using binoculars, she scanned the landscape in every direction.

'Just two minutes, then you eat lunch,' Festo said to the rhino.

Jane paused her vigil long enough to watch what he did next, as she did every time.

Using the broom Festo scratched Douglas's belly. The rhino snorted in pleasure. The brushing drove up clouds of dust and scraped off clumps of dried mud. The keeper worked methodically along the great beast's length, then back along the other side.

'That was your two minutes,' Festo said. 'Now go, eat.'

Douglas waited until he was convinced he wasn't getting any more scratching, then lay down in the shade of the tree, tucking his fore legs clumsily under himself, his rear legs crossed behind. His eyes closed, and his ears twitched. After a few minutes his breathing became regular, blowing up little puffs of dust which hung in the air around his horn like mist around a mountain.

'Not hungry, eh? That's a first,' Festo said, winking at Jane.

He crouched down next to Douglas's great head, which was as big as Festo was. A glistening tear was rolling from the rhino's closed eye. Festo took out a cloth and gently wiped it away. Douglas was a zoo-dweller from a baby, growing up on concrete, and it was only when he arrived in Kenya that anyone noticed he suffered from hay fever.

'Sunburn and hay fever, my friend. Are you sure you're from Africa?' Festo patted the horn. Douglas twitched an ear. 'I'll get you some drops.' He walked away back to the enclosure.

Jane scanned the surroundings again.

In Douglas's enclosure there were many other animals. It was predator-free, protected by serious electric fencing that even the elephants had learned not to walk through. Douglas shared it with two species of antelope, oryx and Jackson's Hartebeest, oddly named with equally odd faces, and with Grevy's zebra. Jane could see oryx, their sharp, straight horns stabbing the sky like victory signs, and zebra from where she stood.

Away to the east in the next paddock were the other two northern white rhino, the females, Uzuri and Neema, Douglas's daughter and granddaughter. They were grazing. Their two guards were in the shade of a tree, silhouetted against the horizon, rifles slung over their shoulders, one with binoculars to his eyes.

Beyond the two paddocks the rest of the Bandari conservancy stretched in all directions. Jane couldn't see the perimeter fences from here, even with binoculars. They enclosed tourist accommodation, a cattle ranch, the ranger station, the kennels, and four hundred square kilometres of savannah that was home to hundreds of species of mammals, birds, reptiles, amphibians, and insects.

Jane lowered the binoculars, looked at the sky, and breathed.

High overhead was a bird, a large one. Forked tail - a hawk or an eagle. It shrieked, a distant but piercing sound.

She saw Festo returning. His smile broad beneath the brim of his hat. He was gentle and slim, from the Kiga tribe in the mountains of Uganda. He had a large bottle of eye drops in one hand and a sack of food pellets in the other. The drier the grass became the more the rhino favoured the pellets. Festo placed the sack on the ground, and Douglas's head came up at the sound.

Douglas was the last male northern white rhino on the planet, and he was in good hands.

————

Tony Kanagi arrived a little before the 2pm shift change. He strode out of the enclosure with purpose, greeted Festo in Swahili, and came straight to Jane.

'There's been a sighting,' he said. 'One of the Ol Faraja rangers driving in for the match. Men with guns on the north side of the C76, walking across an abandoned ranch. He offered to check it out himself. I said we'd do it.'

'You want me to?' Jane said, half a statement, half an offer.

'Everyone else will be at the match. And it will be nothing. It's broad daylight, and the sighting was barely five kilometres from the army barracks. If it is poachers, they aren't smart ones.'

'If it is poachers, we should keep some of the guards back. Anyone with a gun can kill, stupid or not.'

'It's going to be nothing, Jane. But there will be three guards for the duration of the match. I asked for volunteers.'

Jane nodded.

'How long ago was the sighting?' she said.

'About thirty minutes.'

'Where?'

'Two or three kilometres from the Ndaragwa gate,' Tony said.

Behind Tony, Douglas was on his feet, munching pellets.

'Alright,' Jane said. 'I'll go at shift change.'

'Thank you,' Tony said. He seemed to relax. He said something else in Swahili to Festo. Jane had picked up enough to understand what it meant. "Keep them out." Festo kept goal for the conservancy team. 'And you should drive out those owls,' Tony said with a wave in the direction of the enclosure as he headed back to his car.

Jane watched the rhino as he ate. Three years she'd guarded him, eight hours a day, a day off each week, two days off every other week. He was amazing. When awake he was like a permanently hungry tank. Though, as he grew older, he was asleep more and ate less.

Douglas should have had a sixty-centimetre horn protruding from the end of his nose. The vets had cut it off so that he wouldn't be a target for poachers. The compressed hair of the horn was worth much more than its weight in gold on the black market in Yemen, Vietnam, and China. The vets had fitted a radio tracker in the stump, so rangers knew where he was always. The horn was growing back, it was about twenty centimetres long now. The tracker was all but encased.

A few minutes later the next shift arrived. The football match between the two conservancies made it an unusual day. The guards and the keepers were reduced to skeleton crews for the afternoon. But the drones were in the air, the motion sensors on the fences were active, and no animal had been killed inside the conservancy in nearly three years.

The rangers on the next northern white shift were Nathan, Timu, and Jomo.

Timu was first out of the vehicle. Young and enthusiastic, he often volunteered. He was also a keen footballer, the team's star striker. That he'd chosen to guard the rhino, which he did every day, rather than take the chance for glory against Ol Faraja, showed his true passion.

Nathan was next. Also keen on his football, a little older than Timu and very loyal to Tony. If Tony asked, Nathan did.

Jomo was no surprise at all as he'd been on shift anyway.

Like Festo, Jomo was from Uganda and they greeted each other in Bantu.

'How is he?' Jomo said.

'Enjoying his retirement!' Festo said. 'I have treated his skin and his eyes, he has enough food. All you need to do is try not to anger him with your incessant complaining.'

Jomo laughed.

'Play well, my friend,' he said, gripping Festo's arm as he passed by on his way out.

Nathan walked towards the eastern paddock to relieve the guards of the two female rhino. Timu, rifle on his back, took up a position under a tree within sight of Douglas, leaving Jomo with Jane. Douglas kept eating.

'I have to investigate a sighting,' Jane said.

'I know,' Jomo said. 'I should come with you. The drones are up, and the dogs are out. No one is getting in.'

'It will be nothing.'

'Don't look so worried. This is the only place you relax. We should move into the barn,' Jomo said.

Jane smiled at him.

'Have you ever seen me worried?'

'May this day be as uneventful as the last,' he said.

'And more eventful than tomorrow,' she finished.

They touched fingers, just briefly. Then Jane walked away, through the rhino enclosure and out to her Land Rover. As she opened the door, she saw a glint in the sky way off to the south-east. An aircraft. Too small to be a plane. Too big to be anything other than one of the Super Bats, the surveillance drones, patrolling the conservancy, bristling with technology.

She climbed into the driver's seat, settled her rifle in the footwell, placed her binoculars and radio on the passenger seat, and started the engine. When she reached the Ndaragwa gate, she stopped, opened it, drove through, and locked it behind her. She followed the track until it reached the C76 main road. She drove straight across that and followed another track onto the plateau, on the hunt for poachers.

In the sky, a flight of spur-winged geese kept pace with the Land Rover for a little while. Hunters had long avoided the geese because they were poisonous. The species had thrived as a result. But the beetles the geese ate lived in marshlands that had over years been drained to create farmland, and the geese's numbers were dwindling anyway.

Jane thought about the owls in the roof of the rhino enclosure. They were small, not much bigger than pigeons. Their colouring and shape made for camouflage. They were quite beautiful. They ate insects, in the main, and only fed at night. Nothing remarkable.

But in Kenya an owl was an omen. In Kenya the superstition was that an owl in your compound meant someone was going to die.

CHAPTER TWO

JANE STOOD AT THE TOP OF A SHORT RISE WITH AN
unobstructed view of Laikipia plateau rolling out to the north
and east in front of her. She scanned the bush and scrub
through her binoculars, looking for the tell-tale puffs of dust
thrown up by movement.

For a long time, she saw nothing. Then, as she relaxed, her
eyes became more sensitive to smaller movements. Over
there, three tight kicks of dust. Antelope, probably dik-dik.
From the other side of a line of bamboo that marked the
course of a stream, a single billowing cloud. Something large.
A giraffe or a buffalo. A little to the north and east of that, a
brown haze, the after-effect of the passage of several animals.
Possibly zebra.

Nothing unusual.

She kept looking. Further away to the north-east was a
ranch house. It was tiny, even through the binoculars, and she
couldn't tell whether or not it was inhabited. No tell-tale
smoke rising from a stove. The track she'd been travelling on,
which led to a barracks of the Kenya Rifles nestled in a valley

a few kilometres further onto the plateau, snaked empty in either direction. Nothing unusual.

She turned around and looked behind her in the direction of the Bandari conservancy.

The undulations of the land across the kilometres between meant she could not see the rhino enclosure and the inner conservancy, though she could see the outer fence.

It ran for one-hundred-and-twenty kilometres around Bandari, a two-metre-tall palisade with a metre of electrified cords above that. There were gaps every few kilometres filled with low, thick posts set close together to let the migratory animals through. Elephants could step over them, impala, eland, buffalo, giraffe could fit through them, but the rhinos were too short and too wide, so could not leave. Camera traps were set at the gaps. Anything triggering them alerted the control room at the ranger station. If people came through, rangers saw them and found them.

A glint in the sky drew her eye. It was the Super Bat drone again, further to the east now, circling a yellow haze. Something on the ground was kicking up a lot of dust. Something large. Like an elephant herd.

Jane smiled and took out her phone. There were cell towers every kilometre or so on the C76 and the coverage was good.

They are back? she texted, before slipping the phone away.

Using the binoculars, she could just make out the herd, or at least see the individual clouds rising as the great animals moved in a straight line across the savannah.

She felt her phone vibrate in her pocket. She took it out and looked at the message.

They are home ☺, her brother's text said. He knew how

much smiley faces in texts irritated her, and so sent them all the time.

She picked up the radio.

'Ken,' she said.

'Hallo,' he said.

'Are you operating that drone?'

'Everyone's at the football match,' he said, 'so I get to play.'

She didn't say anything.

'It's only fair,' he said. 'I am the boss.'

'Swing it this way,' she said, 'four points off north-east from the Ndaragwa gate, five kilometres straight. I'm on a hill, within sight of the C76 and the fence. Checking out a report of poachers. If you're going to play, play for real.'

'You're no fun.'

'I've heard that before. Out,' she said.

She watched the drone bank, break out of its circling pattern, and head towards her, its course wobbling then stabilising. Jane smiled at the thought of Kennet's large hands trying to master the dual-direction levers on the drone's control panel.

It flew low over her head. The three-metre wingspan seemed larger up close. It pulled up again. Kennet was playing.

Jane waved her arm in a circle, indicating how she wanted him to pilot it. He got the idea and it soared off over the plateau.

Cameras and sensors were strapped underneath the drone. The sensors could detect motion, and changes in heat. They could find and track tagged animals. The cameras could record high-definition video and see in the dark.

The drone made several passes in a five-kilometre-long sweep across the savannah ahead of her. Her phone vibrated.

Zebra, buffalo, dik-dik, eland, giraffe. And the remains of a fire. A lot of heat on the ground here, Kennet's text said.

Jane pressed the push-to-talk button on the radio.

'Where?' she said.

'Here,' he said. 'See?'

Jane looked through the binoculars. The drone was circling the ranch house she had seen earlier.

'OK,' she said. 'Get back to the elephants.' She released the button closing the channel.

She watched the ranch house through the binoculars for another five minutes but saw nothing.

She walked down the rise and got back in the Land Rover, easing it onto the track, driving slowly to minimise dust. It took twenty minutes to get close enough to the ranch. Then she stopped and got out, leaving the door open, taking her rifle.

———

Jane crouched to examine a mark in the dirt. It was the heel print of a boot. There was no way to tell how long it had been there. Possibly up to two years, since the last real rain. Or it could have been made earlier that day.

She stood again, rifle ready, watching the ground and the land ahead of her. She was a kilometre from the ranch building. Nothing was moving. She used the gun's telescopic sight to get a closer look. Nothing. She walked forward.

There were other prints from the same pair of shoes. And a tyre track. The tyre track was recent, as the crushed dried grass was starting to spring back into shape. Within the last few hours. A Pirelli tyre. Broad. Possibly a Land Cruiser, or a truck.

She saw a movement away to her right. Her hands tensed on the gun then relaxed. The wild headdress of a secretary bird bobbed up from behind a clump of grass, its head tilting back, a snake flailing in its beak. The bird jerked forward, letting the snake touch then ground. It stamped on the snake's head, then swallowed it whole in three swift jerks before strutting away to the south.

Jane continued along the track, rifle up.

As she drew closer to the ranch, she could smell the memory of a fire. Just a hint of smoke on the air. There was no other sign of human life.

The ranch included a main building, several sheds, and a large barn. All were in a state of disrepair. The near side of the barn, green corrugated iron mottled with rust, had tilted leaving a wedge-shaped gap between it and the roof.

Jane kept the barn between her and the main building. She approached slowly, treading carefully.

The barn wall had rusted right through in places, and Jane was able to look through one of the holes. There was a flatbed truck, tyres desiccated, windscreen thick with dirt. It had possibly been there for years.

Jane peered around the edge of the barn, a quick glance. All was still, so she looked again more slowly.

The main building had a raised veranda running along the front. Windows flanked a door. The windows were filthy, and the door was open. Jane stood still, rifle raised to her eye, finger on the trigger guard, and watched.

Between the barn and the main building was a shallow pit. Dug recently by the look of it, the earth piled beside it was still dark. The pit had been used as a fireplace within the last few hours. Occasional wisps of smoke escaped from it, and the air above shimmered with heat. Next to the fire was a bottle of Tusker beer. It was half empty.

She heard a sound from inside the main building. She moved her finger to the trigger. She pointed the barrel two thirds of the way up the open door. Chest height on most men.

She heard another sound. A soft thump. She saw movement in the doorway. Her finger increased the pressure. A shadow, then a face.

A large cat walked out, a dead rat in its mouth. The cat was long with spotted fur, big ears, and a small head. A serval. It turned along the veranda, then stopped and looked over its shoulder, straight at Jane.

It was a female, its teats swollen with milk. There must be young nearby.

It held Jane's gaze for a moment, then strolled off the veranda and into the scrub.

'Happy hunting, sister,' Jane said quietly.

Rifle still tucked into her shoulder, confident there would be no people if a cat could hunt in there. She crossed the ground quickly and mounted the steps onto the veranda.

In through the doorway, one step at a time. The ranch was long abandoned. Everything was covered in cobwebs. The cat's pawprints were clearly visible in the grime, as were the claw marks of the rat crossing the room then ending abruptly. There were many rat tracks, on the floor and on other surfaces – a table, an over-turned chair.

A quick search revealed four rooms, all equally unused. No human being had been in this building in a long time.

Back outside Jane checked the ground around the fire. Someone had walked down the track. They'd dug the pit using a tool they must have brought with them and taken away. They'd made the fire out of mostly dried grass, foot-prints led to where it had been pulled up, and, in some places, cut. Dried grass would have burned fast and with little smoke. The person had stood there, drunk half a bottle of beer, then been picked up by the vehicle which had turned around in front of the barn, and driven off in a different direction, north-east, towards the army barracks.

Very strange.

Jane returned to her own vehicle.

As she walked closer to it, the radio beeped. A voice, calling with urgency.

'Jane!'

She started to run.

'Jane!' The voice coming over the radio was Jomo's. It was wild, a fear in it she'd never heard before.

Then she heard a gunshot, and the radio went silent.

CHAPTER THREE

THE SETTING SUN WAS A RICH ORANGE, LIKE THE ROBES OF the Masai, and it lit up the few wisps of cloud with colours of fire. There were still greens in the bushes and trees. Whilst the smallest creeks and springs had dried up, the medium-sized streams had water, particularly the ones draining the snows from Mount Kenya. These threaded the landscape like veins of fat in a haunch of meat.

Jane was driving as fast as the track and the engine would let her. The dust and grit flying from the tyres stretched out behind her like a dirty flame.

She saw vultures, several kilometres away, lazily making huge circles in the air. There were a lot of them, what was the collective noun when circling? Her sister-in-law, Naomi, had told her. A kettle. More joined the kettle all the time. Something large was dead.

'They're over the conservancy,' she said to herself. A chill went down her spine. Jomo. A shot. Vultures.

She pushed even harder with her right foot. She could not drive fast enough.

'Bandari, Bandari ranger station this is *kifaru* two, please acknowledge,' Jane said into the radio, her voice tight, controlled. There was still no response. She flicked the steering wheel to avoid a rock sticking out of the track. The Ndaragwa gate was in sight. The spiralling column of vultures was getting harder to see in the fading light. She drove straight over the C76 without slowing down, causing a truck to brake and blast on its horn.

All the gates in the Bandari boundary fence were tall, strong, and kept locked. There were no cameras on the gates, because poachers wouldn't have keys. Except for the main entrance, the rangers coming off shift met their replacements to let them in.

Today the north-western gate, a kilometre south of the C76 in the direction of Ndaragwa, stood unlocked, unmanned, and wide open. It was the first time Jane had seen this on any gate in the conservancy perimeter. She braked hard as she passed through it, bringing the Land Rover to a stop. The dust wake enveloped the car for a moment.

Despite her frenzied hurry, she pulled a scarf around her face against the dust and leapt out to close and lock the gate. The lock wasn't damaged. Someone had unlocked it since she had driven through earlier in the afternoon.

She was moving again seconds later, the wheels spitting earth and gravel as far back as the fence.

'Ndaragwa Gate camp, Ndaragwa Gate camp, this is *kifaru* two, please acknowledge,' she tried again into the radio. There was no reply. Within a few minutes one of the tourist camps was in sight.

'*Kifaru* two, this is the ranger station,' a female voice

broke through the static. 'How are you this evening, Jane? Was your meal pleasant?' Jane recognised Farashuu, one of the veterinary nurses.

'No time, Farashuu. Get every ranger on shift now,' Jane said.

'Everyone's at the football.'

'Call them,' Jane said.

'I— I can't,' Farashuu's voice was wobbling.

'CALL THEM ALL NOW!'

The shout was too much for Farashuu, and Jane heard her start to cry.

'*Faen ta deg*,' Jane said to herself. The devil take it. She threw the radio into the footwell and willed the engine to work harder, passing the tourist camp and roaring towards the inner reserve.

She reached the inner reserve gate, which also stood open, and slammed on the brakes once inside the fence. She closed that gate behind her too. When she got back into the driver's seat she didn't restart immediately.

The Land Rover was in a slight dip inside the gates, its headlights angling into the sky. Every so often a faint flash of white crossed the beams at the edge of their diffusion. She knew what that was. White-headed vultures. The birds were over the inner conservancy. Something large was dead inside. Where there were usually four rangers armed with assault rifles guarding the residents. Except today when there had been three.

'*Faen.*'

She put the car into gear and drove more slowly. She knew what the vultures were circling and didn't want to get there.

She saw something lying on the ground, picked out by headlights. A body, face down in the middle of the track.

Even though she knew who it was, knew his shape, her mind refused to accept it, forced her not to believe it. She stopped and got out, rifle up, walking slowly.

The clothes were ranger's fatigues. There were two bullet holes in the back of the jacket. A radio lay smashed against a rock close by. One arm was outstretched, the fingers of the hand curled, as if they had been holding something. His rifle was nowhere to be seen. She kneeled beside him, postponing for as long as she could. She placed her rifle on the ground, put one hand on his shoulder, and rolled him onto his side.

It was Jomo. His eyes were still open, but they would not see her again. She looked into them for a full minute before closing them. A tear ran down her cheek and splashed on Jomo's lips. She put both arms around him and pulled him to her chest, held him for a long time. A dangerously long time. Whoever had done this might still be close by.

She eased him to the ground, straightened his arms by his sides, and picked up her rifle. She took one last look at his face and left him there. She got back in the car, driving further into the inner conservancy, past the rhino enclosure, into the paddock.

Jane stopped again, close to where the vultures were descending, by a stream where the animals went to drink. She slipped the wheels over the edge of the bank to angle the headlights down. She opened the door and got out, immediately seeing the carcass that lay on a spit of gravel. Blood from where his horn had been was dripping into the water. Flies were swarming over a bullet-born cavity in his face. The killer had shot Douglas through his right eye.

Jane climbed down through the reeds into the stream and waded across. She dropped to her knees next to the huge body, the stock of her rifle in the water.

She wept. She sobbed. Huge, wracking sobs that shook her whole body. Douglas, in front of her, covered in flies and with a cacophony of squabbling vultures behind him, the birds building up courage to tear the first beak full of flesh. A few hours before he'd been enjoying a scratch with a keeper's broom. Jomo, behind her, shot in the back. A few hours before he'd made her breakfast, done the laundry, run with her through the streets of Nanyuki, over the equator and back.

Jane's sobs grew shallower. Blood was diffusing into the water. She had cut her knee on a stone. She stopped crying. She absorbed, controlled, processed. She converted grief into anger, then controlled the anger, as she was trained to do. She stood up, water dripping from her clothes and hands. Her top half was light with dust, almost white in the neon of the vehicle's headlights. Her trousers were dark with water, reflecting nothing, as if half of her was missing.

She walked to the bank and knelt by the body. She put her hand on Douglas's face and held it there. Touched the blood from his eye, looked closely at the wound. Examined the bloody stump where his horn had been hacked off.

She unhooked a torch from her belt. Waterproof, not for fear of dust rather than water. She checked for tracks. When the vultures got too close, she waved them away. She found the tracker from Douglas's horn about five metres from the body, thrown there by his murderers after they'd gouged it out. It was smashed.

She put the rifle to her shoulder and walked to the second paddock where the other two northern white rhinos, Uzuri and Neema, were. She saw them under a tree, not moving. Uzuri was closer. Jane edged forward, wary. She shone the torch on Uzuri, looking for wounds. Uzuri's ear flicked, then her eye opened. Her horn was intact. She had been asleep. She got to her feet, waking Neema. Both female rhinos were fine.

There was no sign of Nathan who had been guarding them.

Jane went back to Douglas, waded across the river, working out from Douglas's position where the killing shot had come from. She climbed the bank, looking closely at the ground. She found marks, footprints, the deeper dig of heels perhaps caused by recoil as someone fired a large calibre weapon. She took out her knife and placed it beside the marks for scale, taking photographs with her phone, closing her eyes to avoid being temporarily blinded by the flash.

Further away from the bank she found tracks of a vehicle in the earth and the grass. She followed them back a little way. It had not been alone.

There were only two types of vehicles that drove off road in this part of Kenya. All the conservancy vehicles were Land Rovers. These were Land Cruiser tracks. With Pirelli tyres.

A large squabble broke out behind her. The vultures, almost human in their greed for this meal they had not earned, were arguing amongst themselves. Over this noise was another. An engine.

The lights of a vehicle approaching the fence, coming towards her. It stopped at the gate, starting again once it had driven through.

She went to her car and reversed it off the riverbank, turning it to face the gate. She wanted her headlights pointed at whoever was approaching. She left the engine running and got out without shutting the door. The warning noise that the door was open started pinging. She ignored it.

A conservancy Land Rover was approaching. It stopped

by Jomo's body. Men got out. After a few moments two of them got back in and drove to Jane. As it got closer, she saw Festo was driving, with Tony beside him.

Festo stopped and switched off the lights as Tony got out.

'He's been shot,' she said. 'He's dead.' As if to emphasise her words, there was another cacophonous outburst from the vultures behind her.

Festo's face, half in silhouette, registered uncertainty then comprehension. He broke into a run, stopped at the top of the riverbank, and peered into the dark beyond. He took a torch from his belt and swept the night.

'*HAPANA!*' His reaction was pure emotion. Repeating "*hapana*" he jumped into the river, disappearing into the dark with a splash. *Hapana. Nei.* No. The first stage of grief.

'The girls?' said Tony. That he called them "the girls" made her smile even now. Uzuri was eighteen and feisty. Neema was twenty-nine and loved her food. Both weighed two tonnes and could knock a tree down by accident.

'They are fine,' Jane said. 'They were sleeping.' Behind her in the dark the sound of squabbling vultures could not drown out the sound of Festo sobbing.

'The report of poachers?' Tony said.

'A wild goose chase to get us away from the shift,' Jane said, taking one step back into the dark. 'Jomo offered to come with me. I left him here.'

Tony was now looking at the ground with a torch. He crouched down by the tracks she'd examined earlier.

'Land Cruisers,' he said. She nodded. 'Three of them by the looks of it. What about Nathan and Timu?'

'No sign,' Jane said.

He stood up.

'Either they got away or they're dead out there in the

darkness,' he said. 'Why Douglas? Why not the girls? Why not the black rhinos? They all have more horn and less protection. Why didn't they shoot one of them?'

'How do we know they didn't?' Jane said. She turned quickly. 'Festo!' she called, running to the bank. 'We have to check the *kifaru nyeusi*.'

Festo was between Douglas's carcass and the jostling vultures, as though trying to protect him with his body. In the light of her torch, she saw his face, lost. He nodded.

'I'll drive,' she said to Tony.

CHAPTER FOUR

JANE DROVE AS IF THEY WERE BEING CHASED BY THE hyenas of hell. Tony held onto the strap above the door with both hands, and for most of the trip kept his eyes firmly shut. The tracks were smooth enough, but Jane cut corners where she could, driving into the bush, yanking the steering wheel left and right to avoid rocks and holes picked out by the headlights. Thirty kilometres an hour off-track anywhere in the conservancy was dangerous. She was doing sixty.

When they reached the ranger station, Jane hit the brakes and leapt out. Tony was still clinging to the strap. He opened the door and threw up onto the ground. She ran into the station to the tech room.

She had used the small Phantom drones occasionally, but had little experience with the Super Bats. Without thinking, on autopilot, she switched on the control workstations and hit the power up sequences. The heavy remote-control units were snug in their charging docks, but she didn't need them. Outside, she heard the two drones following their pre-set courses, taxiing themselves down their small airstrip in the dark and taking off into the night. They were ultramodern security equipment lent to them by technology companies Kennet had persuaded to sponsor the conservancy in exchange for marketing opportunities with the animals.

Within minutes of Jane's arrival, the machines were in the air and heading north-west to where the black rhino roamed, taking separate routes to cover maximum ground. Jane focused on the monitors. The motion-sensitive infra-red cameras relayed green-yellow images to the screens. Impala, waterbuck, zebra, giraffe. They passed over the river where the hippos were leaving the water to graze.

'The computer,' Tony said. He stood in the doorway. His face looked stretched.

Of course. The black rhinos all had radio-tags. The older ones were collars, big, clumsy things. The younger ones had the newer technology, smaller, punched through their ears. The computer was fed by the signals from the collars, relayed from small masts affixed to trees. She switched it on.

'I don't know how to use this,' she said.

Tony lurched a little as he crossed the room. She stepped back to let him take the keyboard. Pulled up a chair for him. He didn't look well. She thought she should say something.

'Sorry about the drive,' she said. 'We have to know.'

He waved weakly in her direction with his right hand, took the computer mouse and started to click. A window came up, a map of the reserve with dots. The rhinos. He clicked a menu. He clicked an option. 'Security Check'. The cursor turned into a stopwatch. The little hand went around twice, before a window popped up.

Responses expected: 104. Responses received: 104. No unexpected behaviour.

'They're ok,' he said.

A beeping started on the computer.

Tony clicked on another icon. The programme that monitored the radio trackers of the northern whites. As the programme came up it was flashing red.

'It's flashing because of Douglas.'

Tony pointed to three dots on the map, two green, one red.

Jane picked up the radio handset nearest the computer.

'Ranger station to *kifaru* three, copy?'

The static crackled with the unknown.

'This is *kifaru* three, copy.'

It was Festo.

'Super Bats are airborne, the other rhinos are fine,' Jane said.

'Copy,' Festo said. Tony leaned on the desk with both hands, bowed his head. Jane held the radio, breathed. The radio crackled again.

'What happened today?' Festo said. 'Why just Douglas? Why not the other rhino?'

Jane stared at the screen for some moments before answering.

'I have no idea, Festo. I have no idea,' she said. 'I will find out.'

'Death has come to my house. I will mourn until the mountains fall,' Festo said.

'On this sad day,' Jane said.

'On this sad day,' Festo repeated.

Jane replaced the handset.

'Why didn't they go after the black *kifaru*?' Tony said.

Jane didn't answer. She paced and thought. 'This took a lot of money. Planning,' she said.

'The wild goose chase,' Tony said. 'They set up a false report we'd have to investigate. Why?'

'Football,' Jane said.

They'd been the only ones on duty. All the other rangers were at the match. Only the next shift guarding the northern whites had not gone. Someone had picked the time they were at their weakest.

'Nathan and Timu volunteered,' she said. 'I need to find them.'

'They could be dead out there.'

'Or worse.'

'Worse? What could be worse?'

'They could not be dead and not be out there. They could have let them in.'

The images from the drones continued to roll across the screens. Every so often the control stations beeped when they detected another animal moving. Bandari would have been peaceful but for the flashing red dot on the computer screen showing where Douglas's radio tracker had gone offline close to the centre of the inner reserve.

'Why weren't the drones up?' she said.

'I don't know. Kennet was keeping an eye on them,' Tony said.

Kennet. She hadn't thought about him. She took out her phone and called him.

There was a moment before it started to ring. She listened. The ringing from her phone, And the ringing of another phone, not too far away.

She followed the sound, back outside. In the dark, around the side of the building. Ringing. Louder. As she stepped past the corner she stopped.

A patch of darkness was ringing. She turned her torch on.

Kennet was lying on his back, eyes wide, staring at the stars. His mouth was open. Jane dropped her phone and ran to him. It continued to ring, then clicked through to voicemail. She heard Kennet's voice apologising for not being able to take the call as she dropped to her knees. His eyes were bloodshot, his throat bruised and black. She had seen such injuries before. He had been strangled.

She was numb. She could not feel. White static filled her mind. Almost everyone she cared about was dead. Shot, shot, strangled. Jomo, Douglas, Kennet. Three hours ago, she'd been watching a wild cat carrying a rat on her way to feed her kittens.

'Kennet!' Tony was behind her, ran to Kennet's side, knelt. 'Kennet,' he said again. He picked up Jane's phone and used it to call for an ambulance.

'It is too late,' Jane said. 'Too late for healing.'

———

Naomi Haven was a small woman, a good fifteen centimetres shorter than Jane. She had deep brown eyes, braided hair, and the smoothest chestnut brown skin. Kennet used to say her smile lit up the world. She wasn't smiling tonight.

Jane watched as Naomi threw herself on Kennet's body. Tony and Jane had tried to move him, but he was too big, so he still lay on the ground next to the ranger station when Naomi reached them. Jane had closed his eyes, the second pair she'd closed today.

News was travelling. Some of the rangers had arrived, breaking off from socialising after the football match. A faint smell of beer followed one or two of them.

It took four men to get Kennet off the ground and into

the back of a Land Rover. Jane drove, Naomi in the passenger seat, a small procession of other vehicles followed, including one driven by Festo, bringing Jomo's body.

When they reached Kennet & Naomi's villa, six men, including Tony and Festo, carried Kennet's body inside and laid him out on the dining room table. He was taller than it was long, so Jane set up his beloved card table as an extension and rested his head on the green baize. The men went back and brought Jomo to lie beside him, before trooping out and leaving Naomi and Jane with Tony.

Jane looked at her brother. He seemed bigger than ever, as fat as he was tall. She remembered seeing him for the first time in a decade three years before, remembered being shocked at how large his belly had become. 'I don't want the elephants to feel self-conscious when they're pregnant,' he had said, before bursting out laughing, a barbecued chicken leg in one hand and a bottle of beer in the other. He was so large he had to go to Nairobi to buy his clothes.

'I'll call the coroner,' Tony said, and went into another room.

Jane watched him. She was calm. Combat calm. The self-control that descends in the moment the final order comes as the mission goes live. She saw everything in front of her, every detail of the room, the fingers of dawn poking through the window. She heard everything. Birds outside welcoming the new day. Naomi walking up behind her, quiet steps on the worn rug.

'Oh, Jane,' Naomi almost launched herself into an embrace. She caught Jane off-guard. Emotional physical contact was not one of Jane's strengths. It took her a few seconds to raise her arms and reciprocate, not letting her hands touch behind Naomi's back. Jane kept her arms there awkwardly as Naomi cried.

Eventually Naomi pulled away and took hold of Jane's hand.

'I am sorry, I am sorry. He isn't gone. He isn't gone. When I reach over in bed at night, he always takes my hand. For ten years, he always takes my hand. He always took my hand.' Her tears kept streaming over her cheeks, she held onto Jane's hand with both of her own. 'Poor Jomo,' she added, looking at Jane, and then at Jomo. His body seemed child-sized next to Kennet's giant frame.

Jane was staring at her brother. In death, he seemed undiminished. He looked peaceful, as though enjoying one last sunset. But his skin was turning purple. Jane reached out her hand to his face, let it fall without touching.

There was a sound from outside the dining room window. A low growl that slowly grew until it was a roar.

'Lion?' Jane said, certain it wasn't, though that was closest she could think of.

'That's not a lion. That's an elephant. An elephant in distress,' Naomi said through her tears.

The sound came again, a second over-lapping it, and a third, until there was a chorus.

Jane followed Naomi onto the veranda where Festo and the rangers who had carried Kennet and Jomo inside were watching in amazement.

The roar came again, two, three, four, a dozen times. A wall of sound. The herd of elephants, all fifteen of them, were between the ranch and the row of vehicles parked along the side of the mango grove. They seemed even larger than usual in the weak light coming from the ranch's windows and the two gas lamps on the veranda. The great creatures stepped from foot to foot, raised their heads, pointed their trunks to the west, and roared, not in unison, but one at a time. It was deeper, older, and more powerful than the roar of any lion Jane had heard. The sound ached with loss.

'They are saying goodbye,' Naomi said. 'They are saying goodbye to Ken.' Her tears had stopped, and she was smiling, though her eyes were as red as the setting sun.

'Thank you, Bibi,' Naomi said, loudly. The men looked at her in surprise. Jane watched the oldest female elephant in the herd leading the pacing. She moved from foot to foot in a strange dance the herd repeated behind her. As Naomi spoke Bibi stopped. The great creature looked straight at the woman half her height and a tiny fraction of her size. She flicked her ears, blinked her eyes, and briefly lowered her head. As she raised it again, she made a different sound, a low-frequency rumble like the creaking of snow before an avalanche. The other elephants stopped their roars and waited. Bibi turned to her right, walking past the last car in the line, brushing it with her foreleg.

Others of the herd bashed into the same car as they left. The last to trot past was a baby, no more than a few months old. As he passed, he raised his tail and let drop his evening dung.

Eventually the elephants disappeared into the darkness away to the east. The front of the last car was mangled to scrap. None of the other cars were damaged. The air smelt of elephant.

'I have never heard of that before,' Festo said.

'Elephants have senses beyond our understanding,' Naomi said. 'Bibi and Ken were bound together.'

'They knew before he died,' Festo said. 'To get here now.'

'Perhaps,' Naomi said, a smile in her tears.

The door behind them opened and Tony joined them, putting his phone away as he walked out. It took him a moment to take in the scene.

'My car!' he said, running down the steps towards the battered one at the end of the row. He was too intent on looking at the damage to notice the dung.

CHAPTER FIVE

THE AMBULANCE PICKED UP KENNET'S AND JOMO'S BODIES shortly before sunrise. The rangers had to help the men from the hospital get Kennet onto the stretcher.

After that, everyone drifted away until Jane and Naomi were the only ones left. Jane stood on the veranda, watching the sun in the east rising over the cattle pens. Naomi busied herself in the kitchen, making unnecessary noises, repeating unnecessary chores.

Two hours later a conservancy Land Rover came down the track from the north. It was Tony returning. He looked at the wreck of his own car wistfully as he got out of the one he'd borrowed.

'Everything is locked down,' Tony said. 'The police have taken evidence. The Kenya Wildlife Service and the army have been notified, and the bulletin issued to all reserves, conservancies, and parks. No other incidents overnight, nothing. No sign of Nathan or Timu.'

'Are they at home?' Jane said.

'I spoke with Nathan's wife and Timu's mother, and to his girlfriend. Neither went home yesterday.'

'Whoever did this left Jomo dead on the ground,' Jane said.

'I know.'

'Someone opened the gates with a key,' Jane said.

'I know.'

'Why did they kill Kennet?'

'To delay pursuit? To stop the drones coming straight after them? As soon as Douglas died his tracker would have sent an alarm to the station.'

'No,' Jane said.

'No?'

'The trackers don't monitor health, they just emit a location. The alerts at the station were because they'd broken Douglas's tracker, not because they'd killed him. If they'd left the tracker intact Ken would never have known they were here.'

Jane moved, slipped off the veranda, walked purposefully towards her car.

'Where are you going?' Tony said.

'To find Nathan.'

'How?'

Jane shrugged as she climbed into the car.

———

It was nearly half-past nine in the morning when Jane pulled up outside Nathan Jennings' house on the outskirts of Nanyuki. She had driven after the morning rush to school, and the road was quiet.

She opened the glove compartment and took out a handgun, slipped it in her pocket. Nathan Jennings was at the very least a witness to two murders and a wildlife crime, and possibly an accessory or a perpetrator. Walking across the road, she approached the house slowly until she was against the wall. She turned her head and looked through the window.

The door opened straight into a kitchen. There was a woman sitting at a table.

Jane knocked. The woman looked up sharply, stumbled to the door, opening it quickly. When she saw who it was, or more likely when she saw who it wasn't, she deflated a little.

'Oh,' she said.

'My name is —'

'I know who you are. I have seen you. Nathan has talked about you.'

'May I come in?' Jane said.

The woman shrugged and walked back to the table leaving the door open.

'My apologies,' Jane said, raising her hands in a gesture of peace. 'I have to ask you some things, then I will go. May I sit?'

The woman herself had already sat. She shrugged again. Jane took a chair.

'Your name is Saachi?' she said.

The woman nodded. There was a large kitchen knife on the table in front of her.

She looked at Jane, her eyes red from crying. Otherwise, she seemed calm.

The kitchen was ordered and tidy, but for a pile of unwashed pans by the sink, and a plate of ugali and sukuma wiki — cornmeal mash and cassava leaves — under a fly net. The scent of fried garlic hung in the warm air. She had expected him home for dinner last night and he had not come.

'Where is Nathan?' Jane said.

'I told the police I don't know,' the woman said. 'I told Tony Kanagi I don't know.'

'I am not the police.'

'I still don't know. He is gone.'

'How do you know that?'

Saachi's face looked drained. She did not answer straight away. She was attractive, Jane could see. Or would be if her eyes were not red and puffed up. She had a grace to her, and a shape.

'Nathan told me many stories about you. He did not like you. You made him angry. A white woman becoming a ranger. He thought it was wrong.'

'He is not the only one,' Jane said.

'He watched how you are, how good you are at hunting the poachers, and he forgot you were white. He never forgot you were a woman. "Man's work should be done by men," he said. However good he thought you were he was always angry you were a woman.'

'There's not much I can do about that,' Jane said.

'That run you did. Sponsored run. First time I'd heard of such a thing. Raising money for new electric fence at Bandari. You and forty men, ten kilometres, and you won. He was outraged.'

'That was two years ago. There were twenty-three men. And it was twenty kilometres. And I didn't win, I was third.'

'Kamba men, he said, Kamba men. Fastest distance runners in the world. Records in everything. Beaten by a candle woman. That's what he called you. "Candle woman."'

'I run a lot. Twenty-one of those twenty-three didn't,' Jane said. 'The other two beat me easily.'

'You beat him by a kilometre,' Saachi said. 'I was pleased.'

'I don't remember,' Jane said.

'But Nathan, however angry he was, he knew you would not hurt the rhino. Knew it. He said once, if someone hurt the rhino you would kill them. You would hunt them down and kill them without a thought. Is that what you are doing?'

'I just want to talk to Nathan,' Jane said.

'I do not know where he is,' Saachi said.

A silence grew between them. In another room of the house was the sound of a faint creak of springs. Instinctively Jane's hand went to her pocket where the handgun was, but Saachi raised her hand in a gesture of pacification, the most she had moved since she'd sat back down.

'It is my son. He did not sleep all night. His father always tells him goodnight, even when he goes to the bars. He could not go to school today, he was too tired.'

'When did you last see Nathan?' Jane asked.

'I told the police I don't know where he is. I was expecting him home. He didn't come. They told me to call them when he came home.'

'Where might he have gone?'

'I don't know.'

'Where is his family?'

'We are here, in this house.'

'His parents?'

'They are near. They have not heard from him today. I called them.'

'Brothers? Sisters?'

'I told the police. Three sisters. All live here, in Nanyuki. All are married. None have heard from him today.'

'What did he do before he was a ranger?'

Saachi looked at Jane. Her face, drained by tears, was disbelieving.

'You work with him for three years and you don't know?'

'He never said much to me. I know what he told Timu. I want to know what he told you.'

'He is a good man,' Saachi said, and turned a little on her chair to lean back against the wall. 'He says goodnight to the boy every night, even when he goes to the bars.' Saachi seemed to be clinging to that idea.

'He may be a good man, but I need to find him to understand what happened yesterday, and before yesterday. What did he do before he was a ranger?'

Saachi contemplated the tabletop.

'He was a soldier. Kenya Rifles. He was with the UN for a while.'

'Where?'

'Uganda. And Rwanda.'

'Does he keep in touch with any of his... old colleagues.'

'I don't know. He doesn't tell me. He is a good man. He gives me his pay and makes the children laugh.'

Outside on the road a car drove past, its engine loud in the otherwise silent room. Jane stood up and went to the window and looked out. The car's brake lights were disappearing as it turned onto the main road. She went back to the table.

'When he is being himself, where does he go? In the house,' Jane said.

'Attic,' Saachi mumbled.

'Do you mind if I look? To see if there's anything that tells me where he has gone?'

Saachi shook her head. 'No.'

It was a single storey building with a slanted roof. Jane could see a trap door in the ceiling.

'It is a mess. Be careful of the ladder, it comes down quickly,' Saachi said.

———

The ladder slid down on rollers, squeaking. She caught it and eased it to the ground. Had she not been warned, it could have hit her in the face. There was another sound of bedsprings creaking from one of the other rooms.

Jane took a torch from her belt and took the gun from her pocket. She climbed the ladder slowly, a rung at a time. She didn't turn the torch on until she was at the top.

It was a garret that ran the full length of the house with a floor of rough planks. Under the sloping roof were boxes, perhaps once neatly piled, now spilled over and torn apart. In the centre at the far end was a small window under which was a makeshift desk created by a door laid across two piles of boxes of different heights. A kitchen chair was pushed to one side. She listened and looked for some minutes.

A single bare bulb was above her head, the switch a string hanging beside it. She put her pistol away and turned on the light.

On the makeshift desk were a few papers, some pens, and a space with a charging cable running to it. No computer.

She flicked through the papers. Forms. Payslips. Nothing useful, no clues.

Pens. Quite a few pens, but nothing handwritten.

She flicked through the piles again. No, nothing handwritten despite all those pens.

There was a small pile of papers to the right of the space

where the computer had been. She took it over to the light bulb and held it at an angle. Yes. The impression of writing, illegible. *stings... ...law?* She couldn't make sense of it. She looked around the attic a last time. Thought a moment. Felt in her belt.

She took out a small camera. High definition, night vision, battery-powered, with its own SIM card. It could send its pictures straight to her phone. She drove a screw into the wood of a beam and attached the camera, giving it a view of the trap door and the makeshift desk. She checked the image on her phone. It was good. She wrapped the camera in a piece of sack to conceal it and checked the image again to make sure she'd not obscured its field of vision.

She picked up the papers, switched the light off, went back down the ladder. At the bottom she pushed the ladder back through the hole and closed the trapdoor. She armed the motion sensor on the camera from her phone.

———

'What will happen?' Saachi said as Jane walked back into the kitchen. She was sitting at the table, but she had moved because the washing up had been done. The plate of ugali and sukuma wiki was gone, either scraped in the bin or put in the fridge.

'Did he have a computer?' Jane asked, ignoring the question. One of the taps dripped occasionally. She stepped over and tightened it. The drips stopped.

'A laptop,' Saachi said.

'Where is it?'

'I don't know. He takes it with him sometimes. If it's not in the attic he has it.'

'Anywhere else there may have been papers, records, files?'

'No'.

'Where else does he go? Where does he spend his time? You said bars?'.

'A few. Riff's Bar. Dreams he mentioned once.' Saachi stood up, took a towel from a drawer, started drying the pots and pans.

'Riff's Bar? When did he go there?'

'In the evenings sometimes.'

'Are you sure?' Jane asked.

Saachi nodded.

'Do you know who he drank with?'

'I don't know. Other drinkers.' There was contempt in her tone.

'Any he'd known for longer than others? Any old school friends?'

'He drank with the young boy, Gatimu.'

'Timu?' Jane said, surprised. Timu hardly stopped talking but she couldn't remember him mentioning drinking with Nathan.

'Recently, yes. And old army colleagues, yes. Omariba. There's one called Omariba.'

'How long was Nathan in the army?' Jane asked.

'He joined up after school. Was with the UN in Rwanda. And Uganda.' Saachi had finished drying and started putting the stacked crockery in cupboards.

'Do you know Omariba's surname?'

'No. Just that they were in Rwanda together.' Saachi stopped moving, the dish towel limp in her hand.

That was the third time she'd mentioned Rwanda. Jane knew the UN's missions. The one in Rwanda had ended when Nathan was about three years old. He'd not been in

Rwanda, at least not with the UN. Though his wife believed he had.

'Thank you,' Jane said. 'I am sorry I had to disturb you, Mrs Jennings.' Jane moved for the kitchen door.

'What will happen?' Saachi said again. Jane stopped.

'What do you mean?'

'What will happen to me? To the children? Now Nathan is gone.'

'I have no idea,' Jane said.

CHAPTER SIX

DREAMS WASN'T TOO FAR, CLOSE TO THE CENTRE OF Nanyuki between the hospital and the British Army training ground. Jane drove there, parked two streets away, approached on foot.

Unsurprisingly for mid-morning it was closed. A sign on the door said, "Open sunset to sunrise."

Jane peered through the glass in the door at the dimly lit interior. Small booths and small tables. Intimate. She knocked, but nothing changed, no one answered.

She'd come back later.

Riff's Bar she knew. She'd been there once or twice with some of the rangers. It was on the Nyeri road heading out of town to the south, next to one of the airstrips. It did great breakfasts, and amazing coffee. Its lunches weren't bad either. It catered for the people using the airstrip and closed at 4.30pm. If Nathan had told Saachi he drank at Riff's in the evenings, he had been lying.

As she was walking back to her car Jane's phone vibrated. A text from Naomi.

I'm going to lay a stone, it said.

Jane nodded, though there was no one to see. She went back to the Land Rover. Once behind the wheel again she headed north through Nanyuki, turning onto the C76 road into the heart of the shopping district. Local stalls catering for ranchers from Laikipia county nestled alongside tourist shops with the word "Equator" in their name. This close to Mount Kenya it was cool for the time of year, barely twenty-two degrees, and most locals walking by the side of the road wore jeans and coats, hurrying past the shade of the trees. Visitors tended to come from cooler climates, however, and the handful of tourists were in shorts and t-shirts, keeping out of the sun. The motorbikes, cars and trucks on the grey-brown road filled the air with a fine, dry dust that mingled with the exhaust fumes. Jane closed the windows.

The traffic only lasted a few blocks, thinning to the occasional piki piki, motor scooters bearing improbably large baskets of mangoes and avocados to sell at the roadside. The shops gave way to other buildings: the hospital, a new apartment block resplendent in clay-red brick, single-storey, colonial-style local government offices, and more traditional residences. The further from the town centre she drove, the further back from the road the buildings were, giving the impression that the world was expanding as she left the concentration of people behind.

She drove past a copse of trees hiding the sewage plant. Beyond that lay Nanyuki airport and the air force base. A plane was coming in to land, a sleek private jet, probably bringing some wealthy American or Chinese for a safari.

After three more kilometres the route turned sharply west. The Graveyard appeared on the left, set half a kilometre back from the tarmacked road on a little-used track that connected the C76 to Bandari's north-eastern entrance. Jane pulled off the track, stopped the Land Rover next to Naomi's old Subaru, and got out.

The Graveyard surrounded a lone acacia - a fever tree - a symbol so often used to depict east Africa, particularly Kenya and Tanzania, that it had become a cliché.

There were no bodies buried there, but rangers had placed a stone for each animal killed by poachers in the surrounding conservancies and reserves in the last twenty years, inscribing the stones with a record of the crime. There were thousands of them.

Naomi was kneeling in the middle of the stones a hundred metres away. A man Jane didn't recognise was standing some distance behind her, his hands clasped respectfully in front of his waist.

Jane's heartrate quickened as it always did as the number of stones overwhelmed her. She was no stranger to death, and in war death could be so common it became normal. The idiocy of this would never normalise. Killing animals for body parts made as little sense as killing children for their finger-nails. Using guns to do it took as little courage.

Jane walked until she was amongst the stones close to Naomi, at the heart of desolation.

She squatted in the dust. She read some of the inscriptions at random. "Heidi" one simply said. "Male elephant 22.09.02" said another. *"kifaru nyeusi* Feb8". "Three lioness 04.2004. They took their bones." *"familia ya tembo Mwaka mpya* 2010". Family of elephants, New Year 2010.

Naomi was crying, her tears glistening on her cheeks. She was staring at a stone, fresh-placed, that read "Kennet Havn, man with heart as big as an elephant's" in Naomi's neat, block script. Without looking up Naomi reached out towards Jane.

Jane stood and took her hand, and Naomi stood to hold her, sobs coming again.

After a few slow minutes, Naomi's breathing became regular and she stepped back, putting both hands in the pockets of her coat, and pulling out two more stones. She held them out to Jane.

"Douglas, the last male northern white".

"Jomo, lost, found, now lost again".

Both in Naomi's writing. Jane smiled, weakly, and took them, placing them on the ground either side of the Kennet stone.

She stood back. Naomi took her hand again. They stared at the stones for some time.

The Graveyard stood in an area that had once been a British prisoner-of-war camp. Ten thousand Italians captured in Abyssinia and held until 1944; a larger population than that of modern Nanyuki.

Back then rhino and elephant roamed freely on the slopes of Mount Kenya and the biggest human population for hundreds of kilometres had lived behind fences. Seventy-five years on and the most dangerous thing on Mount Kenya was the mountain itself. The surviving animals were the ones behind fences. To the west she could just make out Bandari's border.

The conservancy had originally been called *Patakatifu*, a word that had taken her several days to learn to pronounce when she spoke no Swahili and it sounded like nothing she'd ever heard. 'Pat a cat if you' had helped. *Patakatifu*. The Sanctuary. When Kennet took over, he had changed it to *Bandari*, which he said was a translation of their surname. It wasn't, though it made a good story. They had both anglicised their surnames to Haven as most non-

Norwegians pronounced it that way anyway. *Bandari* meant port.

Haven. Sanctuary. That's what Kennet and Naomi had been building. Jane's job was to protect it.

The cry of a bird of prey, an eagle, came from far above them: a harsh, high-pitched shriek. It jerked Jane out of her reflection. The shadow of the acacia tree was stretching across the stones as the sun rose. Jane turned to the tree.

Some of the rangers, including her, made a scratch in the trunk each time they killed or caught a poacher. Like keeping score. She saw the last marks she'd made, not six months ago. Jomo had been standing beside her as she carved them. Five lines in the bark, weathering now. She walked across and put her hand on them, feeling the texture of the tree.

She stared at the stones and then east towards the distant mountain rising into the clouds. For a moment she saw the mountain as a living thing in a vastness of living things, each one being hunted, all fighting for their own survival. She stood motionless for some minutes, until she shook herself out of her thoughts.

'Oh, Jane,' Naomi managed, her soft voice cracked. 'Jane, Ken is dead.' *Ken er død* her brain translated. She stood on the edge of the sea of stone death-markers listening to Naomi crying. She had no words. He'd sent her a text just a day ago. *They are home* ☺. He'd sent the smiley face to annoy her. He couldn't be dead. And Jomo. That was still too raw.

Overhead the bird shrieked again.

There was another sound, feet moving on earth. She had forgotten about Naomi's companion.

He was a small man about the same size as herself. He was younger than Jane, much younger than Naomi, with an open face. The hint of creases around his eyes suggested he smiled a lot, though not today. He dressed very smartly, too smartly, and certainly an unusual outfit for the Kenyan summer. A deep blue suit, with a silver waistcoat and a tie in a strong red. His shoes were mahogany brown, highly polished, and somehow not dusty.

He saw her looking at him and gave a small bow.

'I am Makena,' he said.

'I am sorry, I should have said. This is my cousin,' Naomi said. 'One of my cousins. I have many cousins.'

'And I have many more,' Makena said, stepping carefully through the stones and offering his hand. Jane shook it. 'My heart weeps for you both on this sad day.'

Jane nodded.

'And if there is anything I can do to help find who did this,' Makena said, 'please simply ask.'

Jane looked at Naomi.

'Makena is a businessman,' Naomi said. 'He has many contacts.'

'And I have many cousins,' Makena said.

Jane thought for a moment.

'The two other rangers on guard last night, Nathan Jennings and Gatimu Obote, known as Timu, have disappeared. They have not been home, they haven't turned up dead. I need to talk to them,' Jane said.

'I shall ask some people I know,' Makena said, with another short bow.

'Do you want me to write down their names?' Jane said.

'Never write anything down. You never know who might read it,' Makena said.

CHAPTER SEVEN

JANE PULLED UP ON PARK ROAD ABOUT A HUNDRED METRES from Dreams on the opposite side of the street. She could see the entrance in the rear-view mirror. It was an hour before sunset.

Jane had spent thirty minutes driving around the adjacent streets, familiarising herself with the neighbourhood. The bar was in a block, backing onto a fish and chip shop which faced onto the next street. The door she was watching was the only way in.

The other side of the block was a busy shopping street, this side bordered the park. There were few people, and only a handful of cars. A young woman was pulling racks of dresses into the clothing store on the corner, shutting up shop. The mobile phone store next to the clothing store had put its lights on, spilling into the growing shadows of the trees across the road.

Before the sun was finally gone a battered Nissan pulled up in front of Dreams and a tall, willowy man unfolded from it. He locked the car and, taking another key from the same bunch, he walked to the bar and unlocked the door. He disappeared inside. After a moment lights came on behind the bar, and another over the entrance. Low lights, enough to see by, not enough to attract unnecessary attention.

Jane waited.

Shortly afterwards two young women turned the corner by the clothing store and walked up to the door to the bar, chattering to each other in Swahili loud enough for Jane to hear. They went in with familiarity, with confidence. Staff, Jane guessed.

Almost at once one of the women came out again carrying a sign with a weighted base. The headlights of a passing car lit it up. The side facing Jane said "Realise your Dreams. Cocktails, 2 for 1, sunset to 8". The woman placed the sign on the edge of the pavement. Once the car had passed it was too dark to read.

Jane got out and went to the bar, walking straight in.

'Welcome, my friend,' said a voice. It was the tall, thin man. He was behind the bar. Unexpectedly, the bar was part metal cage, chrome bars far enough apart to pass drinks through, but otherwise as solid as a prison cell. 'What can I get for you this fine evening?' He reached under the counter and something clicked. Lights came on in some of the beer pumps. The Tusker elephant head was silhouetted clearly.

'Do you get a lot of trouble here?' said Jane, indicating the cage. The man laughed. He continued doing things under the counter, occasionally crouching.

'These were put here long ago, during less stable times,' he said from out of sight, 'They add a certain something, so the owner has not removed them. And, once in a while, they come in useful. What can I get you?'

'I need some information,' said Jane.

The man's face changed. Not dramatically.

'What sort of information?'

'I'm looking for a man. One of the rangers from Bandari. He drinks here sometimes.' Jane took her phone out of her pocket and held up the photo of Nathan from the conservancy website. The man stared at it through the bars.

'I think I recognise the face, don't know him, though. He may have been in here. Why are you looking for him here if you know where he works?'

'His name is Nathan Jennings. He may have been here with Timu Obote.' Jane held up Timu's photo from the website. 'They are missing after an incident. I need to speak to them urgently.'

The door from the street opened and two young men came in, walked to a booth halfway into the room, and sat down. One of the waitresses came from the back and took their order.

'He looks too young to be in here,' the man said, looking at the photo of Timu.

'That was taken a few years ago.'

The man looked closer.

'Maybe. Again, nothing definite, but he may be familiar.'

The waitress came to the bar and stabbed an order chit onto a spike.

'Two Tusker,' she said. The man behind the bar took out a glass and started to pour.

'Nathan, the first one, might drink with someone called Omariba, or Riba,' Jane said.

'No last name?'

Jane shook her head.

'Not an uncommon name,' the man said, sympathetically.

He passed one drink through the bars and started pouring a second.

'He and Nathan were soldiers. Possibly in the Kenya Rifles together before Nathan became a ranger.'

'We get plenty of soldiers here. Kenya Rifles come in when they're on furlough. They come in truckloads from the barracks out towards Ndaragwa. British army from the training ground up the road. If they were soldiers, they could easily have been in. Want me to ask some of the regulars?'

'I would appreciate it,' Jane said.

'Send me the pictures.'

She wrote an email on her phone, including the links to the two photos, and the three names. The man finished pouring the second beer and put it next to the first on the tray. The waitress took the tray to the two men in the booth. The door opened again, and again shortly after that. More customers, twos, and threes. The place started to fill with the low buzz of conversation.

'Where should I send it?' Jane asked.

'behindthebar@nanyukidreams.com. For the attention of Legishon.'

'That you?'

'Yes,' he beamed.

'Jane,' she said, hitting send.

'And now would you like a drink?' he said.

'Another time,' she said, pulling out two five hundred shilling notes and tucking them into a tip jar on the bar. 'Thank you for your help, Legishon.'

'I will be in touch, Jane,' he said, with a smile at the notes.

Jane nodded and turned to go.

The door opened again. This time it was a larger group. All men. They held themselves like soldiers, but they weren't

Kenya Rifles. Five of them were white. British army, possibly, though too old to be at a training camp. They swaggered in as if they owned the place. The one in front would have walked into Jane if she'd not stepped out of the way. She bristled instinctively, put her hand in her pocket, felt her Kubotan, a piece of metal about fifteen centimetres long that, in the right hands, upgraded a punch from painful to lethal.

The men trudged through to the back of the bar and sat at a round table, whistled at a waitress, commanded her over. The accent of the man who called was South African.

Jane stepped back to the bar, close to Legishon.

'Who are they?' she said.

Legishon looked up from pouring more beer.

'Asked them once. Private security, they said. They're not very friendly. Been coming in here for a few months. They're nothing to do with the army. None of them are Kenyan.'

'Thank you,' Jane said. She gripped the Kubotan more tightly for a moment, then released it.

She took one last look at the men in the corner of the bar then left.

She came out into the street and looked both ways, then started walking to her car. She saw a movement in the shadow of the trees behind it. She didn't slow down. She put her hand in her pocket again. She'd left the handgun in the car. She stepped onto the pavement and took the Kubotan out, holding it loosely in her right hand, letting her arms swing, muscles relaxed.

There was another movement, and someone came out of the shadows towards her. She moved in close and fast, in case they were armed, getting too close for them to raise, or let fall, a weapon.

The person's hands were empty. Instead, they jumped back in surprise.

'It's me, it's Makena!' the man said, raising his arms. Naomi's young cousin. The one who had many cousins. Still in his shiny suit.

'It's not a clever idea to lie in wait for women,' Jane said.

'I'm sorry, I thought it best to come quickly.' Makena eyed the Kubotan as Jane slipped it back in her pocket.

'How? No one knew where I was.'

'Bandari conservancy Land Rovers are not difficult to spot,' Makena said. 'A cousin of mine drove past yours an hour ago.'

Jane frowned.

'Why were you looking for me?'

'Because I have found one of the men you are looking for. Gatimu Obote,' Makena said. 'I have found Timu.'

CHAPTER EIGHT

MAKENA'S TRUCK WAS HELD TOGETHER BY THE MEMORY OF its former self. It rattled so violently on the smooth tarmac it felt as if it would disintegrate at any moment. It was thirty years old if it was a day. But the engine was in decent shape, and the tyres were almost new. Jane quite liked it. She'd driven far worse, and far better with less character.

Makena did not look like he was enjoying the ride. He sat in the passenger seat clutching the door handle as if he were afraid the door would fly off and he'd be sucked out. The antiquity of the truck contrasted dramatically with the shiny suit; the old and practical, the new and impractical.

'She's too old to go this fast,' he said, his voice strained.

'You're the one who is insisting on going the long way around,' Jane said.

'I have deliveries to make.'

'Couldn't they wait?'

'I made a commitment. My father always said the only thing a man needs to do to have a successful life is to do what he says he's going to do when he says he's going to do it. I honour my commitments.'

Jane said nothing. The truck rattled on, the tarmac in the headlights seeming grey, endless, and dead. Either side of the road was the plateau, lost in the dark. It was the kingdom of the night hunters now. She eased off on the gas a little.

'Fair enough,' she said. 'Where in Nairobi is Timu?' she said.

'Staying in a hotel.'

'You're not going to tell me which one?'

'I do not know. My cousin will show us which one when we get there.' Makena's grip on the door handle relaxed a little.

Jane glanced at him.

'How are you sure it is Timu?'

'He took an air taxi from Nanyuki airstrip to Wilson airport about three o'clock yesterday afternoon. He gave a fake name, but it was him. The pilot knows my cousin and recognised his picture. From Wilson airport he took a regular taxi to the hotel and checked in. The taxi driver that took him works for a company whose bookkeeper is married to one of my cousins.'

'How do you know he is still there?'

'He is not. He is at a club with some girls.'

'How can you know that?'

'One of the girls is the friend of another of my cousins.'

'Is that a coincidence?' Jane said.

'No, I arranged it,' Makena said.

Jane stared at him for a long time, until a look of increased panic in his eyes made her turn her attention back to the road and straighten the wheel to avoid a car coming the other way. There was the blast of a horn, which moaned in their wake.

'That must have taken a lot of effort,' she said.

'For Naomi, it is worth it,' he said. 'She suffers terribly, losing her husband. I will help find his killer.'

There was certainty in his voice. Jane relaxed a little, eased off on the gas.

———

Nyahururu was a word Jane found very pleasing. It sounded musical, other-worldly, an echo of an ancient sound living on in a changing world. It meant "waterfall", named for the falls on the Ewaso Narok river that flowed through the town bearing the name.

Makena confidently directed Jane through the sleeping streets until they pulled up in front of a two-storey building with a clay-tiled roof. It was split down the middle, a branch of the Women's Microfinance bank on the left, a veterinary clinic on the right.

'I won't be long,' Makena said, and slipped out of the cab. He walked to the front door of the clinic and knocked loudly. Nothing happened. He knocked again.

Jane looked up and down the street. The split two-storey was the first in a long row of other buildings, though most of them were single-storey, and mostly shops. Some of them had chairs and tables leaning against their fronts, stacked, or folded away for the night. All cars she could see were parked. The town was at rest.

A light came on in one of the second storey windows of the clinic. After a few minutes the front door opened and a woman came out, her face a crumpled cross between still asleep and very grumpy. Makena greeted her with a smile and a wave, and went to the back of the truck, pulling the tailgate down and sliding out a large cardboard box which he carried into the clinic. The woman watched him and woke up a bit. She smiled and shook his hand, saying something Jane didn't catch, then disappeared inside. The door closed behind her and after a minute the light upstairs went out.

Makena closed the tailgate before climbing back into the cab.

'Thank you,' he said. 'Let us go to Nairobi.'

Jane started the engine and put the truck into gear, backed out onto the deserted street and headed through the backstreets until they joined the main road once more.

'Let me guess,' she said, 'that was one of your cousins.'

'No,' he said, 'she is a friend of Naomi's, from university. They became vets together. Naomi imports things that are difficult to get in Kenya. She has a big heart. She makes sure they get to places where they are needed.'

————

They drove through Nyahururu heading south along a road Jane had not travelled before. The gibbous moon had been rising steadily and gave good light, revealing the landscape that had been swallowed by the night an hour before. The eastern rim of the Great Rift Valley, the Aberdare mountains, loomed like a row of drunken giants, their heads cast back in silent laughter. Closer to them were hills and thick forests. As the road uncoiled, they rounded a bend and found two moons, one below and one above them. The lower was quivering a little, a reflection on water.

'Which lake is that?' Jane asked. It was long and narrow,

filling the valley. Even in the moonlight she could see it ringed with multiple bands of dried mud showing how low the water level had dropped. Between the road and the lake were farms. On the other side of the valley, beyond the lake, trees came down to the water's edge.

'Lake Olbolosatt,' Makena said. 'It is a war zone.'

'What sort of a war zone?'

'The front line. Between the farmers and wild Africa. That side is Aberdare National Park, this side all those farms. The lake is protected, but it is poisoned by cattle shit, so the animals don't drink there anymore. There was a big thing in the papers. Tourists came for the birds, the birds disappeared as the lake died so tourists stopped coming. Without tourists, the only way to make money is farming. The farmers take more land and water to feed their crops and families, and the lake dies faster.'

'It's not all like that,' she said, though as she said it, she remembered Kennet talking about Olbolosatt, wanting to get involved to try and incentivise the farmers to protect the lake and its wildlife.

'Not yet. But there are more people all over the world buying coffee and tea. The farms need more land. And the tourists who stop coming to see the animals go home where they buy the coffee and the tea that comes from the land taken from the wild. The world has too many people to keep going this way.'

'Aren't most of the people cousins of yours?' Jane said.

It was Makena's turn to stare at her, seemingly oblivious to her weak joke.

'Everyone is everyone's cousin,' he said.

———

They followed the C77 for a hundred kilometres, then turned onto the A104. There was little traffic. Midnight passed. They exchanged few words. Once or twice, Jane thought Makena might sleep, but whenever she glanced to her left, he looked alert, watching the road. Occasionally he checked the text messages on his phone.

After a hundred kilometres they entered the outskirts of Nairobi. The A104 swept round the city to the east and became the Southern Bypass. They passed a turn off to Lang'ata, the maximum-security prison for women. They saw signs for the Nairobi National Park to the south, the world's biggest wildlife park in a capital city.

'Take the next exit,' Makena said.

This exit was for Kibera, one of the districts of Nairobi that qualified as a slum. A million people crammed into two square kilometres, paying rent they couldn't afford on rooms and houses built illegally on land the landlords didn't own.

Jane followed directions, driving slowly, carefully. For a while the road ran parallel to railway tracks. A goods train a quarter of a kilometre-long kept pace with them for a minute before the road wound away leaving the train to plough through the night alone. The truck headlights lit up a pile of rubbish as they turned, startling a dog that had been foraging. It ran a few steps, then slowed and looked back warily.

'We're going over there.' Makena pointed to an alley half-concealed in the gloom. 'Reverse in, there's nowhere to turn.'

Jane did so and switched off the engine.

'This isn't a hotel or a club,' she said. She looked at her watch.

'Timu is going nowhere, do not worry. I have a delivery to make. And I need to change,' he said.

'Into what?

'To look like you.' He took a canvas bag off the back seat of the cab and stepped into the alley. Jane took her own bag and followed him.

Makena pulled out a torch and switched it on. The alley was strangely clean. Or uniformly dirty. The only rubbish were lines of plastic bags against the edges of the buildings. It stank.

Jane touched a bag with her toe. It was soft.

'No toilets in most of these buildings,' Makena said. 'They shit in a plastic bag and when it gets dark, they sling the bag as far as they can. Thing is, everyone does it, so it's every- where. Someone clears them up occasionally. Do you know what the difference is between Kibera now and a city in Europe a hundred and fifty years ago?'

Jane shook her head.

'Plastic bags,' he said, and knocked on the door of a corru- gated shack. The door didn't fit its frame. It had no lock and opened under the pressure of the knock. The number 42 was written on it in whitewash.

'*Hujambo!*' he called in a loud whisper.

There was no answer. Jane looked at her watch.

'It's two in the morning,' she said.

'*Hujambo!*' he called in a loud whisper.

'Makena? *Ni kwamba wewe?*' A tiny woman appeared in the doorway, so frail she might be blown away by the faintest breeze.

'Yes, Auntie. I am sorry it is so late. I have brought you things from my mother. And I need to change. May I change here? And might you ask that my truck be watched?'

'You are on business?' the woman said.

'Yes, Auntie. This is my associate, Captain Haven,' Makena said.

'*Hujambo*,' Jane said, stepping inside. He knew her former rank. How the hell had he found that out? The shack was a single room, sparsely furnished. A cheap table and four plastic chairs; rolls spread out on the floor as beds, three occupied, one recently vacated; light from a bulb, and a small fridge humming in the corner. Electricity, at least. There was a portable stove on a pile of bottle crates against one wall. The air smelt of paraffin.

'Welcome, welcome,' the woman said. 'Come in. Would you like some chai?' She bustled off into the corner to make some before either of them answered. 'It will be good for you, Makena. You drink too much coffee. It weighs down the soul.'

'From my mother, Auntie,' Makena said. He pulled several parcels from the bag he was carrying, some heavy, some light. There were also some bottles, two litre water bottles refilled with something else. Auntie cooed over each one and lined them up on the floor.

'My mother says I am a worthless son and do not visit my auntie often enough,' Makena said. Auntie smiled and embraced him. Then she gestured with energy. 'Change! I shall have Amos watch your truck,' Auntie said.

There was a groan from one of the occupied bed rolls. Presumably that was Amos. Auntie continued pouring water into a tin from a huge plastic bottle, that could hold forty litres was almost empty. She put the bottle down, put the tin on the little stove, and lit the paraffin with a match. The air around it rapidly took on an oily texture that caught in the throat.

'I won't look,' Jane told Makena.

He turned his back on her as he took off his shiny jacket and started to unbutton his shirt.

Jane had not visited Nairobi in more than a year, and had never been after dark. At three in the morning the air was hot and thick with exhaust fumes and dust. It tasted of oily sweat. It needed laundering. The rains could not come soon enough. What she remembered most from her visits in daylight was the noise. The chattering music of voices mixed with the blast of horns, the drilling and hammering of construction, and the chirping of bicycle bells. Almost a solid thing. At night the noise was different, somehow louder, as if the darkened sky was a ceiling that kept the sound in. There were fewer horns and cycle bells, and no construction noise at all. People were still out in numbers. Happy people, revellers, dressed to attract, to impress, to display. Jane and Makena were entering the wealthy north, the party streets.

They were not dressed to impress. At least not in the same way. Makena had changed into desert fatigues and a cap to match Jane's. He'd even brought similar boots. The only real difference between them was that Jane wasn't wearing sunglasses. Makena had put on a pair of Aviators.

'They're part of the disguise,' he said, in response to Jane's raised eyebrow.

There was one other difference. Makena's uniform was clean and crisp, fresh-laundered. Jane's was dusty and worn, long lived in. She hadn't changed in more than thirty-six hours. Hadn't slept.

'Sure you know where we're going?' Jane said, hitting the horn and startling a group of people who'd stepped into the street without looking. The horn sounded desiccated, like an elderly parrot farting, and the crowd had a unity to it, jeering good-naturedly, waving at Jane. Further down the street was the entrance to a night club, two bouncers the size of boulders flanking the door, two other men in identical snapped-black suits and wearing headsets patrolled the line of young people waiting to go in. The line spilled into the street and became less disciplined further away from the entrance.

'We need to get around this,' Makena said. 'Turn down there,' he indicated an alley between two buildings. 'I love cities. They are so colourful.'

The colours of the city were neon and sodium, bright, changing, unnatural. Jane turned the truck into the alley, and they were plunged into darkness.

'Been to many cities?'

'Just this one. And Mombasa. Go straight across and down there.'

They emerged into another street brighter and with even more people than the last. Jane kept the truck in first gear, edging through the crowds, until they were across the street and into the next alley. Halfway down it a large wheelie bin partially blocked the way. Jane nudged it to one side with the truck's grill.

'Stop here,' Makena said.

'Here?'

'This is the back of his hotel.' He checked his phone. There was a new text. 'He is still in the club. He is quite drunk. He is going nowhere.'

CHAPTER NINE

JANE LED MAKENA IN A WALK AROUND THE ENTIRE BLOCK, drawing closer to the hotel on a second circuit, pushing through a corrugated metal gate at the rear to pass the open door to a laundry room and what, from the smell, was a sleeping kitchen.

The front of the hotel was in the middle of the block on a wide road that ran along the edge of an open market two streets from the main bus station. Opposite was a Catholic bookshop. The road was quiet, only the occasional car. The hubbub of the party streets was a background murmur.

They stopped a little away from the hotel entrance. A man waiting in shadow at a bus stop looked at them then looked away quickly.

'We stand out,' Jane said.

'A uniform is a uniform,' Makena said. He took off his sunglasses and rubbed his eyes with his hands, replaced the glasses. He leaned against the doorway of a photography shop, framed prints of the colours of Kenya displayed handsomely in the window. Jane stood next to him and watched.

The hotel was mid-range. A three-star establishment according to its website, which Makena had open on his phone. Not too expensive in the pecking order of central Nairobi hotels, very expensive for a young ranger. Two months' salary per night.

The building was six storeys tall. From the outside it looked cheap and shabby. The photos of its interior on the website looked stylish and glamorous. There was no doorman.

'We should go in and wait for him,' Makena said.

'No,' Jane said. 'Someone could tip him off.'

'My cousin's friend says he can barely walk!' Makena said, waving his phone.

'There could be someone else. Nathan could be in there. He's older. Not so reckless. Might have stayed in the room.'

'Timu travelled alone.'

'Travelling separately would be a sensible precaution. We wait.'

Makena shrugged.

———

'They're on the way,' Makena said, looking up from his phone.

It was another ten minutes before a taxi bearing the livery of the Delight company pulled up in front of the hotel. Two young women got out first. Similar dresses – figure-hugging, just above the knees, one red, one white – and similar faces, the rounded chins and button noses of Kenyan beauty. One with straightened hair, one with braided. Both giggly and staggering, using the car and each other to avoid falling over.

Then a man. Tight jeans and a baggy football shirt, hair

cropped back to his skull, wide eyes, the start of laughter lines just visible on the edge of his sunglasses. Timu. He was far more the worse for wear than the women. He was trying to pull bills from a pocket to pay the driver. He dropped them. The women in the red dress stumbled after them, Timu almost falling over himself trying to reach for the money and the woman at the same time. He missed both.

Finally, a third woman emerged from the taxi. A purple dress, both looser and shapelier than those of the other two, falling to mid-calf where it swished as she moved. Short hair and a face with the grace and elegance of a fox. She moved with complete surety, glancing once across the street, her eyes stopping when they reached the doorway Jane and Makena stood in, nodding once. She turned to pick up the dropped notes, handing them to the driver, and shepherded Timu and the other two women up the steps into the hotel entrance.

After ten minutes Makena's phone beeped again.

'No one else in the room,' he read.

'Let's go,' she said, and started to cross the street.

'Let me talk,' he said.

She stopped and turned back.

'Why? Because you're a man?'

'Exactly. Not about me, about them. They may be fine, but is it worth taking the chance they're not?'

'That's not my problem,' she said. He held her gaze. 'Alright, you talk.' She turned and finished crossing the road.

Makena caught up to her on the steps. When she opened the hotel front door, he marched through it officiously. She followed, watching.

The lobby was air-conditioned in contrast with the heat outside. There was a reception desk, a porter's station, and several armchairs. Not the highest quality, not the lowest either. No one was in sight.

Makena left his sunglasses on and marched to the reception desk. There was an old-fashioned brass bell on the counter. He rang it, brusquely, twice.

A man came out from a room behind reception. He was dressed in hotel livery and had BENJAMIN embossed on a name badge over his left breast. It wasn't pinned on straight. BENJAMIN looked to be in a bad mood.

'Obote. Which room?' Makena said.

BENJAMIN's face showed signs of conflict. The bad mood was telling him to be rude. Makena's attitude, and the two uniforms, were telling him not to be so silly. Eventually the bad mood lost.

'One moment, sir,' he said, with a forced smile. He typed something on a keyboard concealed by the counter.

'We have no one of that name registered, sir,' he said.

'Just came in with three girls,' Makena said.

'Oh, that, gentleman, sir. He'd lost his key. Three-three-seven, sir. I told him he wasn't allowed guests, that it is a room rate per person. He was rather rude.'

Makena nodded, and turned to the doors marked "Stairs".

BENJAMIN said something else. Makena wasn't listening. Jane marched after him, the way a junior officer would.

'That wasn't the first time you've done that, was it?' she said to Makena moments later, on the stairs to the third floor.

'It was,' he said. 'I have watched a lot of Nollywood movies, so I have the equivalent of much experience.'

———

Gatimu Obote had passed out in an armchair in an "Executive Suite" which included a bedroom, a bathroom, and an armchair. It was the shabby best of the middle of the road. Not a lot for two months' salary.

He still wore the sunglasses, tilted to one side by the lilt of his head. His right hand was curled, as if clutching a bottle. The bottle of Tusker it had been clutching had slipped to the floor and landed on the carpet without falling over in a triumph of physics. His left hand was half in his trouser pocket, clutching a wad of thousand-shilling notes. He was shoeless and shirtless, the items discarded on the floor between the door and the chair. The door to the mini-bar fridge was open. Jane closed it with her foot.

The armchair was in a living area away from the queen-sized bed. On the bed lay the two women in white and red, eyes closed, one of them snoring, making a noise like an insect. The woman in red had unzipped her dress and started to take it off before passing out, lying on her side with her arms above her head.

'He was talking big about what he was going to do to us all when he got us back here,' said the third woman in purple, standing at the window.

'Dhakiya?' Makena said.

'Makena,' Dhakiya said.

'How did you get them asleep so quickly?' Makena said.

'I told them to sit down and count to a hundred, that it was part of the game.'

Jane nodded. She started going through the drawers. All empty. She opened the wardrobe.

Inside hung Timu's ranger clothes, still light with Bandari dust. Had he been wearing them when he watched Douglas die? Had he watched Douglas die? Had he watched Jomo die?

On the floor of the wardrobe were Timu's boots, also coated in Bandari dust, and a bag. Jane dragged the bag out and tipped it out on the bed. The woman in the white groaned, stretched, but didn't open her eyes.

The bag held more clothes. No paperwork, no travel documents, nothing else.

Jane checked the pockets of the fatigues in the wardrobe. Empty except a small, orange feather. Hildebrandt's starling. Common in Laikipia.

Jane checked the cabinets by the bed, ran her hand under the mattress, all round, causing the sleeping women to stir but not rouse. She checked the bathroom. The shower, and a towel, had been used, nothing else.

'Get him up,' she said.

Makena helped her get Timu to his feet. He grunted, eyes opened, glassy and unseeing. She went through his pockets, emptying them, throwing the contents onto the bed. Bills, coins, a phone, a set of keys. That was it.

She let Makena hold the semi-conscious Timu upright whilst she shoved his shirt and shoes in the bag, followed by his phone and keys. She took the thick roll of bills and split it in half. She held out half to Dhakiya.

'Thank you for your help,' she said.

Dhakiya looked at the money and shook her head. Jane looked at Timu. 'I thought she was a friend of your cousin, not your cousin.'

Dhakiya put her hand into a pocket concealed within the folds of her dress and pulled out another, smaller, roll of bills.

'I have taken my share already,' she said.

Makena smiled. Jane nodded.

'We take him with us,' she said.

'Of course,' Makena said, pulling out a cable-tie and pulling Timu's hands behind his back.

For the second time that night Jane raised an eyebrow.

'Nollywood,' Makena said, by way of explanation.

CHAPTER TEN

THEY PUSHED THE STILL SHIRTLESS AND SHOELESS TIMU down the stairs to the lobby and out into the street. His hands secured behind his back, he blinked like a rat in sunlight in the weak lighting. On the way past the reception desk Makena slipped the manager four of the notes they'd found in Timu's pocket.

'For the room, and for the cleaning bill,' he said, meaning "we were never here". The manager nodded curtly.

———

Makena's truck moved relatively smoothly on the tarmacked road now that Jane was driving at a more sedentary pace. They took the A2, the direct route back to Nanyuki. Makena had no more deliveries to make.

Jane looked in her rear-view mirror at the slumped form of Timu. He had barely opened his eyes as they pushed him into the alley and into the parked truck. In the middle of the bench seat in the back of the cab, he'd looked uncomfortable but unconcerned. After the engine had started, he quickly fell asleep, trying to use his own shoulder as a pillow.

'Hey. Kid,' Makena said, loudly.

The only reaction was a guttural muttering.

'How drunk is he?' Jane said.

Makena reached back, grabbed Timu's head with one hand, raised one of his eyelids with the other.

'Very,' Makena said.

'It's going to be a while before he'll be afraid of anything,' she said.

'Or he's so drunk he'll just tell us,' Makena said. 'Depends on what mood he was in when he started drinking. If it was a good one, he will currently love the world and want to be our friend. If he was filled with regret and self-loathing, we will only get a cornered hyena snapping at us.'

'Hey, Timu,' Makena shook the sleeping man by the shoulder. He barely moved. 'Hey,' Makena said again, punctuating the word with a slap to Timu's face. Still no response. Makena sat back in his seat, dropped his shoulders. Jane glanced in the mirror. The young man's eyes were closed, his face peaceful.

Timu had only been on her shift a few months. He was the son of a shopkeeper, but his uncle had a farm where he'd spent a lot of time growing up. He knew the plateau well and was a reasonable tracker. He saw the rhinos as animals, saw the job of protecting Douglas little different to that of protecting a dairy cow. What excited him was the technology, and the prospect of a run in with poachers. He learnt quickly, though, and would have made a fine ranger. Jane had thought he was alright, as much as she liked anybody. He was eighteen.

Makena suddenly leaned into the back with startling

speed and hit Timu's face hard with his right hand, the sound of the slap filling the cab.

'*Amka*,' he said, slapping him again with his open palm, 'wake up!'

Timu Obote opened his eyes and blinked.

'Wha—?' He screwed his eyes up and let his tongue explore his mouth. 'Is there anything to drink?'

'No,' Makena said, voice like a shutting trap.

'Blood-alcohol level. Coaxing might work better,' Jane said. 'I thought you were being good cop?'

Timu's face changed when he heard her voice, but he didn't look at her, he just looked confused, as if trying to remember something.

Makena took a bottle of water from the bag in the cab's rear footwell and poured some of it into Timu's mouth. He swallowed and spluttered.

'No, a *drink*,' he said.

'That's all we have, friend,' Makena said. He tilted the bottle towards Timu's mouth again. Glassy-eyed, he nodded, and drank more.

'You had a good evening,' Makena said, looking straight at Timu's eyes.

'Yeah?'

'Quite a party in that room. Your girl not with you?'

'No?' Evidently Timu hadn't realised this. Or had forgotten.

'No, she wasn't. Why don't you tell me what happened?'

'Who are you?'

'We are your friends,' Makena said.

Timu closed his eyes and seemed to be falling asleep again. Makena shook him.

'Hey, get back here. Tell me what happened yesterday.'

Timu blinked, trying, and failing, to focus on Jane. He settled on a spot on the back of the seat.

'Party. Drinking. Dancing. Music. Girls.'

'Why?'

'Big pay day. For doing nothing. Big pay day for Timu.'

'You must have had to do something,' Jane said. 'No one gives money for doing nothing.'

She was watching him in the rear-view mirror. His face paled. He had realised who she was.

'Jane,' he said.

'What did you do, Timu?'

He didn't answer for what felt like a long time. His face took on the sulk of a teenager who'd been caught by his mother at the liquor cabinet.

'Let them in,' he finally said in a tone of admission. He tried to lie back, to get out of the sight of Jane's eyes in the rear-view mirror, but his cable-tied hands made it difficult. He tried to arrange himself a different way, and Makena pulled him back into the middle of the seat.

'Let who in?' Jane said.

'The man. The big white guy,' Timu said, slurring a little at the edges.

'What was his name?'

'Don't know.'

Makena shook him again.

'Hey! That don't feel good.'

'What was his name?' Jane said again.

'I do not know.' Timu was precise in his enunciation as he breathed in.

'When did you know something was wrong? That they were going to kill Douglas?'

'They killed him? I didn't know they were going to do that.' He was lying, and lying badly.

'Who gave you the money?'

There was fear in Timu's bloodshot eyes now. Conflicted fear.

'It's me you need to be afraid of, not someone who isn't here,' she said.

'Nathan.'

Makena rested his hand on the boy's shoulder, an affectionate gesture, like that of a benevolent uncle. 'Tell us,' he said.

Timu cleared his throat.

'There was a phone call. Nathan took it. We drove to the gate, let in these Land Cruisers, three of them. Led them to the rhino enclosures. Then we drove off, out the main gate, to Nanyuki. Stopped Riff's Bar. He gave me the money, told me to lie low for a few weeks.' Timu spoke with concentration but couldn't avoid slurring some of the words.

'What about Jomo?' Jane said.

'We left him with the rhinos, told him Tony had called for help, there was a problem at the main gate.'

'And he believed you?'

Timu tried to hold her eyes in the mirror for a moment then lowered his gaze.

'Who killed Jomo?' Jane said.

Timu's reaction was different this time.

'Jomo's dead?' he said. His face slowly crumpled, and he started to cry, silent tears at first, then the huge, sucking sobs of one both heartbroken and drunk.

They let him calm down. Let the rolling truck and the sun rising over Kiandutu and Thika soothe and soften. Eventually

Timu tried to wipe his eyes and nose on his shoulder, reacting to his bonds crossly, like a child.

'Who was in the Land Cruisers?' Jane said.

Timu didn't answer for a minute. He was swallowing. Makena handed him the bottle of water. Timu took a drink.

'The big white guy was in the second one, on the back seat. Maybe four others, more, I don't remember.' He put his head in his hands.

'Did you speak to them?'

Timu's face seemed to contract.

'No. Nathan did,' he said.

'Would you recognise them again?'

Timu shrugged and made a choking sound.

Silence filled the cab, and Timu's eyelids, already puffy from alcohol and tears, started to look impossibly heavy.

Makena shook him, dragging him further along the bench by his arm so the cable-tie dug into his wrist. 'Concentrate,' he said.

'Why did you do this?' Jane said.

'The money. I wanted to impress my girl.' Timu was crying now, tears leaking from his eyes, forced out by his fear. 'But I don't know where she is. And the money is gone.'

'This big white guy, what was his name?' Jane said. Timu tried to keep his eyes open. His face contracted as if momentarily electrocuted. 'He's going to throw up.'

Her warning came too late. Timu vomited over Makena's arm.

———

They pulled up next to the wreck of Tony's car in front of Kennet and Naomi's villa about two hours after sunrise. Timu was asleep again. Makena was squirming, unable to sit still whilst he was wearing clothes infused with drying vomit.

Naomi emerged onto the veranda before Jane turned the engine off. Her sister-in-law was dressed and alert, though her eyes were red.

Makena climbed out of the cab and straight away asked if he could use the shower. He grabbed the bag with his suit inside and ran into the ranch.

'You got him,' Naomi said, stepping down to the car. 'What did he say?'

'Little of use,' Jane said, pulling the seat forward to reveal Timu sleeping behind it. 'Where can I put him?'

'Shouldn't you take him to the police?' Naomi said.

'I will, but I want to talk to him sober first. He needs some hours to sleep it off. Somewhere he can't run away from.'

'He looks so young, poor thing,' Naomi said.

'He admitted to letting three Land Cruisers into Bandari. Five or six men, including one "big white guy". Says he and Nathan then left. Didn't know they'd kill Douglas, didn't know they'd kill Jomo.'

'What about Kennet?'

'I didn't get a chance to ask him about Ken. He passed out before we got to that.'

Naomi gripped Jane's arm, her small hand surprisingly strong. Neither looked at the other for a moment.

'Do you believe him?' Naomi said.

'Partially. I believe he didn't arrange it or talk to anyone who arranged it other than Nathan. I need to find Nathan.'

Naomi looked at Timu's sleeping face.

'The old stable on the other side of the mango orchard.

The hitching post inside should be strong enough, if you tie him to it,' Naomi said.

Jane nodded.

'Up you get,' she said, yanking Timu's arm.

––––––

After tying Timu to the hitching post and leaving him sprawled on old straw, Jane joined her sister-in-law for breakfast on the veranda. Naomi had made chai, picked mangoes, put out *mkate*, and even made *mandazi*. The *mandazi* particularly smelled heavenly. The normalcy of the layout and the setting felt surreal against the backdrop of dead loved ones.

Makena joined them shortly afterwards, once more fragrant, and resplendent in his shiny suit.

'I hope you don't mind, I put my uniform in the washing machine,' he said.

'Where did you get that uniform?' Jane said.

'Borrowed it,' he said.

'From a cousin?'

'No, from the Bandari ranger station. Farashuu's mother knows my mother.'

Jane ate. Despite everything she ate. She hadn't eaten properly in two days. *Eat when you can.*

'I have to sleep,' she said, suddenly. Without another word she stood up and walked into the ranch, to a guest bedroom whose en suite bathroom was still fresh with the scent of ablutions. She lay down on the bed and closed her eyes.

––––––

She was woken by voices outside the window. She checked her watch. She'd been asleep nearly six hours.

She left the guest room and walked into the ranch's living room. She stopped just inside the door onto the veranda. One of the voices was Naomi's. The other was Timu's.

They were sitting at the table where they had eaten breakfast. Timu's back was straight, his hands in his lap, his head bowed, like a schoolboy admonished by the teacher. Naomi at ninety degrees to him, talking in a low voice. The rope Jane had used to tie Timu to the hitching post lay on the table in front of him next to the remains of a dish of ugali and rice, as well as a large jug of mango juice nested in a box of ice, and several glasses.

Jane hadn't made any noise, but Naomi noticed her standing in the doorway.

'Jane, you have to hear this,' she said. 'Timu, tell her what you told me.'

Jane walked round the table and took the chair opposite Naomi, so they sat on either side of Timu. Timu looked up. His eyes were bloodshot, his face puffy. He looked sorry. He looked down again.

'When Nathan and I let the men in we went across Bandari and left through the main gate.' He paused.

'Go on,' Naomi said, almost kindly.

'We passed the ranger station.' He swallowed. 'We saw Mister Kennet lying on the ground, by the main building. He wasn't moving.'

Jane didn't have time to process the information.

'Kennet was dead *before* Nathan and Timu let those men in,' Naomi said. 'Someone else was already in the conservancy.'

'Did you see anything else?' Jane asked Timu.

He shook his head.

———

Jane took Timu back to the old stable and retied him to the hitching post. He seemed eager to please, as if he sensed a chance at redemption. Jane ignored his eagerness. He'd offered too little real information.

Makena had joined Naomi at the table on the veranda by the time she got back.

'What does this mean?' Naomi said.

'Start with what we know,' Jane said, taking a seat. 'Someone unlocked the Ndaragwa gate, and the inner conservancy gate, and let in three vehicles, most likely Land Cruisers. Shortly after that Jomo was dead, Douglas was dead and his horn cut off, and Nathan and Timu had disappeared. At about the same time, possibly a little sooner, possibly a little later, someone strangled Kennet by the ranger station.'

She paused to pour herself a glass of mango juice, took a mouthful. It was fresh, chilled, and sweet. It was also spicy. Naomi added chillies.

'What Timu has added to that story is that he and Nathan let the vehicles in, that they were Land Cruisers, that they had five or six men in them, one of who was a big white guy, and that once they had let the men in, they left not knowing they were going to kill Jomo. They drove through the conservancy and out the main gate, seeing Ken lying dead on the ground on the way.'

She took another drink. Makena was listening carefully but didn't look like saying anything. Naomi opened her mouth to speak, then changed her mind.

'This is all consistent and raises at least four questions.

The first, is it too convenient that Timu's story exonerates Nathan and Timu from direct involvement in three deaths? Leaves them guilty only of conspiracy to kill a protected species?

'The second is, if Nathan and Timu didn't know anything about Ken's death why didn't they stop and help him? How did they know he was dead from a moving car?

'The third is, if Timu's story is true in the main points, the men they let in didn't kill Ken, so who did?'

'And the fourth, and biggest, is in a conservancy with more than a hundred rhinos, why did five or six men go to great lengths, including planning, expense, and murder, to kill the one with the smallest horn?'

Makena said nothing. His eyes steady, fixed on the jug of mango juice, as if he was thinking. After a few moments he reached for it and poured himself some. Condensation quickly formed on the glass.

'What do we do now?' Naomi said.

'We have to find Nathan,' Jane said.

'Are there other things we can do?' Makena said.

Jane shrugged.

'Not a lot. Try and work out which three Land Cruisers might have been together at the time.'

'That might prove impossible. There are thousands of them in Kenya,' Makena said. Jane nodded.

'Find someone selling rhino horn, see if they've handled any in or from Kenya in the last twenty-four hours,' she said.

'Easier and harder,' Naomi said. 'There have been no other rhino poaching incidents in the last week within three hundred kilometres, I checked. But if...'

'But if they were after horn to sell why leave all the other rhino alone when the conservancy was effectively unguarded,' Jane finished. 'I know.'

Makena took a mouthful of juice, swallowed, and coughed. His eyes watered, and he wiped his mouth.

'Spicy,' he said.

'We need to find Nathan,' Jane said.

CHAPTER ELEVEN

JANE AWOKE TO THE SOUND OF BOOTS ON WOOD. THE SUN shone through cracks above her, and dust particles floated in the light as the planks vibrated at the impact of footsteps. She was wrapped in a sleeping bag with an outer layer of insulated mesh, against the cold of the Kenyan night and against snakes looking for a place to shelter and mistaking her for a stone. A shadow passed overhead as the owner of the boots walked across the veranda and down the steps.

She listened as the footsteps moved from wood to grass to earth. Keys jangled and a door opened and slammed. An engine started, and a car crunched clumsily into gear. She did not move until the sound of the engine had died away. She looked at the time. 06.32. She'd hidden under the porch of an early riser. She'd been asleep for less than four hours.

She checked for snakes. There were none. She eased out of the sleeping bag and rolled it tightly, packing it into her rucksack. She went to the toilet in a bottle, an awkward manoeuvre in such a confined space. She wiped the funnel with a tissue, sealed the tissue in a plastic bag and put the lid on the bottle tightly. She put both bag and bottle into a second bag and packed it in the rucksack. No smell, no trace. She took out a soft nutrition bar and ate it. She folded the empty wrapper tightly so it couldn't rustle and tucked it in a small plastic pot which went into the rucksack. She took a mouthful of water from a canteen with a plunger. As the water level lowered the plunger stopped it sloshing when moving. All the time she was peering through the gap between the steps she was hiding beneath, watching the house across the street, the house of Nathan Jennings.

She'd left the conservancy with one thought in mind: to find him. Timu did not know who had killed Douglas and Jomo. If Timu had just done what Nathan told him, for the money, Nathan would know. She was going to find him.

She'd returned to her apartment and collected some things. A rucksack, water, rations, and from the space under her floorboards, night vision goggles, portable chargers, and three more motion-sensitive wireless cameras, hi-definition, 4G sim cards, just like the one she'd already hidden in Nathan Jennings' loft. She'd left Makena at Naomi's and left her gun in the Land Rover.

She set two of the three cameras when she arrived, a little before 3am. One at the back of the house and the second in a tree in front of it. The third was still in her pocket. During the night, cars driving past triggered the front camera twice. Nothing had triggered the one at the back or the one in the loft. If Nathan had gone home yesterday, he was still in the house.

She could see the front porch, windows either side of the door, patterned curtains drawn. At 07.30 Saachi opened the curtains of the room to the right, the kitchen where they'd talked. Several minutes later she opened the curtains in the room to the left.

At 08.01 Saachi came out onto the porch with two children and locked the door behind her. The elder, perhaps five or six, was a boy. He was stomping his feet, crossing his arms, balling his fists. From her hide across the street Jane could hear Saachi shouting at him. The younger, perhaps three or four, was a girl, who held tightly onto her mother's hand and said nothing.

Another mother, walking along the edge of the road with three children in tow, passed the Jennings' house. Saachi called out, and the little group stopped. Saachi and the girl joined them, and the six set off. The little boy remained stubbornly on the front porch. Saachi waved for him to follow them and walked out of Jane's line of sight. Through her binoculars Jane could see the confused anger on the little boy's face. This turned to fear as soon as he could no longer see his mother and he ran off after her. Jane stayed where she was.

If Nathan tried to come in or go out through the back of the house the camera trap would send the video to her phone. She disabled the motion detection on the camera watching the road as there were too many people walking by and it was alerting her constantly. Through the feed from that camera, she watched Saachi, the other woman, and the five children turn up another street a hundred metres away.

Saachi came back alone at 08.45. Kindergarten and primary school must be close. A kilometre, assuming half an hour to get there with a three-year-old on foot, fifteen minutes to get back unencumbered. She unlocked the door and disappeared into the house.

At 10.07 the camera trap at the back of the house fired an

alert. It showed Saachi coming out of a side door and hanging washing, children's clothing, on a line before going back inside. Jane had the microphone on the camera turned on and was listening through an earpiece. All she could hear was a breeze pushing the damp clothing.

At 10.53 the camera trap around the back of the house fired another alert. A bird. A collared dove, its white wings flashes of light in the camera's vision. It bobbed across the parched grass for a few moments pecking hopefully, grew bored and flew off.

At 12.00 Jane ate another nutrition bar and packed the wrapper in the plastic tub. She had another mouthful of water and pushed the plunger a little lower, packing the canteen away.

At 12.13 a car turned into the street as Jane was watching the footage from the camera in the tree. It was going more slowly than other vehicles that had passed that morning and slowed even more as it approached. She pressed record.

The car drove in front of the Jennings' house. Inside were three men wearing army battle dress uniform. Two of them watched the house as they passed. A little down the street the car turned around. It pulled up at the side of the road facing the Jennings' residence. The men waited.

At 12.44 one of the men got out of the car, walked away from the Jennings' house, and pissed against the first tree he came to. He returned to the car.

At 12.45 a second man did the same.

At 12.48 the third man followed suit.

They repeated this again an hour later in reverse order. They were big men, army uniforms, soft kepis, the obligatory sunglasses. As conspicuous as a washing machine in the jungle.

At 14.15 Saachi came out of the house again. She locked the door and turned down the road in the direction she'd gone in the morning. She greeted a woman, a different one to her companion of earlier, who was passing on the opposite side of the street. They joined up and walked out of sight together. Jane's phone vibrated and flashed a warning on the screen. Battery low.

Two of the three men got out of the car. Jane watched them on the screen until they came into her field of vision, watched them directly as they walked up to the Jennings' front door with the rigidity of parade grounds. They were army for sure.

They tried the front door, which Saachi had visibly locked not three minutes before. They separated and tried the windows either side of the front door at the same time. Locked. They went around the house, one to each side.

Jane switched to the feed from the camera at the back of the house. Her phone vibrated again. Battery lower. Without taking her eyes from the screen Jane reached for her rucksack and the portable powerpack. The rucksack was easy, though the powerpack was just out of reach. She looked up briefly to find it. When she looked back at the screen one of the men appeared at the back of the house. The other did not. The phone vibrated again.

She plugged it in to the powerpack. The man she could see reacted to something she couldn't hear or see and crossed to the other side of the house, before vanishing too.

She guessed what had happened. They'd found the window she'd seen when she set up the cameras in the early hours of the morning. It had been open four or five centimetres. Frosted glass. Bathroom.

It was 14.25. If Saachi were repeating her morning routine

in reverse, she would be back with the children at 14.59. 34 minutes.

The men did not reappear.

14.29. Jane flicked back to the feed from the camera in the tree. The third soldier was still in the car. He had sunglasses on so she couldn't see his eyes, but from the tilt of his head against the headrest she guessed he might be falling asleep.

She adjusted the sensitivity and field of focus for the camera pointed at the soldier and switched the motion-sensitivity back on. If he moved or got out of the car, she wanted to know without having to watch him. She went back to watching the house.

14.37. A boy in his teens passed on the other side of the street dribbling a battered-looking football. Nothing else had changed. The men were still inside. The one in the car hadn't moved.

14.45. The motion-sensor on the camera in the attic triggered. Jane switched to its feed. The head of one of the two soldiers had appeared at the top of the ladder. It was difficult to see clearly through the gloomy footage, but his nose looked broken, his mouth and chin covered in blood. Jane remembered Saachi's warning about the ladder coming down too quickly.

The soldier started a clumsy search of the attic. It took him about five minutes. He found nothing. He disappeared back down the ladder.

14.52. A movement on the edge of her peripheral vision caught Jane's eye. An old couple, she tall but stooped, he short and chunky but straight-backed, were walking in front of the house Jane hid beneath. She switched to the camera in the tree. As they passed the third soldier in the car, he didn't move. He was asleep. The couple, who were each chattering away without listening to the other at all, didn't give him a second glance.

14.56. In three minutes Saachi Jennings and her two small children would reach their front door. The two soldiers were still inside, and their lookout was asleep. They'd waited until Saachi had left to go in, so it wasn't her they were after. If Saachi surprised them... Jane had seen soldiers hopped up on adrenaline before, seen them overwhelmed by testosterone. You could never predict how any individual would react to it. And they would react. Until you'd experienced it you wouldn't have learned the self-control to respond.

14.59. Saachi and the children, in company with another woman and two children, turned onto the street.

14.59:30 Saachi and the children stopped on the street outside the house as Saachi continued to talk to her walking companion.

'*Anakuja!*' Jane heard it through the camera feed in the attic, though distorted as it was coming from the men on the floor below. She checked the other cameras. Nothing in the back; the lookout was still asleep.

'*Anakuja!*' Jane heard again with more urgency, more of a hiss.

Saachi said goodbye to her companion and went to her front door, children running ahead, racing to the porch.

Saachi unlocked the front door and opened it. The children ran in ahead and she followed. After three seconds, Saachi screamed. The scream was cut off almost immediately. The little boy appeared in the doorway again before a hand grabbed the back of his top and pulled him back inside. The door shut.

CHAPTER TWELVE

JANE NEEDED TO THINK QUICKLY. THE SOLDIERS MIGHT have nothing to do with Douglas and Jomo's death. They might be something to do with Nathan's former life in the army. In fact, that would be more likely. The army wouldn't be looking for Nathan, it would be the police.

She was already moving, irrespective of the conclusion she would come to. Saachi's scream had been a primaeval sound. It could either mean "keep away, there's danger" or "help". Jane knew who was in the house, the woman and two children suddenly missing a father. They weren't dangerous. Saachi was calling for help.

Jane crossed the road at a run. Ran around the side of the house to the bathroom window. It was wide open. She checked her phone for the footage from the camera at the back one last time. It showed nothing unexpected. She listened to the feed from the camera in the attic. But she didn't need to now, as she could hear more clearly through the open window. She took out her earphones, put the phone in her pocket, took the Kubotan in her hand, and climbed through the window.

———

She stepped into a bath. She almost put her foot on a bar of Whitestar but noticed it in time. She froze and listened. Saachi's sobs, pleas for her children, protestations.

'I swear, I don't know where he is.'

She heard the voices of the soldiers. Only regular Kenyan voices. They sounded nervous.

Jane stepped out of the bath, took one stride to the door, put her hand on the handle, visualised the layout of the house in her mind.

The front door opened into the kitchen where she had been the day before yesterday. There were two doors out of there. One, that had remained closed, was a storeroom or pantry, utility or laundry. The other she had been through into the hall to get to the attic. Three doors off the hall, and the trapdoor. This was one of those three doors, the last one on the right.

The voices were coming from the kitchen.

She slowly turned the handle and eased the door open, looking to the left.

The door to the kitchen was half open. One of the soldiers, the one with the broken nose and bloody face, was pacing backwards and forwards in front of Saachi who sat in a chair. Jane couldn't see the children or the other soldier, but from the look on Saachi's face and her repeated attempts to stand up and run forward, the second soldier was to the left, in the corner behind the door holding both children.

Neither soldier had a visible weapon. Jane needed the one

she couldn't see to let go of the children.

She took a slow step, staying in line with the door. She could move to the other side of the hall out of the line of sight of the partly open door. That would allow her to get close with less risk, but she would then need to cross the doorway. She was less likely to be seen in plain sight moving very slowly than moving quickly from one side of a door to the other.

A step at a time. Kubotan in one hand. Saachi might have seen her. Would have seen her if she wasn't so focused on her children.

Jane paused when a board beneath her feet creaked. No one in the kitchen was paying any attention.

She reached the doorway, a metre behind the pacing soldier. She stole a glance through the gap between the door and the frame. The other soldier was holding the little girl behind him with one leg and the little boy in front of him with both arms. The girl was curled in a ball and crying, the boy looked angry and struggled against the soldier's grip.

Good work, little man. Maybe Jane didn't need the soldier to let go of the children.

She waited for the pacing one to pass left to right then stepped forward and punched him just below the ear with the Kubotan. He went down like a sack of yams. She pushed the door closed behind her, revealing herself to the second soldier, and, more importantly, revealing him to her. She span round, following through to drive her fist into the man's face, the Kubotan crunching his nose. He let go of the boy as his hands went to staunch the resulting spurt of blood. The little boy took the opportunity to kick the soldier in the shins twice before Jane pulled both children away and pushed them towards Saachi, flying to embrace them. Jane kicked the second soldier in one ankle and the opposite knee, and he fell to the floor in turn. It was over.

'Did they say who they are?' Jane said.

Saachi shook her head.

The second soldier was still moving. Jane kicked him in the ankle again and knelt to press the tip of the Kubotan into his temple.

'Who are you?' she said.

The man's face was a wreck. The top and bottom of his nose were split, and blood covered the lower half of his face. There was blood in his eyes as well, and he was holding his knee and ankle and gritting his teeth. He tried to open his eyes.

He said something in a dialect Jane didn't recognise.

'Did you understand that?' she said to Saachi without looking at her.

'No,' Saachi said.

'Call the police,' Jane said.

She flipped the conscious soldier over onto his front and forced his arms behind his back. He tried to resist, and when he showed too much strength, she rammed the Kubotan into another soft part of him until he gave up. She bound his hands with two cable-ties from her belt. She did the same to the other one. He was unconscious, but alive. His breathing was rough. There was a growing bruise below his ear where she'd hit him, and his face was masked in dried blood.

She went through their pockets. Took phones, cash, and nothing else. Because they had nothing else. She checked the phones. They were protected by PIN or thumbprint. She used their thumbprints to unlock both phones and set her own PINs.

She photographed them both.

'Did they want anything other than to know where Nathan was?' Jane said.

Saachi shook her head, hugging her children to her as if the three of them were one living thing.

'Heard from him since yesterday?'

Saachi shook her head again. Her face was streaked with tears.

'Thank you,' Jane said, and opened the front door.

'Wait,' Saachi said.

Jane stopped in the doorway.

'They asked if anyone else had been. Been in the attic. Who might have taken something. I told them about the police. And about you. I am sorry.'

'No need to be sorry,' Jane said.

'Who are they?' Saachi said.

'I have no idea,' Jane said, and stepped out into the morning, shutting the door behind her.

She walked across the front of the house, intent on crossing the road and returning to her hiding place. She heard a police siren. She looked up and down the road. The third soldier in the car, was awake and looking at her. He opened the driver's door. Then the siren came again, and he changed his mind. He started the engine and made a phone call.

One of the phones Jane had taken from the soldiers in Saachi's kitchen rang.

Jane took it out of her pocket and answered it.

'*Hujambo*,' she said.

The man in the car said nothing. He held the phone away from him to look at the screen. Then he looked back at Jane, taking off his sunglasses. His eyes widened. He threw the phone on the passenger seat, put the car into gear, and screeched off down the street.

CHAPTER THIRTEEN

Jane left the cameras in place and returned to Kennet and Naomi's villa. On the way she stopped by Dreams. It was closed. She checked her emails to see if there was anything from Legishon about Nathan, Timu, or Riba. There was not. She sent an email to him.

Can we talk?

She parked next to Tony's elephant-wrecked car and checked on Timu. He was still in the old stable, tied up and sleeping peacefully on the musty straw.

Naomi and Makena were in the villa. Makena was pacing the kitchen on a phone call. He'd taken off his shiny suit jacket. The white shirt beneath it looked freshly ironed.

'I understand,' he was saying into the phone, 'yes, it's a lot of work. What would make it worth your while?' He waved to Jane with his free hand.

Naomi was sitting in a large rocking chair in the living room. Its seat reclined at full stretch, an extra section supporting the calves and feet. Its cushions were a patch-work, the original material forgotten, the frays and rips and tears of the years concealed by patches in many colours, from the drab leaf-and-earth, to the resplendent reds and golds of feathers in a mating dance. Ken had loved it, dragging it out onto the veranda as often as not to watch the sunset. Rarely the sunrise. He'd never been a morning person. Naomi was engulfed by it, rocking gently, staring into nothing.

Jane watched her for a while. Naomi showed no sign of acknowledging her presence. A tear rolled down her cheek, glistening in the sunlight as she rocked.

Jane thought of Jomo, of Ken, of Douglas, and felt herself clench. She flexed her muscles and pushed past it. There would be time for that later.

She joined Makena in the kitchen, sitting in a chair at the breakfast table. Makena adjusted the route of his pacing to accommodate. She plugged her phone in to charge. Then she took the phones of the two soldiers from Saachi's house from her pockets and put them on the table in front of her. She took a small notepad from one of the pouches on her belt. It had a short biro attached.

She went through each phone, noting anything that wasn't a default setting. There were only three numbers in the address book of each. One of the three in each case was the number of the other phone. The second was the number of the third soldier – she knew that from his call outside Saachi's house. The third was the same for each phone and had not been called from either phone, not according to the call history.

In fact, the history showed no calls at all for one phone, and only the one received outside Saachi's house for the other.

'Burners,' Makena said. He'd finished his phone call and was now watching her.

'What?'

'Burners. Don't you watch any television? Pay-as-you-go phones with no registered owner used by people who don't want the calls to be traced back to them.'

Jane shrugged and used one of the phones to call the third number. There was silence, then a pleasant voice gave her the recorded Safaricom message that the number had been disconnected. She looked at her watch.

'Three hours since he saw me.'

'Who?'

Jane told Makena about the three soldiers who had come to Saachi's house. Nathan's house. And what had happened to them.

'They've cancelled the phones already?' Makena said.

'Exactly. Unless...'

Jane dialled the other number, the one of the third man in the car. Silence. Then it started to ring.

It rang.

Eventually it went to a pre-recorded Safaricom message telling her to disconnect or try again.

'They didn't disconnect that number. Why?' Makena said.

'In case they want to talk to me?' Jane said. 'Or to find me.' She pulled both phones apart and took out the batteries. She stood up.

'What about Nathan?'

'He hasn't come back. I have cameras on his house. If he comes back, I'll know. And I think Saachi would tell me.'

'What if he doesn't come back?'

'Have your cousins found anything yet?'

'Maybe. I'm checking it out first, making sure it's something.'

'What is it?'

'Possibly nothing.'

She stared at him.

'If it's not nothing you'll know straight away,' he said.

She nodded, turned to leave.

'Where are you going?' he said.

'If they can track these phones, I don't want the last place they were switched on to be here. I'm going to switch them on somewhere a little more interesting.'

'And then what?'

'Then wait for them to come and get them.'

———

As Jane pulled onto the main track that led from Kennet and Naomi's ranch to the C76 her phone rang. The caller ID showed "Tony K." Jane answered.

'Tony,' she said.

'Jane, you have a problem,' he said.

'More than one.'

'Bigger than all those. Can we meet?'

'Sure. I have some errands to run, then I'm going to the ranger station. Eight tonight?'

'See you there.' Tony hung up.

———

Jane returned to her apartment to collect another camera. Once up the steps and inside, the sounds of Nanyuki gave her a strange sense of normality. Shouts in the street, traffic on the main road half a kilometre away, birdsong both wild and domesticated. Amongst the birds she recognised two voices: the strangely hypnotic squeaky call of the Superb Starling, and the incessant crowing of a neighbour's mad cockerel. The cockerel not only crowed to welcome the sun each morning, but kept crowing to welcome everything else, and continued crowing through the day until he was crowing to let everyone know it was time to go to sleep. Not for the first time she imagined strangling him.

She was only inside two minutes. Out again, down the stairs to the car.

'Jane,' a voice behind her. She turned, quickly, ready.

'Mr Kaara,' she relaxed. The man from downstairs. Old and lively, once a tailor, now retired and living on the beneficence of his daughters, who were all also tailors. His wife had died of pneumonia the previous winter. He was sitting on the bench underneath the stairs to her apartment, enjoying the afternoon sun.

'I heard,' he said. 'My sincerest condolences, on this sad day.'

'On this sad day,' she said, quietly, instinctively. 'Thank you, Mr Kaara. That means a lot.'

He looked at her, blinking. The wrinkles of his face always seemed to have a piece of thread tucked in them somewhere. Jane wondered if he put them there on purpose.

'The police, they came looking for you,' he said.

'When?' Jane said.

'An hour ago. They weren't looking friendly,' he said.

Jane frowned, then nodded.

'Thank you, Mr Kaara,' she said. 'You enjoy your day.'

'And you yours,' he said.

———

Jane drove to the Graveyard. She screwed a camera mount to the acacia tree at its centre and fixed the camera to it. Switched it on, checked the feed. A view of the memorial stones and the land rolling away to the south-east, including the approach track. Satisfied, she took the first of the two soldiers' phones out and put the battery back in, switching it on. Once it was booted up, she placed it in the centre of the camera's field of vision. She got back in her Land Rover and armed the camera from her phone.

The next stop was in a small gorge just off the C76. It took her a few minutes to find what she was looking for. Then she lay the phone on the ground next to it and found a bush with a direct view. She attached the camera and checked the feed, adjusting until the phone was centre frame. She replaced the battery, booted the phone up, and very gently slid it into a crack in the rock, taking care not to disturb the delicate structure of the paper wasps' nest above it.

Back in the car she armed the camera.

It was time to go meet Tony. She would be early. Being early was always an advantage.

CHAPTER FOURTEEN

THE RANGER STATION WAS A SINGLE-STOREY WOODEN building in the middle of the reserve at the centre of a cluster of huts and sheds. A mobile transmitter rose from its roof. Other than the string of masts along the C76, this was the last point from which the mobile network could be accessed west of Nanyuki until Ndaragwa a hundred kilometres away. To the east she could see the glow of Nanyuki, and the flashing taillight of a late plane landing at the main airport. Other than that, the only light from the east came from the stars.

Jane had been watching the station for an hour. A lamp was on inside the building, shining through the window at the south end of the structure. That was the office Tony Kanagi claimed for his own, though others used it when he was not there.

The front door opened, and a figure came out. Farashuu. Jane had shouted at her on the radio what seemed like a lifetime ago, though it was less than forty-eight hours. Farashuu walked down the two steps from the veranda and crossed the ground to her small car. The engine started, and she drove off down the road towards the C76, brake lights flashing angrily at one point as she stopped to avoid something that bolted across her path.

Eventually the car disappeared beyond the curve of the earth.

No cars remained near the buildings. Tony's was still in front of Naomi and Kennet's ranch, crippled by elephant damage, so if he was there already, he'd not driven himself.

The night was quiet for a minute or two, but for the dull chug of the building's generator and the casual chirruping of conversational insects. A lion roared in the distance, perhaps five kilometres away. It was a lazy roar, letting you know it was there, not the frantic rage during or after a kill.

Jane was sitting in her vehicle half a kilometre away. She wore a pair of night vision goggles, the eyepieces raised while she looked at the light sources of the ranger station and the town. She was satisfied everything was as it should be. It was only seven-thirty. She waited.

She lowered the eyepieces and scanned the bush. They changed everything, from mostly black with hints of shadow, to greens and yellows, as distinct as day without the help of the sun.

The bush was clumpy in most directions. Flat, lifeless earth for the most part, then every two to three metres a clump. Sometimes it was grass, dry and broken. Sometimes it was a bush, deeper roots, still some life. And sometimes it was a tree, or a cluster of trees. Through the night vision goggles, all were yellow and green.

The insects creaked. A bird called. The trembling trill of the scops owl. Jane wondered if it was one of the pair that nested in Douglas's enclosure. Douglas's old enclosure.

Away to the south something moved quickly, just on the edge of her vision. She turned her head too late. It was gone. It had been small, unlikely to be dangerous. A mongoose or a boar piglet.

She heard an engine. The dazzling brilliance of a pair of headlights approached along the track from the main gate, the track Farashuu had left by. Jane slipped the eyepieces up.

It was a Land Rover. It pulled up in front of the ranger station and stopped. It was a conservancy Land Rover, the rhino logo on the front door reflecting the starlight. Tony Kanagi stepped out and looked around.

Jane got back in her vehicle and started the engine, driving slowly through the bush until she pulled up next to Tony's vehicle.

Tony had climbed the two steps to the veranda that surrounded the ranger station. He was silhouetted against the glow of a naked bulb.

'Jane?' he called.

She took off the night vision goggles and put them on the passenger seat. She got out of the car, leaving the door open.

Overhead she heard the engine of one of the Super Bats as it patrolled the night.

'You're early,' Tony said. 'What have you learned?'

'Nothing,' she said. 'I found Timu. He knows nothing. Nathan is gone. What do you need to tell me?'

'Not here,' he said. 'Inside.' He was looking around as if afraid there were spies in the rocks and bushes.

She followed him into the station, to the control room. The computers were on, the lights representing the animals' tracking collars glowing a life-affirming green.

'The police are looking for you,' he said, in a whisper. 'That's what I needed to tell you. I called the Kenya Wildlife

Service this afternoon, to see if they'd learned anything, and they told me. A witness contacted them, said you were one of those who shot Douglas.'

Jane stared at him in disbelief.

'What witness?'

'They wouldn't say.'

'When did this witness contact them?'

'They wouldn't say that either, though I got the impression it was sometime today.'

'Why would anyone do that?' Jane was thinking out loud.

The creaking siren of a nightjar sounded not too far outside the window, hovering on the background noise of a loud vehicle in the distance.

'I know. It doesn't make sense.'

She paced, thinking. Paused. Drummed her fingers on top of one of the tables. She took out her phone and sent a text.

'I need you to do something for me,' she said.

'What?'

'Timu. I need you to take him to the police. Record his statement first. He says Nathan gave him money to let three Land Cruisers into the inner reserve. The killer was a big white guy. I have a recording of it. If you take a statement as well, they can't say I intimidated him into saying it. Make sure you photograph him before you hand him over. Just in case.'

Tony nodded. He would understand why. To make sure he stayed healthy, have proof he went into custody healthy.

'Where is he?'

'At Ken & Naomi's. Naomi will show you.'

An owl twooted somewhere outside, not a scops owl this time, something bigger. An eagle owl, probably. And she could hear something else. Something new. Was that the sound of another engine, closer than the distant highway?

It was the sound of more than one. She pushed past Tony, rushed outside. Tony followed. She could see headlights coming down the track from the main gate. She turned. A second pair of lights was coming up the track from the southern gate. She ran to the end of the veranda. More headlights were coming from the Ndaragwa gate, and a fourth and fifth set on the track from the inner conservancy.

'Those are trucks, not police cars,' she said, spinning, looking at each pair of headlights in turn, estimating travel speeds and distances, arrival times.

She looked around. There was a fifteen-litre jerry can at the far end of the veranda, half full of water.

She ran to her Land Rover, opened the back, rummaged in a bag, took out a few things. She picked up the night vision goggles from the front seat and put them over her head, kept the eyepieces raised.

Tony watched, motionless with indecision.

Jane ran back to the jerry can and carried it to the generator cage at the side of the building. She used a rock to smash the cage's lock, then poured the water into the fuel tank, the engine, and the alternator. There was a fizzing, a few sparks, and the lights in the ranger station went out.

She pulled the night vision goggles over her eyes.

'What are you doing?' he said looking into the dark at a place where she no longer was.

'Making sure they don't know where we've gone,' she said. He whirled round in the direction of her voice, still not able to see her.

'Shouldn't we wait and find out who they are?' he said.

'They're not friendly,' she said. 'You don't approach from four directions at once if you're friendly. Get in!'

She grabbed his arm and pulled him towards her Land Rover, bundling him into the passenger seat. She jumped into the driver's seat and started the engine, turning slowly and moving off into the night, driving without lights. They headed south east into the conservancy through the bush, weaving between rocks, trees, and bushes. Tony watched the headlights of the trucks behind them, occasionally obscured by trees.

'They've changed direction,' Tony said, after a few minutes. 'I think they're coming straight for us.'

'They know where we are,' she said.

'How could they know that?' Tony said.

Jane looked in the mirrors, and over her shoulder. She turned the wheel, ninety degrees to the direction she had been driving.

'They've changed again,' Tony said after another two minutes. Jane checked the mirrors again.

'They're tracking something. Me? The Land Rover? My phone? Not the phone, I took the mast out, there's no signal. The Land Rover, then? Not good.' She changed direction again, following a gap through the bush in a more southerly direction.

Three pairs of headlights were in pursuit. They weren't gaining, but they weren't falling behind either. She could see them, they couldn't see her.

They seemed to know where she was anyway. They changed direction again.

She knew the land she was crossing. She had studied and memorised satellite photos of it long ago. The land wasn't road, and buried rocks and ditches cut by run-off water during rainy seasons had changed the texture of its surface since the satellite had taken the images, since she'd last walked here. Even with the night vision goggles she couldn't risk going too quickly. As if to emphasis the danger, there was a bang as the left front wheel hit a rock and lost its hubcap. This didn't stop her, but she slowed instinctively.

She needed to get on a track. There she would be able to speed up properly. She was only a few minutes from the southern gate. She turned sharply west, aiming to reach the track to that gate.

There was another loud crack, this time from under her as the left front wheel went into a rut and the chassis hit a rock. Tony was thrown forward and banged his head on the windscreen.

Immediately she knew something was wrong. The car stopped responding to the steering wheel and the engine began thumping. Damage to transmission and axle. Pressing the gas pedal did nothing. She braked and left the engine running. She got out and shut the door. Tony did the same.

'If they are tracking the car, they're going to find it,' he said.

'And if they're not then they're tracking one of us, so we need to split up. Go east and then north, get round them, back to the station. Get your car and get out of here. Find Timu. Record what he has to say.'

Tony nodded. A gesture she wouldn't have seen if it had not been for the goggles. He looked green through them. Behind him the bright flares of the headlights of the pursuing trucks stabbed her eyes.

'Go!' she said.

'Good luck,' he said, and he was off.

She went to the passenger side. Tony had left the door

open. She took her handgun from the glove compartment, checked the clip, though she knew it was full.

She started to run. South west, straight for the southern gate. If she was lucky her pursuers would find the truck pointing due west and assume she had headed that way. Unless they were tracking something other than the truck. How had they known which way she was going? Think!

She found her rhythm, arms and legs punching. *Concentrate on breathing out, watch the ground, don't worry about what's behind you, keep running. Count to sixty, start again, count to sixty, start again.*

After four minutes she saw lights overtaking her. One of the trucks had gone back to the track and was heading for the southern gate. It was going to get there before she did. Had it guessed that was where she was going, or did it know?

She stopped dead. Caught her breath.

Behind her the lights of another truck were visible a long way off. They hadn't found hers yet.

A snort not so far away caused her to tense. There was a footstep, another footstep, a stamp, the sound of teeth on teeth. Just behind her. She walked forward carefully and turned slowly. Not three metres away was a ghostly shape in the green of night vision, its breath a cloud, like smoke from a dragon. It was a zebra. There would be others with it, sleeping standing up in a group. This was one of the sentries. The herds moved in and out of the main conservancy as they roamed the Rift Valley in search of food.

Stupid.

She wasn't in a vehicle anymore. She didn't need to go through a gate. There were gaps in the fences all around the conservancy to let migrating herds through. She'd trigger the motion sensors, but no one could be monitoring them because the ranger station had no power.

She nodded in thanks to the zebra sentry and started running again, heading ninety degrees from the southern gate, towards the first gap in the fences.

She ran through it a few minutes later. She kept running for a minute to put some distance between her and the gap, stopped again.

She worked out where the slight breeze was coming from and set off into it. She ran for five minutes until she reached a shallow gully. She dropped down and listened. She could hear a truck engine. More than one. And shouting.

She looked back the way she had come. The headlights of three trucks were uncomfortably close. Had they seen the motion sensor alert? Could they have restored power to the station that quickly? It didn't seem likely.

She breathed, slowed her breathing. There was another sound, a whoosh, overhead.

Suddenly she understood. When she'd been in the control room and seen the Super Bats were in the air, she'd not seen something else. Something that wasn't there to see. The heavy remote units for the drones weren't in the charging cradles. The bastards were following her with the conservancy's own anti-poaching equipment. She lay back on the ground, breathed, calmed, let the adrenaline subside so she could hear properly. There it was again, the whir of a Super Bat somewhere above her.

Faen. It was a trap.

How had they got the remotes without Farashuu noticing? Or had she noticed? Had she known?

Jane closed her eyes to get her bearings from the map in her mind. This gully ran south east, against the wind. She knew where she was, and where she was going. She set off again at a crouch, following the lower ground, keeping where the trucks couldn't follow. They might know where she was, but if she was on foot and they were on foot, she didn't rate their chances, however many of them there were.

Behind her the shouts had changed. The beams of torches were waving into the sky. She slowed and looked over the edge of the ditch. One of the trucks had stopped half a kilometre away and a line of soldiers were spreading out from it, silhouetted in the beams of the headlights, guns held high and poorly. The other two trucks were moving slowly at each end of the line, headlights on full beam to act as search lights. They were coming towards her in a giant crab-claw. She kept going, quick and low.

After a few more minutes she stopped by a tree to breathe and listen. Lights of trucks and torches were still out there, though some were a little further behind now. The occasional shout sounded, but nothing else disturbed the chirruping of the crickets. Except... a growl in the darkness. A low, lazy growl not far ahead of her.

She froze. The growl was answered by another growl that tailed off into a yawn. Lions. A breath of wind confirmed it. She could smell the meat of fresh dung.

She couldn't keep going forward into a pride of lions. They would be about to start their nightly hunt. And if the soldiers came this way, they'd shoot the lions.

She ran through the map in her mind. She needed to go back the way she'd come and turn east to get around the lions. Worse, to prevent the lions being shot she needed the soldiers to know about her change of direction. Which meant she might get shot.

To get away cleanly she needed one of those trucks. And to disable the others.

That would take too long. She looked back at the torches bobbing her way. She estimated the distances. She had perhaps eight minutes before the soldiers stumbled onto the lions and all hell broke loose.

What could she do in eight minutes? Not a lot with a handgun, a phone with no signal, a Kubotan, and some cable-ties. And whatever she did, if they didn't find her, they'd not stop looking for her, and then they would find the lions anyway.

Jane made a shallow scrape in the earth at the foot of a tree and emptied her pockets and belt into it, covering everything with stones. They might miss it in the dark. She switched off her phone and buried it four metres due east of the rest. All she kept with her was the Kubotan, its metal warmed by her hand.

A more urgent growl came from the dark behind her. The soldiers would hear it soon. She had to move.

She ran towards the nearest waving torch, quickly and quietly, so she'd be as far away from the lions as possible when the shouting started. The men were walking in a bad line with large gaps and she could have slipped through easily, but that wasn't the plan. She needed to be captured to save the lions. She wasn't going to just surrender. At least one of these amateurs was going to have a headache in the morning.

She ran at the holder of the torch as fast as she could and landed a blow with the Kubotan just below his ear. He went rigid before slumping to the ground. The torch fell from his hands and she ducked in to catch it. She hadn't given him a chance to cry out.

She took off her night vision goggles and threw them and

the Kubotan – she had several, though that one had been a favourite - away into the dark. She placed the torch on the ground so its light showed her face and yelled as loudly as she could. She dropped to her knees, put her hands behind her head, and waited.

CHAPTER FIFTEEN

THEY THREW HER INTO THE BACK OF ONE OF THE TRUCKS. She pulled herself to her knees, turned, and leaned against the back of the cab, watching. They hadn't tied her hands. That was a mistake, but it would not have made that much difference. Eight soldiers climbed in the back with her and sat on the benches, four on each side. All were armed. Four had their guns trained on her. The two nearest she could disarm in a heartbeat. The other two would get a shot off before she reached them, assuming the other men in the truck didn't stop her first. She waited.

There was a lot of shouting, barked orders, loud and ill-disciplined conversations into radios with handsets bigger than bricks. She saw the man she had incapacitated carried off on a stretcher towards another truck. One of the stretcher bearers was congratulating him loudly for catching the "rhino-killer" - though the hero was still unconscious.

They'd not even searched her. She needn't have thrown away the Kubotan, though one of the soldiers had a knife with a ten-centimetre blade hanging from his belt. That would do.

A lion roared in the middle-distance.

'Good hunting, sister,' she whispered.

The soldier sitting nearest to her looked as if he was about to speak, but he didn't.

Men got in the cab. The engine started, though the truck didn't move. It sat in the darkness. The light from the cab behind her attracted insects. Something buzzed close to her ear. A cheetah moth fluttered past, its orange and black wings almost blue on the edge of the night. One of the soldiers swatted at it and missed.

Another pair of headlights flashed away to the north, raking the sky unevenly as the vehicle bounced through the bush. Jane could not see the other trucks as they were behind her, but she could hear at least one driving away. The one she was in was waiting for whoever was approaching.

He stepped from the Cruiser with the confidence of a conqueror, chest out, shoulders back, walking as if he had a brush-tailed porcupine shoved backwards up his arse. He was wearing the burgundy beret with crown insignia of a major. He made his walk to the truck last as long as possible as if this would increase his power over her rather than increase the number of his teeth she was planning to knock out when she got him alone.

When he got to the back of the truck the soldiers sat at attention. There were suddenly no guns trained on her. It was all she needed.

Two blows and the soldier to her right was too busy trying to decide whether his leg or his stomach was causing him the most pain to notice she was now holding his rifle. But she froze before she raised it. With remarkable reflexes the major had pulled out a pistol and was pointing it straight at her. In the confines of a corridor of soldiers in the back of a truck no one would miss. She slowly handed the rifle to the soldier to her left.

'Tut, tut, tut,' the major said. 'You are a prisoner of the Kenyan Rifles. There is no escaping. Bind her,' he ordered two of the soldiers.

She put her hands in front of her, but they turned her round and tied them behind her.

'And her feet,' the major said.

All of his teeth.

Sitting down again was far less pleasant. Not only could the soldiers not tie knots, they did it very uncomfortably.

Another officer, a captain, strolled up to the major and said something to him quietly.

The major laughed.

'No, my friend. She is to stand trial. Justice will be done by the courts. Let the magistrates judge her,' he said.

The Captain said something else Jane could not hear.

'Put her in solitary. Tomorrow we will take her to the police,' the major replied. The tone of his voice changed from warmth to ice. 'And the killer will find justice,' he added, looking straight at Jane.

The captain walked away, and the major slapped the side of the truck twice. It started to move. Jane watched him, memorising his face as he diminished behind them, standing alone in the shallow pool of light cast by the cruiser, an increasingly small piece of flotsam on an ocean of night.

————

She'd driven past the barracks several times on her way to Ol Faraja, a wildlife conservancy north of Nanyuki. She'd never imagined it held such salubrious accommodation.

The solitary cell was only a metre and a half square. It wasn't big enough for her to lie down straight, which was the point. The floor was concrete, and she hit it hard with her shoulder as one of the soldiers shoved her inside. There was quite a collection of rat droppings a few centimetres from her nose. She sat up as best she could, given her bonds. There wasn't much of the night left so she wouldn't have to keep herself awake too long.

The door slammed behind her and a key turned in the lock. Several sets of footsteps walked away, carrying chatter and conversation with them. Another door shut, and she heard nothing.

For the next three minutes she freed herself of the ropes round her wrists and ankles.

She was expecting visitors. Other than a bit of rough-handling and a poorly aimed punch to the stomach, none of the soldiers had touched her. Maybe they were nice boys who didn't hit women. Or maybe they'd been ordered to leave her alone. If the latter, they'd come later that night after alcohol when it would be easier to pretend orders mean nothing. And it had to be the latter. Nice boys, or girls, didn't last long in any army.

She had two things in her favour. The cell was so small they could only come at her two at a time. And she had some rope. She had split the original two lengths into six and spliced each into a small, double-ended lassoes. It is very difficult to fight in a confined space with one hand attached to someone else's.

She settled down to wait, back against the wall, face to the door, listening.

The barracks were very quiet. Occasionally she heard a door open and close, boots on packed earth, an order given and received.

But they never came. She'd slept for nine hours in the last eighty.

———

Dawn arrived quickly, but it was still two hours before she heard the outer door open and footsteps coming in her direction. Three sets. She got to her feet.

A key hit the lock and turned. The door opened. Two soldiers had guns out and pointed at her. The third had a pair of handcuffs. She heard a fourth person moving further down the corridor.

'Hands!' ordered one of the men with the guns. A corporal.

'Easy, sergeant,' she said to the soldier with the handcuffs. But she offered him her wrists. He motioned for her to turn around. She did, and he cuffed her hands behind her back. They didn't seem surprised her hands were no longer bound. Perhaps they didn't know they had been.

She was marched out of the detention block and into a parade ground where a truck was waiting. There were six soldiers in the back of it, and two more in the cab. The major who had spoken to her the previous night was watching from the other side of the ground.

Two of the soldiers lifted her into the truck and shoved her against the back of the cab. She left the barracks the same way she had entered them.

The road to Nanyuki passed within sight of the ranch she'd been sent to two days before, the one with the remains of a fire, half a bottle of Tusker, and the cat with a dead rat.

There was no smoke rising above the ranch today.

Four days ago, Kennet had still been alive.

Kennet. Douglas. Jomo.

Someone was setting her up. Was it part of the plan of the big white guy Timu had seen in the Land Cruiser? Or was it someone she knew? Could it be someone she knew? No one she knew had the money to pay off Timu and Nathan, or to bribe the police, let alone the army. She only knew rangers. And poachers, but she never knew poachers for long.

What mattered was finding Douglas's killer. And Nathan was the person who would help her do that. She'd find him and send that major to the dentist another time.

The truck joined the C76 and headed to Nanyuki.

———

Jane was pulled out of the truck and pushed towards the police station by one soldier, flanked by two others, their rifles held ready. She must have convinced them she was dangerous.

The first time she'd been here, three years ago, she'd brought a group of poachers caught in the north after tracking them for five days. There'd been four of them, semi-professional, in it for themselves, but insufficiently funded to be properly armed. That group three years ago had given their presence away by shooting at, and missing, an elephant within sight of a Jeep-load of tourists. The elephants had stampeded, giving the tourists some impressive photos. Timu had shown them to her months later on some social media site. The driver of the Jeep had radioed it in, and the chase had begun.

She'd not been long in Kenya at the time. She remembered picking up the trail, leaving the Land Rovers and setting off on foot through the bush. Of the two men with her, one hadn't been able to keep up. The other had and they'd caught up with and disarmed the poachers with ease. She'd roped them up, led them back to the cars, driven them to this police station, and handed them over to the desk sergeant, a significantly overweight man, like the stereotype of a Zulu king on a throne bought from Ikea. The would-be poachers had been freed with a fine within a week. Attempting to kill an animal wasn't seen as much of a crime back then.

The soldier holding her arm pushed the station door open. The first thing she saw was the desk sergeant. Same man, in the same chair. But he'd lost weight. A lot of weight.

'You look good, Sergeant,' she said.

'Hardly. Alcohol allergy. On a special diet. Doctor's orders. Wife's bloody beaming.'

'Sorry to hear that.'

'Specifics,' the sergeant said, pushing a clipboard and a cracked biro towards the lead soldier. The soldier started to fill in the form. The sergeant swivelled a little on his chair, to face Jane straight on.

'Gamekeeper turned poacher, is that how you say it?' he laughed. 'We don't get many poachers as pretty as you, girl.' His leer was awful. Not that it inspired awe, that it was a bad leer, as though he'd never tried one before. Either he had wanted to say something like that every time he'd seen her previously, or he was putting on a show. She found herself imagining splitting his lip open with something heavy. It didn't fit. She didn't want to do it. Benefit of the doubt. He was putting on a show. He didn't want to show any sympathy towards her in front of the army.

'You don't get out much,' she replied. The sergeant smiled with his eyes, as if to say, *it's ok, I don't believe them.*

Two policemen led her through to the cells. The soldiers stayed with her all the way, until the heavy door shut and locked behind her. This cell at least had something you could call a bed. As soon as she was sure she wasn't watched, she slipped her legs through her cuffed hands in a trick they'd taught her in training. She remembered the day she'd learnt it, in a wooden shack on the edge of a fjord a decade and more back. She looked around for something to pick the handcuffs with. Nothing. She sat on the bunk. No mattress, just a thin blanket.

CHAPTER SIXTEEN

NAIROBI. LANG'ATA MAXIMUM-SECURITY PRISON. TWENTY-four hours after the army left her at Nanyuki police station Jane arrived at the securest facility in Kenya in the back of a van. Two female police officers sat opposite; two male officers sat in the cab. Her hands were both cuffed and tied with a nylon restraint. Overkill but effective. During the journey to western Nairobi nothing was said. If she had not been told where they were going, she would not have known. There were no windows in the van, no opportunities to see landmarks.

The van slowed, indicated, stopped, its engine idling. She heard voices, a request for identification. It started moving again but at walking pace, before stopping again. The engine was switched off. The driver's face appeared at the grille between the cab and the back, said two words she didn't catch. The panel closed again, the front doors opened and slammed, the back doors opened. One of the female police officers motioned Jane out.

It was night, though bright white spotlights made it like

day. They were in a fenced yard. Watch towers with armed guards stood at three corners. A welcoming committee of female prison guards was waiting, three of them, grim-faced, their hands on the handles of their batons. The police held out a clipboard. One of the guards signed it. Jane was handed over and the police left.

Lang'ata was laid out like a prisoner-of-war camp. Rows of identical single-storey buildings separated by fences and gates, two-storey guard towers with floodlights on all sides scattered throughout. Lots of guards, lots of guns. Lots of shadows.

Jane was led into a building slightly larger than the others. The handcuffs and cable-tie were removed, and she was told to strip. She was showered, searched, and examined by a doctor. She was given what looked like a pair of striped pyjamas and an orange tank-top and told to put them on. A guard handcuffed her again, and led her out of the processing block, through the maze of fences and gates, into block K.

Inside, block K was lit by fluorescent tubes. It was open plan but for a control booth inside the only door, and the cages. Each cell was a cage with a metre between them on all sides. In each cage were two low cot beds to either side, little more than planks. A lidless steel toilet and sink opposite the door, and between four and six women to a cell. Most of the women lay on the floor.

Jane saw eyes on her as she was led to a cage halfway down the block. One guard barked at the four women inside to move against the back bars. The second unlocked Jane's handcuffs. The third held two cans of pepper spray – liquid chilli concentrate in a can – one in each hand: one pointed at Jane, one into the cell. The first guard shouted to the control booth and the cage door was unlocked, swinging open under its own weight. Jane was handed a thin grey blanket and pushed inside before the door was locked behind her.

The guards marched off, their boots smacking the concrete floor like hammers.

Jane remained standing. She tensed herself for confrontation. But none came.

The four women she'd been put in the cage with looked tired, drained, as if it were the end of a long and exhausting day.

'You want a bed?' one of them said.

Jane shook her head.

'They're as uncomfortable as the floor anyway,' the woman said. But she lay on one, one of the other women took the other, and the remaining two lay on the floor parallel to the beds.

'What time is it?' Jane said to the woman who had spoken to her.

The woman shrugged.

'Past lights out,' she said.

Jane looked at the lights suspended on wires directly from the roof beams. They weren't that bright, but half of them were still on. It would be difficult to sleep in here if it never got any darker. Which meant most of the women would be easily woken. Getting out at night was going to have its challenges.

'*Lala chini*!' a voice said through a loudspeaker. One of the other women tugged at the legs of Jane's striped trousers, urging her to the floor. Jane took one last look around her, taking in the guard in the booth at the end, the rows of cages, the concrete floor, and lay down at right angles to the other four women. She stared at the lights.

Jane was awake in an instant. She'd been dreaming she was with Kennet and Naomi whilst Naomi looked after Uzuri as she gave birth. Uzuri, Douglas's granddaughter. Uzuri, one of the only two northern white rhinos left on earth. Uzuri, who would never give birth, who would watch her mother, Neema, die, who would one day be the last of her species, and then, nothing.

What woke her was a rattling racket, like a metal spoon on a soup tin, which is what it turned out to be. One of the guards was walking down the corridors between the cages, banging away.

'Good morning, ladies, wake up. Today is shower day in the wonderful world of the block K holiday camp, so let's go, let's go.'

Many of the inmates were greeting the guard with surprisingly friendly sounding 'Good morning, Officer Chepkemoi.'

Despite lying on a concrete floor, Jane realised she'd just been woken from the first decent sleep she'd had since Kennet died. Better than the previous night at the police station where the footsteps of cockroaches had kept her awake.

'Good morning,' said the woman who had offered Jane the plank bed the night before.

'Good morning,' Jane said. The woman was probably in her fifties, weathered skin, twists of grey in her dark brown hair. She had the age lines and wrinkles of someone who smiled a lot, and the callused hands of someone who worked in fields and with weaving and wood. What was she doing in here?

'I am Florence,' she said, standing up and offering her hand.

'Jane,' Jane said, rising to shake.

Two of the other women in the cage joined them. Esther and Rose. Jane shook each hand, looking at their eyes as she did so. She sensed no malice in them, no concealed intent. She looked at the remaining woman, who wouldn't meet her eye.

'That's Angweng,' Florence said. 'She'll get used to you.'

The cages were being opened in groups of three or four, depending on how many women were in each one. Two guards led those inmates out of the block before returning five minutes later for the next. Jane and her cage mates got in line and were led out, through the rows of huts, and into a shower block where they took off what they were wearing, showered, dried on towels as soft as sandpaper, and were given clean clothes.

The next stop was a similar march to a mess hall where a simple but surprisingly edible breakfast of ugali and irio was dolloped onto tin trays to be eaten with wooden sporks.

'What are you learning today?' Esther asked Florence over a spork-full of mashed beans and potatoes.

'Compiling,' Florence said, her mouth full.

'What is that?'

'Taking what we've written and turning it into a programme. Testing to see if it compiles, and to see if it runs.'

'You're learning computer programming?' Jane interrupted, unable to conceal the surprise in her voice.

'Three days a week,' said Florence.

'She's good at it,' said Esther. She took another mouthful. 'And I'm learning baking and how to run a cake shop. What classes will you go to?'

Jane shrugged. The world locked out and the opportunity to learn something new. In some ways, this would suit her. If she wasn't already planning her escape.

———

But "maximum security" turned out to be thorough, and within two days Jane came to the conclusion that the only way she was escaping was with help from outside.

The first visiting slot she was given was two days after her arrival at Lang'ata. At breakfast she was told she would have a visitor. Later in the morning whilst she was at her wood-working class, a craft for which she had minimal skill, she was interrupted by two guards. They led her to the gate between the workshops and the main compound, handcuffed her, then escorted her through two fences and two other gates to the visitors' block.

Individual cubicles were set up, separating prisoner from outsider with two sheets of mesh fifteen centimetres apart. Two guards, one with the prisoner, one with the visitor, were present. Naomi was waiting for her and stood up as she came in.

They could not touch, but they pressed their right hands together separated by the mesh and the gap between.

'Sit down,' one of the guards said. 'Fifteen minutes,' she added. There was a large clock on the wall. The hands were at precisely ten forty-five.

They sat. Naomi had tears in her eyes.

'How are you, little sister?' she said, her voice close to breaking. That was what Kennet used to call her. Jane felt her throat swell. She heard his voice repeat the words in her head.

'I'm good. Really. It's not so bad here,' Jane said.

'How can you say that? In a prison with murderers and psychopaths.'

'No psychopaths. A couple of murderers. But most of them were convicted for the illegal distillation of alcohol. They're just people. It's more civilised in here than in politics.'

'Are you alright?' Naomi dried her eyes on a handkerchief.

'You already asked me that,' Jane said. 'I am alright. I've been in worse places, believe me. In some way I feel safer here than I do outside. I can sleep.' It was true. Despite the eternal fluorescent lighting, the changing of the guards, the noise of nearly a hundred other women snoring and coughing, and sleeping on a blanket on a concrete floor, that first night had not been unusual. She slept more deeply in that cage than she had in a long time.

'What's happening?' Jane prompted. As she said it, she knew she should have said "How are you?".

'There's going to be a trial,' Naomi said. 'Some major in the Kenya Rifles, he's adamant you killed Douglas and paid off Nathan and Timu. I got in touch with a lawyer, but he says you can see the bruising on Timu's face in the video you took of him saying Nathan paid him, which backs up the major's story you intimidated him into making his confession.' Jane thought back to the slap Makena had given the boy in the back of the cab. Had that caused bruising? She didn't think so. 'Then he said it doesn't matter anyway. Told me he wouldn't let me waste my money. What matters is who paid who, and he heard someone's bribed the magistrate, so evidence is irrelevant.'

'Isn't that expensive?'

'Not compared to rhino horn.'

Jane was silent for a moment, processing.

'At least the lawyer didn't take your money.'

'No,' Naomi said, swallowing, as if trying to clear a bad taste.

'What?'

'He... suggested other things he would... take from me instead of money.' Naomi looked down at the ground.

'Ah. What did you do?'

'Made him another chai and put laxative in it,' Naomi said, looking up with a flash of ferocity.

Jane nodded. Part of her brain was telling her this was worth a smile, but she couldn't find one.

'Ten minutes,' said the guard.

'What else?' Jane said.

'Makena said to tell you he has found someone you would like to talk to. He'll tell you more when he sees you.' Naomi looked with subtlety, but pointedly, at the guard. Jane nodded.

'I'll talk to him soon,' she said, as casually as if she were talking about the weather. 'Has a trial date been set?'

'Yes, Monday.'

'That's quick.' Jane thought for a moment. 'Can you go to the Norwegian Embassy? Get them involved. Tell them a miscarriage of justice has been bought against a Norwegian citizen. Tell them who I am.'

Naomi nodded.

'Go today, straight from here. Don't let them tell you they are too busy, or that you have to wait. Will you do that?'

'Of course. Of course. I don't know why I hadn't thought of it already. Stupid of me.'

Naomi seemed to change from being upset to being angry with herself. That was better.

'Five minutes,' the guard said.

'And two other things I need you to do for me,' Jane continued.

'Of course, Jane.'

'I need you to go to my apartment. On the right-hand side of the fridge at the bottom is a sticker that looks like a serial number. Ignore the letters and the rest of it is a phone number. Call it. Leave a message saying Jannike Havn is planning a surprise party. OK?'

Naomi nodded.

'What's the second thing?' she said.

'I need you to get hold of an up-to-date book on Java computer programming and send it to this prison for prisoner Florence Subati.' Jane spelled the surname. 'She's studying for the qualification and the books in the library here are a few years old.'

'Java?'

'Like the place the Javanese rhino comes from. It's a programming language, apparently.'

'Who is Florence?'

'One of my cell mates.'

'In for distilling alcohol?'

'No, in for stabbing her boyfriend to death with a pair of flower scissors.'

Naomi sat back.

'You want me to buy a book on programming so a murderer can get a qualification.'

'From what she's told me about her boyfriend, she should get a medal. But a book will do.'

'OK, Jane, I will. Consulate, bookshop, phone call.' She put her hand on the mesh as the minute hand moved closer to eleven. Jane did the same, two sheets of mesh and fifteen centimetres of space separating them.

'Don't do anything silly.' Jane said in reply. They stood up. They looked at each other for a moment. Naomi turned away to hide her tears.

The guard took Jane's arm and led her out of the room before either could say anything else.

As she was being led back to the workshop Jane realised she had never asked how Naomi was, despite thinking she should do so. And they hadn't talked about Kennet or Jomo, or funeral arrangements. She balled her hands into fists.

———

Back in woodworking class, Jane messed up another piece of the chair she was making. She couldn't judge the angle right and kept shaving off too much. It was so frustrating. She could stick her pocketknife into a human body in sixty different places, many of them designed to miss vital organs by millimetres, with absolute accuracy every time. But she couldn't shape a chair leg. It was just practice. And she wasn't going to let the concept of chair legs win. When she got out of here, and found who killed Douglas, and who killed Jomo, and who killed Kennet, and dealt with all of them, she was going to make a chair she was proud of.

'Who was your visitor?' said the woman next to her. Angweng, the fourth woman she shared a cell with who hadn't said a word to her before now.

'My sister-in-law,' Jane said.

'Why does your brother not come?'

'He is dead,' Jane said.

Angweng kept working, turning, shaping, smoothing a bowl she was making.

'I had four sisters,' said Angweng after a while, 'two are dead.'

'I am sorry,' Jane said.

'It was not your fault, so I cannot thank you,' Angweng said with what might have been a smile. 'They were cruel to me.'

They worked on the wood for a little more time.

'*Faen!*' Jane said in frustration. This chair would only bear the weight of ghosts by the time she was done.

'You work too angry. Let the wood tell you how it wants to be.'

Jane stopped herself asking "how can wood talk to you?" and breathed.

'Show me how to listen to the wood,' she said instead.

Angweng took the emerging chair leg and wood chisel from Jane and picked up a piece of fibreglass.

'Ease the shape out of it. Follow the grain.' Angweng's hands worked the fibreglass over the wood with the gentleness of a lover, and Jane saw.

'Thank you,' Jane said. Angweng handed the chair leg back.

'What did your friend say? You are not convicted, yet you are here. That is unusual. Someone has paid. They won't get you out.'

'She said there's a lawyer, but he hasn't been to see me.'

'He won't if you will be convicted. Why would he bother?'

'Because he's been paid to defend me?'

'Here, it is not the lawyers you pay, it is the magistrates, the judges. Most people can't afford a lawyer. They say you killed a rhino. It doesn't matter if you killed a rhino, it matters if someone paid a magistrate to make it so you killed a rhino.'

'What did they say you did?'

'That I poisoned someone I never meet. At the trial the prosecutor didn't say anything other than this man dead, he died of poison, I gave him the poison. The judge said ok.'

'That's not right,' Jane said.

'That's justice,' Angweng said, and lapsed into silence, smoothing her bowl.

Jane watched. She willed Naomi to make that phone call as soon as possible.

CHAPTER SEVENTEEN

Jane was led into the courtroom with her hands cuffed behind her. Metal cuffs with a long, heavy chain. When they reached the dock, one of the guards unlocked a wrist, moved the chain in front of Jane, and re-attached the cuff to a hoop set into the metal table in front of a thin metal chair. Both were bolted to the floor. He checked the other cuff was secure on her wrist, and as he did so he slipped a small piece of folded paper into her hand without looking at her face. He barked at her to sit. She concealed the paper between two fingers and sat.

She'd been in Lang'ata less than a week, but it felt like longer. Her need to act, to hunt down Nathan, to find the killers, was gnawing at her, racing around her brain like a caged animal. She had to let it out. She had to get out.

But the prison discipline and routine had provided some respite, like a refresher course in the army. She'd recharged. She'd used the exercise yard to stretch her muscles. She'd used the confines of the cell to remind herself how to stay still, how to focus. She felt unthreatened and continued to sleep better than she had in a long time even though she slept on a concrete floor in a cage under fluorescent lights in full view of a hundred other women.

And she'd learned how to listen to the wood.

The courtroom smelled of new wood and old sweat. It had a high ceiling but was only a single storey. The dais on which the magistrates would sit was raised above the floor by half a metre, everything else was on the same level. No balcony. The background murmur of voices grew as more people entered. The air was warm and churned up by four large suspended fans. The closest one squeaked as it turned.

There was no jury in this trial, just three magistrates who were yet to arrive. The room was almost full. The defence and prosecution were set up on opposite sides of a central aisle like a bride and groom. After the lawyer Naomi had tried to engage had refused her money and left clutching his bowels, the court had appointed another. He had visited Jane yesterday. A young lad, just out of university, whose enthusiasm in no way made up for his lack of understanding of Kenyan law.

Naomi sat in a section towards the back reserved for "guests" and gave a little wave and a brave smile when she caught Jane's eye. Next to Naomi was a woman in a smart suit, with straight hair in a ponytail, and Scandinavian features, fine cheekbones, and an accurate nose. Jane assumed she was from the Norwegian Embassy. Tony Kanagi, in dark-green jungle fatigues as if he'd just come from the conservancy during rainy season, was seated a few rows behind the prosecutor's desk and watching Jane, his face betraying nothing. He nodded when he saw her looking at him.

And right at the back of the court, several rows behind Naomi, was a woman Jane recognised. An old colleague. A friend.

They were here.

Jane pressed together the two fingers that held the paper she had been handed. She breathed.

Most of the others in the guest section looked like reporters, a greedy pack waiting for easy prey. Naomi had told Jane Douglas's death had made the international press, and that Jane herself was generating huge amounts of hysterical interest. Norwegian, ex-army, female, accused of poaching the last male of a species, an animal she was paid to protect. It had prompted all flavours of outrage from those who had decided she was guilty and those who had decided she was being set up.

No phones or cameras were allowed in the courtroom, but notebooks and pens were in many hands. Jane wondered how much of the story of the trial had already been written. In her orange tank-top and striped prison uniform she felt she was a prop on a stage, the performance about to start.

There was a curtain-raising hush as the clerk of the court announced the magistrates. Jane's defence lawyer failed to stand and had to be reminded.

The magistrates walked in through a door at the front, three men, two tall and fat, one short and slim, two of them with army uniforms under their robes. Jane could predict the ending based on that alone. Her accuser was in the army. The army controlled this. She was going to be found guilty.

The magistrates walked to their seats on the dais, seats that rose like the thrones of kings. Each stopped in front of their allotted position, turned to face the room, and sat in formal order. The central and most senior magistrate, one of the two in an army uniform, sat last. At a bark from the clerk, the rest of the people in the room sat, and the trial began.

'The accused shot and killed a rhinoceros on the Bandari conservancy near Nanyuki on the eighteenth of this month. She removed his horn, presumably to sell on the black market, where it is more valuable than gold,' the prosecutor opened. No "this court shall prove", just assertion of fiction as fact. 'The rhinoceros, who was known as Douglas, was a particularly valuable animal as he was the last male of the northern white subspecies, and as such a strong draw for tourists.

'The accused also shot and killed an employee of the conservancy, Jomo Zimurinda, as he tried to protect the rhino. The accused is further suspected of involvement in the death of her brother, Kennet Haven, who is likely to have been killed by her accomplices.'

The prosecutor was a man so well-groomed Jane could almost feel the warmth left by the trouser press. His suit was immaculate. His shirt had the smoothest surface possible. The knot of his tie was symmetrically perfect.

Jane's defence lawyer was picking his nose and didn't seem to be paying much attention. He'd looked young in the prison visiting room, but in the courtroom and in a suit he looked like a child at a wedding. He had been picked to lose this case.

'Objection: speculation only,' her defence suddenly said.

The court went quiet, and the prosecutor stared at his opposite number in disbelief. The senior magistrate looked at the young defender coldly, then nodded to the prosecutor to continue.

'The accused is a blood-thirsty killer, having been in the army and served in Chad, Mali and Afghanistan,' said the prosecutor with oiled words.

'Objection: a statement of opinion only,' parried Jane's defence, as if sparked into life by something. 'The deployment to Chad was to drill wells and that to Mali was to provide security during the construction of a field hospital built to treat civilian victims of the civil war.' In truth, Jane had never been to either Chad or Mali, those elements of her service record being fabrications to conceal missions of more sensitive natures. But she was more interested in where he'd got the information from. She'd not discussed it with him.

She noticed Naomi was smiling, and the woman Jane had assumed was from the Norwegian embassy was looking grim but on the verge of satisfaction.

'The accused had opportunity as she was on duty at the time the animal was killed, and the two other rangers on that shift have not been seen since,' said the prosecutor.

'We have a witness who says the accused was nearly twenty kilometres away during the window the crime occurred,' said her defence schoolboy.

The lead magistrate was doing his best not to look furious. The prosecutor was bemused. This was not following somebody's script.

The prosecution rolled out several witnesses. Jane had never seen any of them before. They held minor positions in significant departments, or significant positions in minor departments, in the central government, and one of them even in the Kenya Wildlife Service. None of them had been to Bandari. They were simply there as men of "good character" offering their opinion. The way the world had been for centuries. Though not like this, not like this around here.

Time dripped by, like water from a leaf in the moments after the last downpour of rainy season. The chair she sat on had started out uncomfortable and went rapidly downhill from there. She ached through her flesh, her muscles, her bones. Her whole lower body was in the wrong place between sore and numb. She longed to run.

The woman she knew from her old life stood up, made her way along the row of seats, her "excuse me" inaudible at this distance. At the end of the row, she turned and left the court, but another old face came in through the door as the other left. She took the same seat. She stared at Jane with a slightly raised eyebrow, as if to say, "what do you think you're playing at, Marple?"

Jane wasn't sure where Marple had come from. She'd forgotten that's what the woman staring at her called her. It had been years, hadn't it? Five? More? Years since anyone had called her that.

The witness on the stand on the other side of the magistrates' dais was dismissed. He was a whiskery man, his face slightly ovoid, not unlike a vlei rat, though without the charm. Jane liked rats. She thought they got a bad press. She far preferred to be thinking about them than about the type of people processing through the witness box. Principles exchanged for money. And what did they exchange the money for? Nothing worth a soul.

Whiskery not-rat turned out to be the last witness for the prosecution. Her work-experience lawyer stood up in his ill-fitting suit – either he had borrowed it for the occasion, or he was hoping to grow into it – and called his only witness. Gatimu Obote.

Timu.

Jane had known him for two years, and in all that time

only seen him in his work dress. Khaki pants and a green t-shirt for the first eighteen months, transitioning to the fatigues of a ranger for this season. Until a few days ago. She had the image of him passed out in the armchair in the hotel, shirtless, the bottle of Tusker he'd been drinking standing unspilled on the carpet where he had dropped it, his hand clutched in the shape of its memory. He'd been so inebriated he had barely been able to stand. She and Makena had had to hold him up as they guided him down the stairs. She remembered the hot, greasy feel of his skin after a night of nightclubs and alcohol. She remembered the smell of him, as if he hadn't washed for days, the smell of mistake layered on mistake.

He walked into the court with the swagger of a car salesman. He was clean and bright, his eyes sparkled, his suit was well cut. She would not have recognised him if his name hadn't been read out by the clerk. He seemed like a different person, sober as a judge, suited and booted, and primed to tell his story.

Timu told the absolute truth with wide-eyed innocence. Jane wasn't there when they let in the men in the Land Cruisers. Timu didn't see them all, but he thought the guy in charge was a large white man. Nathan Jennings gave him the money in Nanyuki that evening. He hadn't seen or spoken to Nathan Jennings since.

The prosecution lawyer stood up.

'You have worked with Jane Haven for some time, have you not?'

'Yes, sir,' said Timu.

'Is she open and friendly?'

Timu looked confused. He took his time answering.

'Well, she...'

'Let me put it another way, Mr Obote. Does she have secrets?'

'Objection!' said the defence teenager, jumping to his feet. One of the magistrates waved him down again.

'I think she can be secretive, yes,' Timu said, cautiously. 'But I have every respect for her.'

The prosecution lawyer, in his immaculate suit, smiled and sat down.

The summing up was brief. The prosecution asserted someone had killed the rhino and his view was it was Jane. He pointed out that Timu, who admitted to being bribed by a third member of the conservancy staff, had every respect for the secretive Jane, and was, as such, probably simply covering up for her in the hope that she'd do the same for him.

The defence meticulously repeated the structure of his case. Jane was not there at the time and he had proven where she was, he had presented a witness to that effect. Someone else did it, he had provided a witness who confirmed that. Release her now and get on with catching the real criminal.

The magistrates sat back as one. The central magistrate nodded to the clerk. The room slipped into silence.

The magistrate to the right, the only one of the three not in army uniform under his robes, spoke first.

'Not guilty,' he said. The room didn't react.

The magistrate to the left, the first in army uniform, spoke next.

'Guilty,' he said. The room held its breath. The woman Jane knew in the back row of the court stood up and edged her way out of the room. Jane watched her, keeping her hands flat on the desk, concentrating on the paper between her fingers.

The clerks and security guards were watching the crowd,

trying to control it with serious expressions. At least one reporter looked as though she was sending a message on a phone she shouldn't have.

The central magistrate, the second in army uniform, spoke last.

'Guilty,' he said. The reaction was anti-climactic. The pressure that had been building up hissed towards the ceiling to be dissipated by the slow-throbbing fans. On paper, justice had been served. Reporters started to shout questions at the lawyers. Other reporters ran out of the room to tweet the news. The defence lawyer calmly shook hands with the prosecutor, picked up his briefcase, and walked out through the barrage of noise, his face empty, his suit hanging loose.

The guard came and reversed the ritual with the cuffs, unlocking the one attached to the table, slotting it around her free wrist, re-locking it. Not quite the reverse – when she'd entered her hands had been cuffed behind her, not in front. She was led to a small holding cell behind the court room and locked in it, as she had been before the trial started.

It was smaller than a broom cupboard, about a metre square. It contained nothing but a plastic chair, the sort of garden furniture you found outside cheap, roadside cafes. Jane sat, and the door was closed and locked. There was nothing plastic about the door. Steel, five centimetres thick. A window in it with a grille over it. A slot for passing food and drink through. The slot was closed, the grille was down.

Jane unfolded the paper between her fingers using only the hand that held it. She didn't look at her hands in case she was being watched. She raised that hand to sweep a hair behind her ear, glancing at the paper as she did so.

There were two words written on it.

'*Ensom midnatt,*' it said. Lonely midnight. For the first time since she'd heard the lions in the dark, she allowed herself to smile. She wasn't alone anymore. Things were about to get interesting.

CHAPTER EIGHTEEN

Unlike Makena, Jane wasn't particularly familiar with the movies of Nollywood. Nor the movies of Bollywood, Hollywood, or even of Norway, though she could have told you who Ivo Caprino, Bens Hamer, and even Erik Poppe were. But she had been in enough army camps with enough prison movies on in the background to know that all you had to do to get sent to solitary was to pick a fight with the meanest-looking inmate in the queue for dinner and the guards would be all over you in a twinkling.

She was returned to Lang'ata within an hour of the end of the trial. She was transported in the same way she'd arrived a few days before, in the back of a van with two stony-faced guards. They'd spoken to each other in Swahili on the way, either not knowing, or not caring, that Jane understood them, just about. One was perplexed that such a high-profile case had been tried in a magistrates' court. The other was more circumspect.

'Judges are more expensive,' she said.

The same routine as before. The van slowed, indicated,

stopped, its engine idling. Voices, a request for identification. The van started moving again but at walking pace, before stopping, engine off. The driver's face at the grille, two words. The panel closed, doors opened and slammed, the back doors opened. The guards climbed out and motioned for Jane to follow.

They were in the main entrance yard. The watch towers with their armed guards stood at three corners. No welcoming committee this time, just the two guards from the van, grim-faced, their hands on the handles of their batons. The driver held out a clipboard. One of the guards signed it. The driver got back in and left.

Lang'ata was like a prisoner-of-war camp. Rows of identical single-storey buildings separated by fences and gates, two-storey guard towers with floodlights on all sides scattered throughout. Lots of guards, lots of guns. Lots of shadows.

And, over towards the back wall, on the ground floor of the only two-storey building in the prison compound, was solitary. Cells for those under punishment, and for those too dangerous for general population.

Ensom midnatt, the note had read. Lonely midnight. Be in solitary by midnight.

The sticker on her fridge, on the bottom right-hand side, had a bar code and a serial number, letters and digits. The letters meant nothing. The bar code was for an electric toothbrush or something equally irrelevant. But the numbers were a phone number. A phone number in Sweden, for reasons Jane didn't remember. If you called the number, and left a voicemail using certain keywords, software would trigger messages to a select distribution list. There'd be one waiting in Jane's secure inbox.

Her unit had set the phone number up after a particular

mission. A mission that almost went disastrously wrong. They were one of two units sent to— well, it didn't matter what they were sent to do. Their unit comprised two pairs, code names Laidlaw and Reacher, Walker and Marple, names assigned through a process born of a long-standing regimental joke. Jane was Marple. A frayed rope, an alert sentry, a couple of lucky shots and Jane was down, Walker captured. Protocol was to leave Walker there, for the others to complete the mission. They were all trained what to do if captured, how to withstand torture. Nothing was to jeopardise the mission.

But Jane had seen some of the men who captured Walker. They weren't soldiers. They were animals. No way was she leaving her to spend the night with them.

The unit broke protocol. They broke Walker out. They killed seventeen men doing so. But they completed their mission on schedule, so no one complained.

And they enjoyed it.

Lang'ata prison, Nairobi. Maximum-security. The unit would see that as a challenge.

————

Florence, Esther, Rose, and Angweng were in the cell when the guards left her there. It was late afternoon, between the end of workshop and evening meal. Florence was lying on one of the bunks reading her book on Java programming. Esther sat on the floor, leaning her back against one of the beds, drawing. Charcoal on soft paper, a picture of a tree that had more detail, more character, than most real trees. Rose was also on the floor, her legs crossed in a half-lotus position, eyes closed in meditation.

Angweng was lying on the other bed, eyes open, face screwed up like a cloud before a downpour.

Florence looked up as Jane walked through.

'We heard about the verdict,' Florence said.

'No surprise,' Angweng growled.

'Ignore her,' Florence said. 'Someone broke her chair. And not on purpose, so she couldn't get angry at them, so she's angry with everyone instead.'

'I am sorry,' Jane said.

Angweng said nothing, just glowered.

Evening meal came soon enough. The guards came, marching the prisoners across the yard a cell at a time, waiting until they were through the airlock into the food hall, then returning for the next cell. At the other end of the food hall a similar system operated to return the prisoners to their cells as they finished eating. They had twenty minutes to get their food, sit down, eat it, scrape their trays, and get in line for the return journey.

The problem with this system for Jane's immediate purposes was that it was quite difficult to run into someone she didn't know in the food queue. She started by being at the front, pushing ahead of Florence, who usually took point. Florence made way for her without a murmur, indeed, with a smile. Jane was Florence's favourite person since Florence had worked out who sent her the book on Java programming.

The woman in front of Florence was Anisa, one of Florence's friends from the next cell. Not only did she greet Jane with a big grin, which she had been doing since she'd learned the same thing about the book, she was also about the size of, and as cute as, the improbably named local rodent, the Delectable Soft-Furred mouse. Anisa was not the start-a-brawl-in-the-dinner-queue type.

Jane looked along the line at the other women from Anisa's cell. She knew each of them. They were all friendly, most of the time. They all looked up to Florence, on the simple grounds that many had abusive relationships with men: fathers, uncles, brothers, husbands, lovers, and they had all at some time dreamed about doing what Florence had done. Not necessarily with a pair of florist's scissors, but in the same anatomical location, and usually with the same fatal conclusion. Because Jane had helped Florence, she was as popular as she had ever been.

Jane pushed back down the line, past Florence, Esther, Rose, and then Angweng who was sulkily bringing up the rear. Angweng was so wrapped up in her own gloom-cloud she simply stepped aside to let Jane take her place at the back.

Jane waited for the occupants of the next cell to join the queue behind them. Ahead she saw Anisa pick up her tray, and Florence reaching for hers. Time was growing short.

The inner door to the airlock opened and the occupants of the next cell filed in. These women Jane didn't know, at least not their names and not to talk to. She had seen them around. One of them was in wood shop with her and Angweng. Jane had seen her working on a three-legged foot-stool. She was about Jane's size, slightly chubbier, with short-cropped hair and a scar running from the top left of her forehead to just above her right ear, passing within millimetres of her right eye. She was hardly a thick-necked, bodybuilding, roughhouser sporting prison-tats depicting the emblems of right-wing biker gangs, but she would do. She had got the scar somehow.

Jane waited for her to catch up, running through some of the trash talk she'd come across during her decade in the forces.

The woman with the scar gave Jane such a welcoming smile Jane couldn't do anything beyond wait in line, take her tray, and hold it as rice and leaves were spooned on by the trustees who did the cooking.

Seated at one of the bench tables with the rest of her cell mates she asked them.

'What do you have to do to get put in solitary around here?'

Florence looked up from her rice.

'Segmentation? Beat up a guard. Talk back to a guard. Make a guard look bad. Irritate a guard.'

'Ah,' said Jane. She stood up and threw her tray at the nearest guard.

———

Solitary. The cell was not what she had expected. It had a bunk with a mattress. It had a toilet and a sink. It was only two metres square, but she didn't need more space. As the guard locked the door behind her Jane found herself wishing she would be here longer than, by her reckoning, seven hours.

It was seven in the evening. The note had said midnight. But the code said never say what you mean. Midnight meant she needed to be in solitary by midnight. The rescue would come later than that. She just needed to be ready.

As the clang of the closing door echoed around her, she lay on the bunk. It was much more comfortable than the cell floor she'd been sleeping on for the last few days. If the rescue didn't come, she'd engineer it, so she got to stay here.

She settled. She got the angle of her neck right. She stretched her arms. She breathed.

Jomo.

On the banks of that stream, she'd put her hand on Douglas, what was no longer Douglas, the body that had held his life. Once his life had gone, it was just a case of bones and dead flesh. Before that, keeping him alive had been her job. She had failed. She had failed because others had conspired to make her fail. She would find them.

Kennet. Her brother. He had been her entire childhood. She remembered him so much more clearly than their parents. He'd given her a confidence that had stayed with her. It wasn't a personal thing. It was a belief thing. He'd believed. Like a religion. He'd believed that what he had been doing was right. He'd left Norway, moved to South Africa, spent some time in Mozambique, ended up in Kenya. He'd carried a stereotype, the white man in Africa, but he'd been himself. He met everyone as an equal. He wanted to change things. He'd wanted to find those who wanted to change the same things. He'd told her once, after much barbequed chicken and many beers, that he was only necessary because of the colour of his skin. The colour of his skin meant he could raise more money from others with the same skin colour. If money wasn't a problem, Africa wouldn't need him.

He was dead. Killed. Strangled. Murdered.

Jomo.

Douglas. As she lay on the bunk, she imagined her hand touching Douglas's skin. That first time, three years or so ago. Rough everywhere, except behind his ears. And his face. His head weighed more than she did, and when she scratched behind his ears, where the skin was soft, he smiled, didn't he?

Jomo.

The cell was two metres by two metres by three metres. It was tiled, like a bathroom. She lay on the bunk, stared at the tiles. Thought about Kennet and Douglas.

Footsteps in the corridor. Slow and bored footsteps. This wasn't the rescue. This was a guard. She lay still. They would pass.

They didn't. They stopped.

She heard keys, in the lock, opening the door.

'Governor wants to see you.'

It was a guard she hadn't seen before, a big woman, strong. Arms like anchor ropes. An X26 Taser and a truncheon hung on her belt, keys in her hands. There was a second woman behind her.

'Now?' Jane said. It was already dark outside.

'Now,' the guard said.

Jane got up.

'Face the wall,' the guard said.

Jane did so, put her hands behind her, she knew the drill. Her hands were bound. Cable tie, not cuffs.

She was pushed through corridors, then up some stairs. By her reckoning she ended up in a room above her cell.

The room was an office. Sparse, no luxury. A desk, a few chairs, a threadbare carpet.

The governor was behind the desk.

The governor was a woman.

She hadn't expected that.

'Sit,' the governor said, indicating a chair.

Jane sat awkwardly, her hands bound behind her back. The two guards took up positions a step either side of her.

'I run a peaceful prison,' the governor said.

Jane said nothing.

'I've read your file. I watched your trial. I think,' and she emphasised "think" heavily, 'that running a peaceful prison is going to be difficult with you in it.'

Jane said nothing.

'What they convicted you of is going to be ten years. Minimum. If you want ten years in solitary, that's fine. But, if you want a little more freedom, you need to–'

The governor's speech was interrupted by a noise. A loud noise. A noise so loud it blocked out everything. An explosion, monstrous, way away on the far side of the prison. It couldn't be a coincidence. They were early. They were never going to be there at midnight, but she'd guessed they'd be later. She had been wrong. And she was in the wrong place.

The governor was on her feet, shouting into a walkie-talkie. Many voices were answering, confusion, panic.

Come on, come on, Jane thought.

'Take her back to her cell,' the Governor said. Finally.

The guards behind her pulled her to her feet and bundled her out of the office door into the corridor. Jane stumbled as the larger of the two women pushed her too hard. As she stumbled there was a second noise, not as loud as the first one, but far, far worse. It made the building shake.

'Earthquake?' one of the guards said.

There was a repeat of the noise, and the building shook even more than the first time. Jane took the opportunity to sit on the floor, ostensibly to avoid falling over. In reality to get her hands in front of her.

There was a shout from the Governor. The smaller of the two guards ran back into the office. More shouting. The larger guard who'd stayed looked towards the door.

Jane stood up in a single movement and slipped the Taser and truncheon from the guard's belt, flicking the truncheon up so the guard instinctively went to catch it as she turned back, then jabbing the Taser into her ribs and pulling the trigger.

Nothing happened. The Taser wasn't loaded. And the guard was now not in a good mood. And had the truncheon.

Jane took a step back, dropped, swept her leg round hard and fast, catching the guard's ankle hard with her foot as the truncheon came towards her head. The guard stumbled, Jane raised her bound hands to block the truncheon which caught on the cable tie. A single yank and a flick and Jane had the truncheon. She jabbed it into the guard's stomach, then smashed the handle into her face. As the guard's hands went to her eyes Jane grabbed the keys from her belt and ran.

The door to the stairwell was locked. It took precious seconds to find the key. The other guard had come out of the office and turned towards her with a shout. She drew her Taser. Odds on this one would be loaded.

Jane unlocked the door and pushed herself through it, taking the time to lock it behind her just as the second guard reached the other side of it.

She ran down the stairs. At the bottom she unlocked the next door. Then she was in the corridor. She had to hurry. There were shouts on the stairs.

Back at her cell she found the right key and opened the door.

Her cell had changed. Two metres by two metres by three metres was now inaccurate. The back wall was missing. In its place was a bulldozer. A figure all in black, including a black balaclava, was just climbing over the blade of the bulldozer to leave the cell. There was an automatic rifle over their shoulder. The figure looked back as Jane opened the door.

'Where in the name of the devil have you been?' said a woman's voice. 'Move your arse, soldier.'

CHAPTER NINETEEN

MWAI ODINGA EMERGED FROM THE CABIN OF THE JET AND stood at the top of the steps. He looked out across the runway of Nanyuki airport and took in the morning. It was sunrise and the world glowed a soft orange. The occasional thin strip of cloud looked as if it had been painted onto the sky. It wasn't yet light enough for sunglasses. He took off the pair he was wearing and slipped them in his trouser pocket. A bird circled high in the sky. A tawny eagle, lazing on the thermals.

'Home,' he said, smiling effusively at the bird. 'The most beautiful place on earth.'

The airport looked sleepy. This was probably the first plane to land today. A man was climbing into the cab of a fuel truck way over by the tiny terminal building. The hangars of the Kenyan air force to the north east of the runway were silent and motionless. The most noticeable sound was a metallic ping from the Lear jet's cooling engine.

Private jet from Freetown. Just to talk. This client had more money than sense.

A Range Rover appeared around the side of the terminal building and pulled onto the tarmac. Mwai continued to watch the morning, the sun rising behind him, as the vehicle closed the distance between them. It stopped at the foot of the steps and a woman got out of the back on the passenger side.

She was clipped and precise, from the cut of her trouser suit to the rhythm of her walk. She carried an electronic tablet in one hand.

'Mr Odinga, so good to see you again,' she said. Her accent was Kenyan but had an unmistakeable gallic softness sharpened to an edge. University education in France, he guessed. Either that or from a well-to-do family in Mombasa.

'Again?' Mwai said, walking slowly down the steps. When he got to the ground, she offered her hand. It was tiny. She was tiny. At least compared to him. He reached out and shook it with a smile. 'I don't believe we have had the pleasure. I would have remembered. I hope that didn't sound too creepy. I simply mean–'

'It's quite alright, Mr Odinga. Perhaps I am mistaken. You look familiar somehow. Have you ever been to Paris?' she said.

'No, never been to Europe,' he said.

She shrugged.

'I am Kioni,' she said. 'Shall we?'

Kioni swept one arm towards the car in welcome. Mwai nodded. There was a driver. Mwai and Kioni climbed into the back. The Range Rover moved as smoothly as if it was gliding. Much more money than sense.

'Where are we going?' Mwai said as they approached the airport exit.

'To meet the boss,' Kioni said.

'As in–' Mwai motioned to the jet behind them.

The driver hit the indicator, pulling onto the C76 to head north east.

'No, Mr Odinga. Assuming everything is satisfactory you will be working for the Head of Security, not for Mr Andrews directly. Mr Andrews is at home today, but you are unlikely to see him. He won't even know you're here. The interviews are conducted in the bunkhouse, not the main house.'

Mwai nodded.

'Klabu Viziwi, right?' he said.

Kioni looked at him with a brief widening of her eyes.

'You've done your homework, Mr Odinga. Yes, Klabu Viziwi. It's an old ranch, I believe. Mr Andrews bought it last year.'

'It's an old hunting lodge,' Mwai said. 'The name means The Deaf Club, a sort of joke because one of the most frequent hunters to patronise it in the forties and fifties went deaf and claimed it was due to the number of times he'd fired a gun, punishment for the number of trophy heads he had mounted on his wall in London. It was a nickname for a long time, but the lodge burned down in the sixties, and when it was rebuilt the owners decided to rename it formally. Then the government banned hunting and it was empty for twenty years before it was converted to a ranch.'

Kioni was looking at him with less concealed astonishment.

'How do you know that?' she said. 'That's not on the internet.'

'My granddad told me,' Mwai said. 'He used to work there.'

'You're from Nanyuki?' she said.

'Born and raised,' Mwai said.

'What did your grandad do there?'

'He was a butcher. He handled the kills. And the trophies.'

'You remember the details very precisely,' Kioni said, in a tone Mwai took as high praise.

'Everything is made up of details,' he said.

There was almost no traffic. The car windows were up and the air conditioning on. Mwai opened his window to let in the air. The driver switched the aircon off.

'Do you know what that is?' she said, pointing away to a lone tree and the arranged stones around it set back from the road. 'I've passed it many times, but no one has been able to tell me.'

'It's a monument. The rangers from reserves around Nanyuki have made it in memory of animals killed by poachers. A stone for each animal.' Mwai said.

'Looks like hundreds.' Kioni stared at the stones as they drove past. 'Which animals?'

'Sorry?'

'Poachers take for meat every day. No one could know how many. That's too few stones for that. What criteria? What does the animal have to be to deserve a stone?' she said.

'I don't know for certain. Elephant, rhino, lion at least. I put some there myself, some years back.'

'No foxes, rabbits, or frogs, then?' Kioni said.

Mwai looked at her with a slight turn of his head. She had surprised him.

'Not that I am aware of.'

'Interesting.' There was a large bird in the tree at the centre of the Graveyard. 'Is that a vulture or a stork?' she said.

'It's a night-heron,' he said. 'Are you testing me?'

She looked away, smiling gently.

The rising sun brightened the sky until it looked newly washed, fresh, and crisp ahead of the day.

———

Mwai had been close to Klabu Viziwi before, once, a decade and more ago. In pursuit of poachers who had tried, and failed, to kill an elephant. When he'd come across their trail it had been two days old. It took him four days to catch up. About two days into the chase, he'd followed their trail across the sprawling estate of Klabu Viziwi. He'd only seen the buildings from a few kilometres distant.

A decade and more later the buildings had been embellished, and work was still going on. The main compound was a single-storey building that covered half an acre, surrounded on two sides by a three-metre stone wall topped with razor wire. There was a construction crane rising high from within that compound, sleeping now, but evidence of ongoing work. The Range Rover passed the entrance and pulled into a secondary compound, this one entirely enclosed by a chain-link fence, also topped with razor wire, and with electric current running through three cables set at one, two, and three metres from the ground. They hummed.

'Someone's paranoid,' he said.

'Mr Andrews is a wealthy man. He takes his personal security very seriously,' Kioni said. Mwai was uncertain whether or not the two sentences were meant to be connected.

The Range Rover stopped in front of another single-storey building, much smaller than the main ranch house, but still of impressive size. Three hundred square metres, or thereabouts.

'The man you will be meeting is Mr Andrews' Head of Security,' Kioni said. You said that already, Mwai thought. 'His name is Icarus Crewe.'

There was something about the way she said the name that made Mwai take it as a warning. There was a tension in her voice, a hint of fear.

Kioni led the way from the car into the building. He could see through the windows. Bunk beds. The bunkhouse. It had a large reception area with corridors leading off in two directions. There were doors to the left and right ahead of a set of glass double doors that led out onto a shaded area with a long table and half a dozen chairs.

'This way,' she said, and pointed to the door on the right. She stepped ahead of him and knocked.

'Yes?' a heavy voice said. Even with a single syllable Mwai recognised the Boer-tones of Afrikaans. Growing up Mwai had been taught this was the accent of the bogey men, that they were the last people on earth to work out that skin colour told you nothing about a person other than which shade of Band Aid stood out most on a cut. Grown up he'd learned that generalisations like that were meaningless. But the things you were told as a child were difficult to shake, even when you knew they weren't right.

Kioni opened the door.

The guy on the other side of it looked completely out of place. He was sitting behind a desk that was too small for him, in a chair that was too small for him. That said he wasn't overly big. He stood up as Kioni and Mwai entered. Mwai guessed the guy was a good seven or eight centimetres shorter than Mwai himself, though Mwai was close to two metres tall. The guy was broad, but not as broad as Mwai. He had a little bit of a gut which he tried to conceal with a baggy shirt. Mwai guessed the guy weighed no more than a hundred and ten kilos. Mwai had ten kilos on him. And no gut.

'My, aren't you a big one,' the guy said. Mwai instantly filed him under "Bogey man."

'A big what?' Mwai said, with a smile.

Mwai was good at smiling. He prided himself on his smile.

The South African checked himself. Mwai saw a flicker in his expression, a flicker of conflict.

'Recruit, sir, recruit. You come highly recommended. My name is Icarus Crewe. Call me Rus.' Rus extended his hand. Mwai shook it. Rus evidently liked a firm handshake. Mwai equalled it.

'Take a seat,' Rus said.

Kioni moved a chair from against the back wall. Mwai took it from her, carried it to the desk.

Kioni nodded to Rus and left, closing the door behind her.

'She's a beautiful woman,' Rus said.

Mwai said nothing.

'Thank you for coming to see me,' Rus said.

'Private jet, Range Rover from the airport, a few thousand dollars for the inconvenience, hardly a burden,' Mwai said. 'What can I do for you, Mr Crewe.'

'Please, call me Rus.'

'Mr Crewe, I appreciate there's a little sweetener in the way I have been treated so far, and I'm sure you'll tell me why. But the job is the job, and if I am going to be working for you in my usual capacity there will be a chain of command. Chain of command is a chain of respect. If I have people I am responsible for, I will expect they call me Mr Odinga when on duty. So, with respect, I shall call you Mr Crewe when appropriate. Currently, it seems appropriate.'

Rus stared at him. Mwai could see him processing the words. Then he laughed and nodded.

'You are so right, sir, you are so right. Let me get to it, then. I work for Clive Andrews, as you already know. Mr Andrews is a very wealthy man. Pharmaceuticals and newspapers. Worth more money than I could ever dream of—'

'Eight point six billion dollars according to Forbes' latest calculation,' Mwai said.

This seemed to throw Rus for a moment.

'If you say so,' he said, getting back on topic. 'Mr Andrews is developing some additional interests, one of which is in conservation. He bought this property a year ago just to have a place in the sun —'

'In Laikipia County?' Mwai said. It rained here as much as it didn't. At least, it did when they weren't in the middle of a drought.

Rus didn't seem to know how to deal with that either, so simply continued.

'A place in the sun. Then he learned about poaching, and what it is, which animals get killed and why, and he got interested. He doesn't like it. Frankly he's nervous about heavily armed gangs roaming across his land on the way to kill elephant and rhino. It's a security risk. He's tasked me with stopping it.'

'Stopping poaching?'

'Yes.'

'In Laikipia?'

'In Africa.'

Mwai — momentarily - lost his self-control. His face must have shown it. Rus didn't seem to notice.

'A single man wants to stop poaching in Africa?' Mwai asked, keeping his voice calm.

'Yes.'

Mwai stared. Every government in sub-Saharan Africa had tried, and failed, to stamp out poaching in their own national parks. Not their countries, their national parks. Clive Andrews was either an idiot, or Crewe was lying to him.

'How is he proposing to do that?' Mwai said.

'Start small, roll out. Northern Kenya first. Make some examples, send out some scary messages.'

'Go on.'

'A few weeks ago, the last male northern white rhinoceros was killed in the Bandari conservancy a few kilometres south of here. The perpetrator was caught and convicted, but then escaped. Mr Andrews wants her recaptured.'

'Her?' Mwai knew already but played the hand anyway.

'Yes. I know. A woman, right? But this is a dangerous individual. Norwegian. Ex-army. Unbalanced. She was one of the rangers paid to guard the rhino she killed. The day she was convicted she broke out of Lang'ata prison. She had help. Presumably from others in the poaching network.'

'I read about a breakout from Lang'ata. A couple of weeks ago. Blew up the main gate as a distraction, drove two bulldozers through the walls at the back, eight guards shot with rubber bullets made from condoms stolen the day before from an anti-AIDS charity, right?' That last detail had tickled him.

'That's it.'

Mwai sat back.

'So why am I here?'

'Mr Andrews wants her recaught.'

'Why me?'

Rus opened a drawer in the desk, took out a file. A cliché of a file, a brown, buff, piece of light card folded not quite in the middle. Mwai hadn't seen one of those in, well, he couldn't remember.

Rus opened the file. It had a CV on top, with a photo. Mwai could read upside down and quickly. It was the service record of Jannika Havn. Black rectangles all over it. Heavily redacted.

'Because you were trained by Special Forces. She was Special Forces. Takes one to catch one.'

'Why me?' Mwai repeated, looking straight at Crewe's face, at his eyes. 'She's Norwegian. I can see that from her name. She's Jegertroppen. Never come across them, but I was trained by the British SAS. Not the same thing. I learned how to fight in jungles, and how to kill. She learned how to fight on glaciers, and how to kill. You don't need me to catch her.'

'Yes, I do, Mr Odinga. Because you caught the Naidoo Syndicate. Tracked them all the way from Kruger to Durban. And that's where she's headed. Durban.'

The Naidoo Syndicate. That had been nasty. They had been nasty. Traffickers in animal parts. Skin, scale, tooth, horn, tusk, bone. They'd treated people the same way, as if people didn't matter, as if all lives were nothing but irritants that came between the Syndicate and their profits. Mwai hadn't caught the Naidoo Syndicate. He'd destroyed it.

'OK,' Mwai said.

CHAPTER TWENTY

NIGHT. KENYAN NIGHT. CLEAR SKIES, STARS ABLAZE. JANE looked up, then back at the villa. She'd been in a bush watching for six hours. She had the patience to watch forever. Walker did not, and had fallen asleep shortly after sunset, curled up almost foetal, wrapped around the bush's main trunk, her long, rust-coloured hair splayed out in the red-brown earth. As it was dark, Jane couldn't see the colours. She nudged Walker with her foot.

Walker grunted, moved, and exclaimed.

Jane had been standing on her hair. Jane moved her foot.

'I was dreaming. I was just getting to the good part,' Walker said.

'We can go,' Jane said. 'No one's here other than Naomi.'

'I forgot you're always business,' Walker said. 'Should have left you in that cell.'

Jane ignored her, and stepped out of the bush, walking quickly across the two hundred metres to the ranch, slipping up the steps onto the veranda and opening the door without any noise.

Naomi was inside, sitting on a chair, staring at the dining room table. She didn't react to Jane opening the door, but she did react to Walker banging her foot on one of the steps and swearing quietly in Norwegian.

'Jane! I — who is–' Naomi started as Walker followed Jane through the doorway. Jane closed the door.

'This is–'

'Call me Brigit,' Walker said, closing the distance between the door and Naomi in a trice. Naomi stood up and Walker embraced her. 'I am so sorry for your loss. Kennet must have been a great man to put up with Marple here as a sister.'

Jane scowled, but Naomi smiled.

'I am very pleased to meet you, Brigit. Welcome to my home. Can I get you some refreshment?'

'We haven't time,' Jane said.

'Chai would be lovely,' Brigit said.

Jane scowled again, as Naomi embraced the opportunity to make herself busy.

'The police are looking for you,' Naomi said, walking to the kitchen. 'Very keenly.'

'We saw,' Brigit said. 'The cautious one here had us wait outside since before they arrived to make sure they didn't come back. Don't see why. There were only three of them.'

'Where?'

'Some bush out that way,' Walker raised a hand.

Naomi paused from pulling spices from a cupboard.

'Who are you?' she said.

'Friend of Marple,' Walker said. 'Ooo, mangos. Can I have one?'

'Help yourself,' Naomi said, looking at Jane. 'Are you going to introduce us?'

Jane thought for a moment, then shrugged.

'Walker and I used to work together,' she said.

'Call me Brigit,' Walker said, 'Walker's my work name.'

Naomi's eyes narrowed.

'Are you Jegertroppen?' she said. Brigit beamed. Jane scowled, again. Naomi turned to face her. 'Kennet told me. Told me what you did before you came here. I thought when you escaped you might have had some... help.'

'She certainly did,' Walker said. 'Though she forgot to be in the right place at the right time. Nearly had to leave her behind.'

'The news said people died in the escape,' Naomi said.

'The news was wrong,' Walker said. 'No one died. We know Marple's peculiar about that sort of thing, so we took precautions.'

'Precautions?'

'Rubber bullets. Made from condoms. Precautions,' Walker said, splitting a mango skin with her nail and drawing right round it then peeling it back until one half came off in her hand. She licked her fingers. 'Wow,' she said. 'That's the finest mango I have ever tasted by a long way.'

'Thank you,' Naomi smiled. 'I grow them.'

Walker nodded, beaming, her mouth already full.

'I need to talk to Makena,' Jane said.

Naomi filled a kettle and put it on the stove.

'Do you want me to call him?'

'No. His phone might be tapped. I need to know where he is.'

'Why would his phone be tapped?' Walker said through a mouthful of mango. 'This isn't America.'

'Never assume,' Jane said, looking at Naomi.

The kettle started to hum.

'He's staying at his mother's. On the other side of

Nanyuki. I have the address,' Naomi said.

'OK,' Jane said. 'Let's go.'

'No! I haven't finished my mango and I haven't had my chai yet. It's my first time in Kenya, Marple, and I want to fully experience the hospitality. And you wanted to charge your phone.'

Naomi smiled. Jane shrugged and sat down, tapping her fingers on the table. She took her phone out, the one she'd buried just before she was captured. Naomi passed her a charger. Jane plugged it in.

———

Makena's mother's house was a single storey building on the north-east edge of Nanyuki. Looking south east from the lot, all Jane could see was Mount Kenya, the blunted tooth of the earth giant gnashing the sky. In the starlight it was haunting.

'I liked her,' Walker said.

'Quiet,' Jane said.

'We don't need to be quiet, Marple, we're the threat.'

Jane turned and grabbed Walker's arm.

'My brother is dead. Jomo is dead. Douglas is dead. Someone went to vast expense to arrange that. We are not the only threat. Until we know the nature of the other threat, we must be invisible. And we are white, and women. Anyone who sees us will remember us here. Anyone. We will not be seen or heard until we choose to be.'

Jane watched Walker's face as she processed the speech.

'I've missed you, Captain,' Walker said.

'Good enough,' Jane said, and turned back to look at Makena's mother's house.

'Who was Jomo?' Walker said, quietly.

Jane didn't answer, stared at the house, kept her eyes wide open, but a tear fell.

'A friend,' she said.

Walker grabbed Jane's arm and squeezed it, nodding.

'Happy for you, sister,' she said.

Jane looked at her in surprise. Walker squeezed again.

'He's gone,' Jane said.

'He's not gone. Marple. Ten years I've known you. More, right? Never saw you shed a tear for anyone before. He's not gone. You've got him. Right there.' Walker patted Jane's chest, over her heart, twice, with a clenched fist. 'I'm with you. I owe you. But even if I didn't, I'd be with you because of that. Right? You're always alone, you work alone, even in the unit, you always did. I'm telling you right now you're not alone till this thing is done.'

Walker moved her hand, stepped away, looked at Makena's mother's house.

'Let's go,' she said.

Jane smiled, despite herself.

————

'MAKENA!'

'I'm right here, mother.'

'There are white women in my house!'

'They're standing right in front of me, mother, I can see them. And they are my friends.'

'Are you sure? That one has red hair!'

'It's fine, mother.'

'Your mother calls you by your surname?' Walker said.

'I'll explain later,' Makena said.

'She spoke!' Makena's mother said. 'And why didn't the

goats warn us?'

'They're asleep,' Walker said. 'And we were quiet. And we are Makena's friends.' She said this gently, and Makena's mother seemed soothed by it.

The kitchen was tiny, as was Makena's mother. Makena wasn't a large man himself, but with the four of them in the room it felt packed.

'I'll take the air,' Walker said. 'Join me,' she said with emphasis to Jane and Makena.

Walker walked in front of Jane out into the dark and the dirt. Jane and Makena followed. A hundred metres from the back door they stopped.

'The police are after you,' Makena said. Jane ignored him.

'You told Naomi you had some information,' Jane said.

'Nathan's in Malawi,' he said.

'How far is that?' Walker said.

'Other side of Tanzania. Sorry, who are you?'

'I'm Walker. You're Denis Makena. You have many cousins. How far is Malawi?'

'A few hours in a plane. He's got a job. Security guard for a government building. Under a different name.'

'You've good information.'

'I have many cousins.'

'I have two. If any of yours are like either of mine, you have my sympathy,' Walker said.

'How do we get there?' Jane said.

'I have a cousin who's a pilot,' Makena said. 'He'll take us to the top of the lake. After that we'll have to make it up as we go along.'

Jane nodded. 'We borrow a boat,' she said.

'I have no experience of boats.'

'I have,' Walker said, with a grin. 'This is going to be fun.'

CHAPTER TWENTY-ONE

'WE CALL IT "THE KILLING HOUSE",' CREWE SAID.

'You're not the first people to do that,' Mwai said.

'No, but it helps avoid confusion,' Crewe said.

From the outside the building looked like a tatty ranch house. It stood in the middle of ranch land, fenced off a kilometre back from the building over a slight rise. The building wasn't visible from the boundary.

The boundary was also secure. They'd passed through a locked gate, and though the fence looked rickety Mwai saw wires along it, carrying electric current, and a camera hidden in bushes, or at least it would have been hidden if the drought hadn't left the leaves wilted and limp. There would be others he hadn't seen.

'I'll show you around,' Crewe said, locking the car from the key fob. They were many kilometres from the nearest village. The only other people there were men from Crewe's team removing crates from the back of two big four-wheel drive vehicles. There was a third one close by, its doors shut. Crewe was paranoid.

Crewe walked towards the house across the dusty yard. Mwai followed. To the left of the ranch, two hundred metres back in the scrub, Mwai saw a movement. Dik-dik. Antelope. It must have jumped the fence. Then again, dik-dik were not very big. Perhaps there was a gap. The animal had seen them and frozen. It was watching Mwai with wide eyes. He lost sight of it behind the house.

The inside was also tatty but with some subtleties. The windows had what looked like brand new blackout blinds above them. The floor and walls looked as though they'd all been the subject of recent attention. One partition was partially slid back. The ceiling was missing, there were runners in the rafters. There was a hatch in the floor that opened into a dark space below.

'When we're finished, we'll be able to restructure the entire interior based on whatever the target building is. We'll be able to black it out completely. Move the walls, change the material of the floor and ceilings, change the windows. We can train units to move through here as if they were moving through the target building. In pitch black. We scope the target site, mock it up, run drills, scenarios, events. By the time we've finished, our units, including you, will be able to move through it by instinct. You will know your way around target buildings better than those who spend time in them.'

'I've used something similar before,' Mwai said. 'Is the security controlled from the basement?'

Crewe looked at him.

'What do you mean?' he said.

'The cameras and motion sensors on the fences.'

'Ah, no. They're fed to a different centre. This facility is not manned all the time.'

Mwai nodded. He walked to one of the partially drawn-back walls, tested its strength with his hand.

'When will it be ready? Do you plan to use it for Durban?'

'It won't be up in time for that,' Crewe said. 'Durban will be improvised.'

'You want to try and take down a Special Forces soldier on the run with an improvised plan?'

'No, *you're* going to take down a Special Forces soldier on the run with an improvised plan. But don't worry, we have a confirmed location, and the team is assembling. You'll set up observation posts, gather intel, and only go in when you're good and ready.'

Mwai nodded. Patience and homework, followed by an intense period of speed, aggression, and surprise. That suited him. Mwai walked over and looked down the hatch. It was dark. He took a torch from his belt and shone it into the hole. The beam revealed a ladder, metal, looked new. The hole was deep, four metres, and the floor at the bottom appeared to be newly boarded. He saw stacks of crates. They looked new too. The men from outside were bringing in more of them.

'That's the good stuff,' Crewe said. 'Mortars, heavy machine guns, mines. We've got one hell of a budget.'

'Why do you need mortars to catch poachers?'

'You can never have too much firepower,' Crewe said. There was the spark of something in his expression. Either glee or madness.

'Where has the information come from?' Mwai switched the torch off. 'That she's in Durban.'

'The police got some information out of a man caught selling ivory in Mombasa. Spilled all he knew in exchange for a smaller fine. Said she was going there to meet with dealers for goods she has. The animal's horn, as that wasn't found when she was captured.'

'How did you get the information from the police?'

'You know how these things work. We sponsor the local force. They provide us with information from time to time.'

'Tusker sponsor the police round here,' Mwai said. But it was credible, a billionaire bribing local officers, calling it sponsorship. 'And what's your view on the reliability of the information.'

'Could be bullshit,' Crewe said. 'He could have said what he thought they wanted to hear. But the SAPS in Durban confirmed the company he named is on their suspect list. I have my own contacts there. We check it out. If it turns out to be bullshit, we go see the guy in Mombasa.'

SAPS. South African Police Service. Mwai knew them too.

Crewe looked at his watch.

'They're late,' he said. Then he looked up at the ceiling, head on one side, listening. Mwai had already heard it. The distant thwap of rotors. A helicopter.

'The chopper will take you to an airfield north of here. There's a plane that'll take you to Addis Ababa.'

'Then Joburg, then Durban?' Mwai nodded. He'd made the trip before. 18 hours at least. 'Hope it's not economy,' he said. The seats were so small.

'Nah. Mr Andrews is generous with his security budget. Business.' Crewe reached into his pocket and took out a wallet of travel documents, handed them to Mwai. 'You'll be met in Durban. They'll be holding a sign for Langa Amambo.'

'Subtle,' Mwai said.

Crewe looked confused.

'Why?' he said.

'Chief Langalibale of the Amambo people took in survivors of a Dutch East India Company ship in 1686. Taught them their language. Ended up selling them the Bay of Natal.'

'It's the name of a cab company,' Crewe said, with a frown.

'A cab company that knows its history. It will be easy to remember. Helpful,' Mwai said.

The sound of the rotors was louder. The helicopter was coming from the north, or the north east. Mwai took a last look around, then followed Crewe outside.

They waited by the building as the helicopter came in to land about a thirty metres away. It was an Agusta. Expensive. Retractable wheels. Very aerodynamic, for long distance. As the wheels came out of the under carriage during its descent Mwai noticed there were three-wheel tracks in the ground close to where it was landing. It had been here before.

'One other thing,' Crewe said. 'That's Mr Andrews' helicopter. He's very particular about cleanliness. Don't get the seats dirty.'

The machine touched down. The pilot waved with a "come here" gesture. Crewe slapped Mwai on the back and ran to his car. Mwai didn't think they had a slap on the back relationship, but he let it go. He crossed the ground to the helicopter, consciously not crouching as he approached. Everyone does it instinctively, rotors turning at a lethal rate. But even with his height they were comfortably over his head. And crouching hurt his back.

He opened the door and pulled himself in.

There were three guys already inside, other than the pilot. One of them favoured Mwai with an expressionless nod, the way a high school kid would greet someone they've not worked out the status of yet. Mwai treated him to a grin. The others ignored him or stared straight through him. Three men. At a guess two South African by their haircuts, and the third from somewhere in West Africa as he was holding a rifle issued exclusively to the Sierra Leone police. Mercenaries. Didn't matter how different the countries they came from are, you'd think they all went to the same finishing school for bad asses.

He shut the door behind him and settled into a seat, fixing the belt. The seats were of a soft, white, leather. There was music playing. Rodriguez. Definitely South Africans present.

Mwai settled in as the craft rose into the sky.

CHAPTER TWENTY-TWO

'I FORGET HOW BIG THIS CONTINENT IS,' WALKER SAID, studying a map on a tablet device. The small plane jumped and bucked as it passed through pockets of warm air rising from the arid earth of southern Kenya. 'Two and a half thousand kilometres. He's fled two and a half thousand kilometres to get away from you,' she said with a pointed look at Jane. 'That's like going from Tromsø to Berlin. And you found him despite that.' This last with a look at Makena.

'People tell me things,' said Makena, happily.

Jane watched the landscape through the plane's window. Far more farms out here. Tea plantations, coffee plantations. Little left of the wild.

'How are we going to deal with the Tanzanian border?' Walker said.

'The way poachers do,' said Makena. 'We're going to ignore it.'

'Twice? And Mozambique?'

'We're not going through Mozambique. We're going to go down the lake,' Jane said. 'Let you show us your seamanship.'

Walker grinned and went back to her map.

'This little plane going to get us all that way?'

'We change planes,' said Makena. 'This one will get us over the border.'

'Who's paying for all these planes?' Walker said.

'People like to do me favours,' Makena said. He said it simply. Jane couldn't tell what he meant, but Walker was looking at him with almost hypnotised curiosity. She seemed to consciously shake herself out of it.

'Alright, what do we know?' Walker said. She flicked to another app on her iPad and started to read aloud.

'Nathan Jennings, thirty-two, born and educated in Nanyuki, Kenya, left school to join the Kenyan army, basic training in Laikipia County barracks, nine brigade, forty-two Kenya Rifles, posted to Uganda during the civil war. Claims to have been posted to Rwanda too, but the UN ended their mission in Rwanda when he was ten. Left the army soon after returning from Uganda for reasons that are missing from his service record. Became a ranger, got married, fathered two children, took a bribe, fled to Zomba, Malawi. How do we know he is in Zomba?'

'He was an unlisted passenger on a flight from Nanyuki airport to Wilson in Nairobi. He took a taxi to Kenyatta airport and flew to Nampula in Mozambique. From there he took another flight to Chileka airport near Blantyre in Malawi. There he took the minibus to Zomba where he is now working as a security guard at the National Statistics Office under the name of Hastings Mnthali. He's staying in a small house about three kilometres from where he works. He's driving a fifteen-year-old metallic lime-green Nissan Micra,' Makena said.

'How do you know all that?'

'I spoke to the man who arranged his travel, explained I had a similar need, to disappear. He told me he'd have me flown from Nanyuki to Wilson, I would need to make my way across the city to Kenyatta, and from there to head to Mozambique. I found the pilot of the plane he took to Nairobi and bought him some beer. A cousin of mine found the taxi driver who took him to Kenyatta from Wilson. He used the same name on the flight from Kenyatta he is now living under. I have a cousin who works for Kenya Airways as an IT analyst. He is extremely good at looking at data he should not know how to look at, and he found the same name again on a flight into Chileka.'

'You have a lot of cousins,' Walker said.

'And how did you find out about the lime-green car?'

'I made that bit up to impress you,' Makena said, with a laugh.

'What about the job? Why would someone with a big payday go straight for a menial job? Why not blow it all like the boy Timu did?' Walker said.

'There's something we don't know,' Jane said.

'We can ask him,' Makena said. 'We can ask him tomorrow.'

'Patience,' Jane said. 'We need to watch and learn first. We need to know his habits, contacts, hang outs. We need to know his motivation. His wife, she said he's a good man. The men that searched his house. What were they looking for? There's something we don't know. They didn't come for their phones. They're still where I left them.' She tapped her own phone on her leg.

She lapsed into silence and went back to looking at the landscape below them. The shadow of the plane followed them south east.

'Where's the apartment?' Walker asked Makena, zooming in on a satellite image map of Zomba. Makena stroked his finger across the screen.

'Here, off the Old Naisi Road.'

'Have you ever been to Malawi?'

'Never left Kenya, ma'am.'

'You just did,' Jane said. 'Kilimanjaro.' She pointed at the mountain rising to the heavens in front of them like a blunted tooth. Away to the west lay the Serengeti, from which arose huge billows of dust. The wildebeest were on the move. Their pilot adjusted course to avoid the herd-generated clouds.

———

The Old Naisi Road turned out to be four kilometres long. The morning traffic coming the other way was mostly flatbed trucks filled with people or produce. There were women by the side of the road, gathered in clusters in front of buildings, selling fruit and vegetables from woven baskets. Some had just arrived and were unloading their baskets from the backs of trucks. Most wore headscarves against the sun. One had a green umbrella to shade herself as she waved a bunch of bananas at Makena behind the wheel. There were large gaps between the building plots. There were a lot of trees. The former capital city of Zomba slipped past in lazy slow-motion.

Makena had hired the camper van in Nkopola. That was after he had hugged the beach when they came ashore. He'd never been on a boat before, and Walker was to boats as Jane was to cars. Makena claimed he'd never felt so ill in his life.

The camper van was large enough for them and the equipment they had brought and bought; large enough for Jane and

Walker to lie out of sight in the back watching through high-definition cameras mounted on the rear-view mirror and against the back window. Jane didn't want to find out if two white women in a van with a black man would attract attention, so she and Walker stayed hidden. They had driven the hundred and fifty kilometres from the southern end of Lake Malawi on empty roads in the relative cool of the pre-dawn hours.

Makena in the front was dressed in farm clothes, doing his best to blend in. He looked uncomfortable out of his suit, the way others do in them. His sunglasses had been upgraded using equipment from under Jane's floorboards.

'I heard a rumour the quartermaster found some inventory anomalies when you de-mobbed,' Walker had said when she saw the glasses. Jane had ignored her.

'It's coming up,' Walker said from her position of concealment in the back. The other two heard her through their earpieces. She spoke quietly. 'On the left, set back. Indicate, turn here. Thirty metres and stop. Off you go.'

Makena got out. The heavy-looking sunglasses had two tiny cameras set in the frame. Jane and Walker could see what he saw, with a wider field of vision.

They saw his feet first as he jumped out of the camper. Packed red earth marbled with sandy grey. A path led from where they were parked down to a building set in a man-made depression over a metre deep. Only two-thirds of the structure was above ground level. That would keep it cool. There was a wide walkway along the front that continued down both sides. Four doors evenly spaced, all closed. Between the first and the second was an old brown sofa. The roof of the block was corrugated metal painted brown.

'Looks like a stable. Go straight to the door and say hello,' Jane said in his earpiece.

'Hello!' Makena shouted dutifully, knocking on the door post of the nearest door.

'Try them all, same way,' Jane said.

When Makena had finished with no reply, she had him walk around the building.

'It was a stables, look,' Jane said. Beside her in the van Walker nodded.

Makena's walk revealed a fence along the back of the building separating it from a large colonial-era house that had seen better days.

'We need an eye on that house,' Jane said. Walker nodded again and made a note. 'Go back to the doors and open one.'

'Aren't you worried someone will come?' Makena whispered.

'It's zero nine hundred hours. Six vehicles have passed since we stopped eleven minutes ago, all farm trucks. We didn't see anyone walking along the side of this road. Security guards at the National Statistical Office work shifts, either zero six hundred to fourteen hundred or fourteen hundred to twenty-two hundred. No one is in which means he's at work and will be for another five hours. No one's coming,' Jane said. 'Good,' she added as Makena walked through the first stable door.

It was dark inside, there were no windows. Makena propped the door open for light, but he also had a torch in his pocket.

'Slowly sweep the whole room,' Jane said. Makena systematically moved his head to follow the beam of the torch.

'There's no one here? Why don't you just go look yourself?' Walker said.

'Patience,' Jane said again, watching the screen.

It was a stable, an individual stable, and it now stabled a man. There was an army camp bed set up against the back wall, a blanket rolled up as a pillow, taut with discipline and hospital corners. An unfolded towel on it the only thing that looked out of place, that wasn't precise. There was a gas lamp on the floor next to the bed. Three cases of Carlsberg Brown, the top one open, were stacked at its foot.

'What's that, pull it out,' Jane said. Makena reached and pulled a suitcase from under the bed. It was half-full of clean clothes. 'And next to it?' Makena squatted on the floor and swept the torch under the bed. Dirty clothes.

The rest of the stable was empty.

'Try the other doors.'

The other three doors led to identical stables, but without signs of habitation. Or, rather, signs that the last creatures to live in them weren't people. Strands of grass used for feed. In one a mouse scuttled out of the beam of the torch. In one a pitchfork lay on ground thick with dust.

'He's tidy,' Walker said. 'No empty cans. And good taste in beer. All the best things come from Scandinavia. Where's his water? If this was a stables, there will be a stream or a pump or something.'

There was a hand-pump a little away from the building. A tin bucket with a bar of soap sat on the ground beside it.

'Let's go,' Jane said. 'We'll come back later, when it's darker. Set a watch.'

'Why set a watch? Why not just ask him?' Walker said.

Makena got back in the van. He turned it round and pulled back onto the Old Naisi Road.

'What did that all mean?' Walker said.

'That's not the palace of a well-paid master criminal,' Jane said. 'It's the sort of place you go to avoid being seen by anyone.'

'Why the job?' Walker said.

'I don't know. To stop himself going mad from boredom?'

'As a security guard?'

'Is it about the job? Does that give him access to something?' Makena said.

'NSO website. Latest publication on agricultural numbers, last big thing last year's census.'

'Let's just ask him,' Walker said. 'If he's gone to these lengths to not be seen no one's going to miss him.'

Jane was thinking.

'We need to get his laptop out of his car,' Jane said.

'Where did that come from?'

'He had a laptop that he brought with him. His wife said so. There were soldiers searching his house for something they didn't find. And there was no laptop in that stable. Therefore, it's in his car.'

'How will we know which car is his?' Makena asked.

'It will be the one he drives back to that stable tonight. But it will also be a metallic lime-green Nissan Micra. Won't it?'

Jane could not see Makena's face, but she could see Walker turn her head to look at him.

'Alright,' Jane said. 'Let's just ask him.'

CHAPTER TWENTY-THREE

DURBAN. ETHEKWINI. THE CITY. A HUNDRED THOUSAND years of human history. The port of South Africa, nestling on the Indian Ocean, trading with India and the east beyond.

Mwai had mixed feelings about Durban. He had known a woman here some years ago, oh, yes. He remembered her athleticism with arousal. A crazy two months centred on a waterfront apartment that had stretched him physically and emotionally. But during the same two months he'd been employed in a role he remembered with distaste, distaste that had built over time until he'd expressed that distaste to his employer by knocking him unconscious with a single punch. His employer had responded, when he regained consciousness, by sending three men to kill Mwai. Mwai had reacted poorly to that. The three men had just been following orders. Killing someone who doesn't have being killed in their set of life goals carries risks. The three men had accepted those risks. But Mwai hadn't needed to do to them what he had done.

His only consolation was, when he confronted his former

employer that one final time and expressed a degree of displeasure about the fate of the three men sent to kill him, his former employer had revealed things about himself and the three that eased Mwai's conscience.

Mwai stared at the Indian ocean and wondered if his former employer had been fully eaten by the fish yet.

He turned away.

What the hell was his name? The one Crewe had said was in charge. Imran? Sounded possible. No, Imran was the name of the taxi driver that had brought them from the airport. Mwai had chatted to him. The other three had sat in silence, as if they had no time for people. Mwai had time for people. What was all this about, if not about people.

François. Why had he thought Imran? François was Crewe's delegation of authority. Mwai was to do what François said. Yeah. And François already didn't like him. Mind you, from the little he'd seen of François that was true of everyone.

Mwai looked along the Golden Mile. Wealth unthinkable half a century ago. He looked at the port. The warehouse that was their target was not visible from here. The warehouse where he would catch Jane Haven. Or not.

It wasn't hot, but he was sweating. The humidity.

'Let's go,' he said.

His partner was half his size. Typical Special Forces, wiry and all endurance. He was American. And called "Budd". He was from one of the rectangular states, Mwai didn't remember which one.

'I'm in charge here,' Budd said.

'OK. What shall we do?' Mwai said.

Budd thought for a minute, looking towards the port.

'Let's go,' he said.

'Good decision.'

———

The warehouse was innocuous, just one of hundreds on the dock front. Goods went in, goods came out. They came from container ships, they left on lorries. But some went the other way. Fewer, certainly, but a two-way street.

'How long has the surveillance been in place?' Mwai said.

'Two days,' Budd said.

Mwai nodded, for want of something to do. He suspected Budd was lying. There were six of them in total, and three had arrived with Mwai. Budd and the other guy would have had to pull two twelve hour shifts each to have been watching the place for two days. One pair of eyes missed things, anyway. This was a risky mission. He hoped there wasn't anyone with Special Forces training in there.

The street was deserted. Their watch point was from the cab of a truck a hundred metres from the warehouse entrance. There was another team of two on the roof, and a third team of two watching the back.

'She's not in there,' Mwai said.

'Intelligence says this is where she's headed,' Budd said.

'Explain,' Mwai said.

'Just do as you're told,' Budd said.

Mwai breathed. And watched.

Two hours later no one had gone in and no one had come out. The sun had set, and the street had changed, from a busy worktime thoroughfare to a sleepy night-time nothing.

'It's time,' Budd said.

No, it isn't, Mwai thought. But he put on his night vision goggles all the same. There was a camera attached to the side.

What he saw was being live streamed to a command centre. A secret bunker, no one on the team knew where, Mwai had been told. He could make a good guess.

———

The infiltration went to plan. With one exception.

Mwai and Budd exited the truck and crossed the street. They tried the warehouse door quietly, and found it locked, as expected. Budd affixed a charge, as per plan, and when the lock blew, they went in.

The other two units went in at the same time, one through the back door, one through a skylight, abseiling down.

They had expected to find a security guard and Jane Haven. The exception was, there were six men in the warehouse, not one, and by the time Mwai got to them, they were all dead.

Mwai and Budd went through the front door, quiet. The warehouse was like most warehouses Mwai had been in – large, open, split into channels, into columns, into zones. Mwai and Budd moved into the first zone in tandem, weapons out, ghosts, the world green through the goggles.

They heard shouts, as the lights were cut, but that didn't matter. The shouts were deeper in the warehouse, not close.

They moved into the first channel, stacks of crates reaching almost to the ceiling. There was no one. They kept walking, their boots making little sound on the concrete floor. They reached the top of the channel, near the right wall. A forklift was parked at an untidy angle. Mwai looked down the side of the building, giving cover as Budd turned to his left, into the second channel. Mwai was following Budd by sense, keeping his eyes front, trusting Budd to cover him in the same way. Their training was the same, instinctive.

Mwai stepped into the second channel, following Budd, but walked backwards for the first few steps, making sure no one was following. Then he turned, looking down the channel. Budd was three metres ahead of him, walking slow, his weapon up, tight into his shoulder.

There were more shouts, then a bright flare, like a flash of lightning in the goggles. Someone had found a torch and was shining the beam at right angles to the channel they were in.

They heard shots and the torch went out. Bang, bang. Bang, bang. Bang, bang. Double taps. Mwai knew those. He'd been trained in those. They were kill shots, not capture-and-question shots. They left him thinking.

Mwai and Budd continued down the channel to its end, then paused. They had still seen no one themselves. Then more shots. Bang, bang. Bang, bang. Bang, bang.

'Rear quadrant clear.' Through the headset. Backdoor team. Scottish accent.

'Central quadrant clear.' A different voice, another South African, François who he'd met on the helicopter, the one Crewe had put in charge.

'Front quadrant clear,' Budd said. Mwai heard it in stereo, both from Budd and through the headset a fraction of a second later.

When they got to the bodies in the main area of the warehouse, the skylight team wasn't there.

'What's going on?' Mwai said.

'We got 'em,' Budd said.

'Who?'

'Them.'

'Who are they?'

'Does it matter? We got 'em.'

'Everything matters,' Mwai said, looking at the faces of the dead.

'Nah.' Budd waved his arm and walked off.

'Where's Jane Haven?' Mwai called after him.

'Who?'

'The person I was sent here to catch.'

'She ain't one of them?'

'They're all men.'

Budd shrugged, and disappeared behind a stack of crates.

After two or three minutes, the warehouse lights came on. Grey neon light flickering from fluorescent tubes high in the ceiling. Mwai removed his night vision goggles, put them back in a pouch, into his rucksack. Whoever was seeing what he had been seeing was seeing it no more.

Mwai crouched down, went through the pockets of the dead. Nothing, as the saying went, but loose change and lint. Yeah, and car keys and folding money, couple of phones, couple of wallets. He pocketed the phones and the wallets. He studied the faces.

Budd returned with a clipboard, concentrating on it with such fury he didn't notice one of the corpses and tripped over it, stumbling. The clipboard went flying. Mwai caught it and had read the first eight lines before Budd grabbed it back. Manifest. Crate numbers. Crate contents. "Used household goods and personal effects". The crate numbers were easy to recall. Two letters, six numbers. Mwai looked at the nearest stack. Each crate was labelled, some neatly printed, others hand-written. He walked along the stack, reading the labels.

Halfway down the second stack Mwai found one of the crates on Budd's manifest, three up and beneath three others. It would take the forklift to get it out. Mwai pulled the stack over. The top two crates cracked as they hit the concrete, but the others landed intact. He righted the one with the matching number on and looked at it.

'What you doing?' Budd said.

'Satisfying my curiosity,' Mwai said.

Budd shrugged.

Mwai looked at the crate lid. Nailed shut. He stooped and picked it up to guess the weight. Forty or fifty kilos. It would take a crowbar to get the lid off. Mwai raised the crate over his head and threw it onto the ground.

It split from bottom to top. Its contents spilled out all over the floor.

It was full of bones.

Mwai knelt next to them and picked one up.

'What are they?' Budd said, perhaps curious despite himself, despite Mwai acting under his own will.

'Lion bones,' Mwai said. 'On the manifest as "household goods and personal effects". This is a smuggling operation. They're trafficking illegal wildlife parts. Is that why you killed them?'

'I didn't kill no one. Find the rest of them,' Budd said, flinging the clipboard at Mwai.

Mwai caught it. He nodded. He did. It took him two hours.

At the end of the two hours there were twelve broken crates, and a pile of lion bones, pangolin scales, elephant tusks cut into fifty-centimetre-long pieces, and rhino horns.

By Mwai's calculations he was looking at the remains of two hundred dead animals. At least. Difficult to estimate the number of pangolins from a pile of scales.

He looked at the dead men, now moved to the side in a line. Two Asian, probably Vietnamese. Three Africans, two likely Zulu, one more northerly perhaps from East Africa, Tanzania or Kenya. The last one was white, perhaps eastern European. He photographed them, then found a desiccated tin of boot polish in a drawer in the office and used that to take their fingerprints.

'What you doing that for?' Budd had been leaning on a crate chain-smoking thin roll-ups and watching him for the last hour.

'You can never have too much information,' Mwai said, numbering each set of prints with the order the bodies lay on the floor, then carefully slipping the pieces of paper into a plastic bag. 'What now?'

'Burn it all,' Budd said. 'I gotta video it for the boss.'

It took Mwai another twenty minutes to find an accelerant. Kerosene for an ancient heater in the warehouse office. He poured it over the pile of animal parts.

'Got a light?' he said, standing well, well back.

Budd took out a phone, switched video on, took a drag from his latest roll-up and flicked the glowing butt at the heap.

It went up instantly, like the fires of hell. Mwai stepped back further. The flames were shooting six or seven metres up. Not reaching the ceiling, but a simple shift in the air current and they could spread sideways.

They didn't. The bones, horns, tusks, scales, burned. Budd filmed. The dead men were in the background of the shot.

Mwai could only watch for so long. He went to sit in the truck.

CHAPTER TWENTY-FOUR

JANE WATCHED HER PHONE SCREEN AS NATHAN JENNINGS, coming off shift, walked into the Malawi National Statistics Office car park and into the range of the cameras in Makena's sunglasses. As soon as he was sure Nathan had seen him, Makena jimmied the boot of the metallic, lime-green Nissan Micra and grabbed the laptop bag from the otherwise empty spare wheel cavity.

Unbeknownst to Nathan the laptop bag was already empty, and the laptop was with Jane. The sunglasses cameras saw Nathan give a yell before Makena turned his head and burst into a run across the car park, bolting through a hole in the rotten fence and out onto the Chimbaya Road.

The afternoon was pleasantly cool, and Jane envied Makena the run. She hadn't run in too long and felt out of shape. As soon as this was over she was going to run until she hurt.

Makena kept looking over his shoulder to check Nathan was behind him. He sprinted across the Chimbaya road in front of an oncoming truck, which blew its horn in half-hearted remonstrance. Once across he raced down a track into the forest, heading away from the city centre, little puffs of dust flying up as his boots beat the ground, hanging a moment in the still air behind him. Nathan was gaining. Nathan was much fitter than Makena. It had been part of the risk.

Nathan crossed between two cars, holding his hands up to slow them down. His uniform, and the gun holstered on his belt, gave him authority over the traffic. He flew down the track on Makena's heels, thumping the packed earth with his heavy boots, spraying gravel behind him with anger.

'You see him?' Jane said quietly into her headset.

'I see him,' Walker acknowledged.

Makena turned right into an empty compound. The buildings once there had been bulldozed; he could see the scars in the earth. Any material left behind had been removed or pilfered. It was little more than a bare patch of uneven ground. Makena stumbled over the broken surface, Jane's feed jerked and showed nothing but the earth for a second. Makena was hardly a gazelle. Nathan ran on this sort of surface all the time and was barely three metres behind when Makena looked back for the last time.

Makena concentrated on going forwards. Jane could hear his breathing from the microphone in the sunglasses. He was trying to take air into his lungs in huge gulps. He headed for the shrubs and tangles of young trees fighting for sunlight on the edge of the forest that surrounded Zomba. Makena tripped through them, righted himself, and kept going. He had no idea how close Nathan was behind him. Jane did. She could see him with her eyes now. He would be able to grab his prey in seconds.

Makena lurched out of the other side of the shrubs into a

smaller compound, old, abandoned, overgrown. Jane could see her own hiding place in the feed from Makena's cameras. A single storey building, the roof rusted through in many places. Next to the building was the skeleton of a truck, from the days of the Republic if not older. Shrubs and young trees pushed up wherever they could, a balsam sapling bullying its way through the crumbling bonnet. She turned the phone screen off and put it on Nathan's laptop by her feet.

Makena staggered on, and as he passed the building, he threw the laptop bag through the window. He stumbled round the side of the building and collapsed out of sight.

Nathan Jennings went for his laptop first, abandoning his pursuit of Makena and running into the building. The bag was in a pool of light on the floor of the ruin. He picked it up, realised it was empty, and swore.

'Hello, Nathan,' Jane said from behind him. He tried to get his gun out of its holster, so she took some small satisfaction in breaking his arm. He screamed and dropped to his knees.

She took the gun from him, flicked the bullets to the ground and threw the weapon through an empty window frame into the undergrowth in the yard.

She stepped behind him and pushed him to the floor, patting him down, removing things from his pockets. Money, an ID, a phone. The ID was in the name of Hastings Mnthali. The photo looked nothing like Nathan.

'Who is Hastings Mnthali?'

Nathan whimpered, his face screwed up, clutching his hand. She'd broken the radius, nothing more. The wrist, rather than the arm. He opened his eyes, looked at her with something close to terror.

'Lots more bones to go,' Jane said. She looked at the phone. It wasn't one she was familiar with.

Makena walked in through the doorway, breathing heavily.

'This–' he said but ran out of breath.

'Can you get into this?' Jane said, holding out the phone.

Makena breathed heavily for another minute, put his hand out for the phone and took it.

'Need his fingerprint to unlock it,' he said, breathing better.

Jane took the phone back and grabbed one of Nathan's hands, pressing a finger on the phone button. Nothing happened.

'Could be any of them,' Nathan said. 'Any finger, I mean.'

Jane tried them all. Nathan screamed again when she grabbed the hand with the broken wrist. The thumb on that hand unlocked the phone.

'I don't know how to use this,' Jane said, after a moment of staring at it. Makena took it from her again.

'It'll take a few minutes,' he said. 'Messages first, then calls, then everything else.'

'How are we looking?' Jane said. Makena looked at her, but then went back to the phone. She had spoken to Walker through the microphone in her headset. 'Good.'

Jane waited, standing over Nathan, who lay on the floor clutching his wrist, tears on his face. She stared at him, her face blank.

'Did you kill Jomo?' she said.

The question hit Nathan like a bucket of water.

'No,' he said. 'No, how could I? How could you ask?'

The question seemed genuine.

'You let in the men who killed him, which is as good as the same,' Jane said.

'He wasn't supposed to be there,' Nathan said.

'He was on shift. He was the only person supposed to be there.'

Jane walked over to a bag she'd brought from the car. Pulled out a Beretta M9. It was a weapon she'd had for many years. She didn't have favourites. They were just tools. But, as with all tools, she had guns she knew. Maintained, used many times, understood. They were familiar to her hands. This one was one of the most familiar. And besides, she'd stolen it from a US Marine who'd called her a dyke, and every time she used it there was the possibility that someone would get a ballistics match on a casing that would lead back to him.

She pointed the barrel at Nathan's head, for a moment. And then at his knee.

She said nothing.

'I didn't kill anyone,' Nathan said, his eyes wide, his face serious. 'I just took the money. They threatened my family.'

'If they threatened your family why would they give you money? And why would you leave your family in Nanyuki and run here alone if they were the ones being threatened? Try again. Think it through this time.'

She flicked the safety catch to "off". The gun was rock steady.

Walker's voice came through the headset.

'Jane, there's a truck pulling into the adjacent lot. Construction dumper. Two males.'

'Copy,' Jane said. She flicked the safety back on. 'Do not move,' she said to Nathan.

She walked over to the window, looked out. Through the

bushes she could see the truck. Yellow, patches of rust. It was just sitting there.

'Late lunch stop, looks like,' Walker said.

'Copy.'

Jane went to Makena, watching Nathan as she did.

'Anything?' she said.

'Possibly. There's some numbers in the address book we could try, but they all look like his family, unless he's being cute and has a business contact under an entry for Auntie Jemimah or something. The call log is no help – the last three inbound calls on the day of the killings are all from a withheld number.' Makena held up the list. Jane read it. "Withheld" called three times that day, the first time shortly after she'd left the conservancy, the second and third close to each other an hour later. 'There are no interesting emails or text messages I've seen yet. But he doesn't have a network contract in Malawi, only in Kenya, so he hasn't been able to make a call or collect his messages since he got here. He probably switched off the phone in Nanyuki and didn't switch it back on till he arrived, so anyone trying to track him through his phone would follow a trail that dead ended in Nanyuki.'

'How did you get in touch with them?' Jane said to Nathan, holding the pistol by her side, barrel pointed at the ground. She reached across with her other hand and flicked the safety to "off" again. He was watching her hands.

'I didn't, they got in touch with me,' Nathan said, watching her finger moving onto the trigger. He knew how she fired, how she trained her finger to hold at one third pressure, two thirds pressure, ready to fire at a fraction of a second's notice. He'd asked her about it the first time he'd seen her kill. Asked her how she'd fired so fast. She gently squeezed, one third pressure. She felt him watching her.

'On the day, perhaps. But you must have had a way to get in touch with them. You arranged things with them. That mission was planned.'

'I didn't, really.' Nathan's eyes seemed to be getting wider.

Jane walked closer, squeezed the trigger a little more. Enough to make him think she was about to shoot.

'Timu said you did,' Jane said. 'Timu said a lot of things. I didn't have to break any of his bones, either.'

Nathan's reaction wasn't quite what she expected. He didn't look particularly surprised or worried.

Walker's voice came over the head set again. She was whispering.

'It was just a lunch stop, but one of them got out to take a piss in the bushes. Saw the campervan. He's walking round it. The other's still in the truck.'

'Copy.'

Jane moved quickly to the window, putting a finger to her lips as she did so, signalling to Makena to be quiet. She stopped still out of sight then gently leaned forward to get a view.

There was a man walking around the campervan, peering inside, holding his hand up to prevent the sunlight reflecting off the glass. He was dressed in overalls more suited to a decorator than a construction worker. He suddenly looked all about him, to see if he was being watched. For a moment he looked straight at Jane, though he didn't see her concealed in the shadows. He stared into the bushes, and towards the trees between him and the main road. He reached his hand up to the campervan door handle, but hesitated, scanning the trees once more. Then he turned on his heels and walked quickly back through the bushes. After a moment Jane heard the truck's engine start, and it moved away.

Through the headset Jane heard Walker laugh.

'What?' Jane said.

'Man said he felt like he was being watched as he got back in the cab.' Jane imagined it. Walker watching, through the sniper scope of a Remington rifle. The two men eating their lunch in the crosshairs. She wasn't sure what there was to laugh about.

'We need somewhere a little more private,' Jane said.

CHAPTER TWENTY-FIVE

MWAI AND BUDD GOT OUT OF THE RANGE ROVER IN FRONT of the bunkhouse. Night had fallen during the drive from the airstrip, and Klabu Viziwi was lit up by dozens of brilliant spotlights, the whole of the main compound circled in a comforting moat of light. Beyond it the Laikipia plateau was black. There could be an army out there, hidden in the darkness. In the distance was the sound of frenzied yipping and barking.

'What's that?' Budd said, freezing and looking in the direction of the noise.

'Wild dogs. Hunting.'

Budd watched the darkness for a moment, then led the way inside.

Crewe was in his office behind the too small desk. The only light in the room was a desk lamp, the bulb too bright for its size.

'Well?' Crewe said.

'We got 'em,' Budd said.

'I know that,' Crewe said. 'I was watching. Where is she?'

Budd shrugged, looked at Mwai.

'No trace,' Mwai said. He put the bag with the boot polish fingerprints in it on Crewe's desk.

'What's this?'

'Fingerprints of the dead. I assume you've got the resources to run them through the SAPS database, through Kenyan police?'

Crewe nodded, taking the sheets out of the bag, and putting them on his desk.

'Only two of them had IDs,' Mwai continued. 'One's Ugandan. Joseph Kamoga. Address in Kampala. One's Ukrainian. Name of Andrei Petrov. Address in Mombasa. Both had phones, both locked with PIN codes so I've not been able to get in them. I'll keep them charged.'

'Why?'

'In case someone phones.'

Crewe nodded.

'Good idea. Give them to me, I'll get someone to work out the PIN codes.'

'I left them at the hotel,' Mwai said. Budd looked at him, then looked away.

'What next?' Crewe said.

'If that's the extent of your intelligence then we go to Mombasa,' Mwai said.

'Why?'

'Because your source came from Kenya, and Andrei Petrov is the only one who lived here. In Mombasa. Your source may have known Andrei. Andrei has an apartment. There may be information in it.'

Crewe nodded.

'Bring the phones here before you leave. I'll arrange transport.'

'I have one question.'

'What's that?'

'Where did the other four guys go?'

'They had another mission,' Crewe said, taking out a phone and photographing the boot polish fingerprints. They were dismissed.

———

As they climbed back into the Range Rover Budd said, 'We didn't stop at your hotel.'

'And you didn't mention it.'

'Not my business.'

'Where shall I drop you?' the driver said.

'I'm staying at the Rustic,' Budd said.

'Le Rustique, nice,' Mwai nodded. 'Just drop me in town, I fancy a drink.'

'Where you staying?' Budd said.

'With an old friend.'

Budd shrugged, and looked out of the window.

The Range Rover pulled out of the compound and into the night.

———

Mwai got out first, stepping on the pavement outside the Hemisphere, a bar he'd not been to before. He waited as the vehicle pulled away before turning and walking in the opposite direction, across the street and down Laikipia Road.

When he got to the block with the church he turned left,

his feet beating parched earth that should have been five centimetres of mud by now. He passed a handful of corrugated shacks and turned into Chep Road. A little further on the right was a house concealed by a six-foot wall, which was itself half-concealed by a well-maintained hedge growing on both sides. There were double gates in the wall, their tops disappearing into the hedge. Mwai tried the handle. It wasn't locked.

He slipped through, closed the gate behind him.

The yard hadn't changed at all. The car parked by the house was the same. The tyres were probably the same, though he couldn't see them in the dark. The house itself, with the green copper roof that amplified the rain when there was rain, sat neat and kempt, as it always had.

He knocked on the door.

'Come in.'

He went in.

———

It's the smell you never normally notice that hits you first when you walk into a room you're familiar with after a long absence. A mixture of furniture polish, soap, laundry detergent, a hint of sawdust, and the aroma of the inhabitants. In this case, the inhabitant.

The door opened into a room that was most of the house. At one end the kitchen, at the other, an old armchair. The walls on three sides were covered floor to ceiling with shelves, and those shelves were filled with books.

In the old armchair was a man. Twenty-five years older than Mwai, and not as tall, but still a tall man. He was reading. His hand had always seemed empty without a book. He looked up, eyes bright behind small, round glasses.

His face split into an enormous smile and he was on his feet in an instant. Mwai covered the distance in two strides, and they embraced, a fierce hug.

'Hi, Dad,' Mwai said.

'What a surprise, what a surprise!' His dad held on for a little longer then stepped back.

'You've got bigger,' he said.

'You always say that.'

'I just remember you...'

'As a little boy, I know, Dad.'

'Why didn't you say you were coming?'

'I didn't know when I'd be free. Here on a job. Nipping about a bit. Mombasa in the morning.'

'Where are you staying?'

'Here, if that's alright, Dad.'

'Of course, of course. Where are your bags?'

'I didn't bring any. I have things here.'

'You do, you do. Oh, this is a wonderful surprise.'

'Aren't you going to tell me off for not visiting in too long?'

'Take the pleasures when you can, son, don't ruin them with regret. Sit. Let me make some chai. Or would you like some beer? I have a case somewhere. And there's one in the fridge.'

'Share a beer with me, Dad,' Mwai said.

'Yes, yes, I shall do that. I would like that.'

Mwai's father walked to the kitchen end of the room, taking out glasses, opening the fridge. Mwai took a chair from the kitchen table and brought it next to the armchair. He sat, ran his eyes over the books, old friends. They were neatly ordered, all his father's medical books on the wall inside the door, his history books on the shelves behind the armchair, and everything else along the far wall. Mwai had read many of the history books himself.

His father returned with two glasses and a chilled bottle of Tusker, putting them on a small table next to the chairs. He took a bunch of keys from his pocket and used one to take the cap off.

'I haven't had a beer in, oh, let me see.'

'The last time I was here?'

His dad laughed.

'You're probably right. In fact, I think this is the one you made me put in the fridge because the one we shared wasn't cold.'

Mwai smiled, remembering.

His dad sat in the armchair and poured the beer into the two glasses. He handed one to Mwai.

'*Afya, vifijo,*' he said.

'*Afya, vifijo,*' Mwai echoed, clinking his glass against his dad's. They drank.

'You going to see your brother?' his dad said.

'If I get a chance, of course I will. How's he doing?'

'Well. He's making good money. He says business is booming.'

'I'm pleased for him.'

Mwai took another mouthful. His dad put his glass down.

'What brings you home?'

'A job. I've got to find someone. You may be able to help me.'

'Me? Are they a patient?'

'No, a ranger.'

'Surely you're more likely to know them than me.'

'I've never met them. Are you still friends with Sergeant Mburu?'

'Andy? Of course. We play chess in the park every other Saturday. He was terribly ill. Lost all the weight. Allergy to alcohol. He was devastated. Says chess is the only pleasure he has left.'

'How did Mrs Mburu take that?'

'I don't think he says that when she can hear.'

'Could you call him? Ask him to come over? I'd like to talk to him. Don't mention I'm here.'

'Of course. But I don't have a phone. I never used it, so I got rid of it.'

'Do you have his number?'

Mwai's dad nodded and went to the kitchen table, opening the drawer underneath it. He took out an address book, thumbed through it, held it out.

Mwai took out his phone and typed in the number. As soon as it was ringing, he handed the phone to his dad.

———

Sergeant Andy Mburu had changed dramatically since Mwai had last seen him. How long ago was that? Five years? He must have lost over forty kilos, and it didn't entirely suit him.

His reaction on seeing Mwai was initially confusion, then recognition.

'Mwai, what a surprise!' He stepped from the door and shook Mwai's hand effusively. 'Decided to stop neglecting your old dad, eh?'

'Less of the "old",' Mwai's dad said.

'We're aging, my friend. No denying it.'

They settled round the kitchen table. Sergeant Mburu

looked at their glasses of beer with a wistful expression before accepting Mwai's dad's offer of chai.

'Mwai's the reason I called you, Andy. He has something to ask you. About a ranger.'

'Jane Haven,' Andy said, sipping his chai.

'How did you know that?' Mwai said.

'Who else could it be? She's all the news at the moment. First rhino killed at Bandari since she started working there three years ago. And she's the one on the run for killing it!'

'Sounds like you don't think she did?'

'Never in a million years,' Sergeant Mburu said. 'You know her brother was killed in the same raid? And one of the other rangers who she was, er, close to.'

'Close?'

'They shared an apartment. An apartment with only one bed, according to my Akinyi. I know she's a gossip, but it's not a great leap. And I met Jane many times. She brought in dozens of poachers, from Bandari, Ol Faraja, MKW, Laikipia Wildlife. She's a natural ranger, a tracker, a real soldier. A bit distant, perhaps, but she slowly warmed up over the years. I like her.'

'No chance she lost control?'

'I doubt it.'

'So why are you after her?'

'I'm not!'

'The police, then?'

'Not really up to us. She was convicted, so we have to treat her as a fugitive. Makes no difference. No way we could catch her.' Sergeant Mburu suddenly looked around and lowered his voice. 'One of the other rangers, Nathan Jennings, you know, Zawadi's boy?' This last was to Mwai's dad rather than Mwai. 'He told me that about a year ago they received a report of poachers, five or six of them, coming across the plateau armed with everything you could imagine. Out of Somalia, funded by the gangs, you know. After the elephants. Fifty cals, saws for the tusks, the works. He and she were sent to investigate. Not protocol, two against six. Bandari would usually call in the Wildlife Service for that. But she didn't blink.' Sergeant Mburu took a sip of his chai. 'Nathan told me they found them, at least their trail, way out towards Ol Faraja, like twenty, thirty kilometres from Bandari, and she went after them by herself leaving Nathan to guard a ford on the river. She came back ten hours later, muddy and with blood on her trousers that wasn't hers. Nathan guessed she caught up with them, killed them, buried them. Said she wouldn't tell him what happened.'

Sergeant Mburu sat back.

'I haven't said so much in an age. Usually don't get the chance with my Akinyi. Well, you know.' He smiled a big smile.

'Thank you, Sergeant, that's interesting,' Mwai said.

'Please, Mwai. You're all grown now. Andy is my name.'

'Andy. What I wanted to ask you was, well... A team has been put together to find her. The team was given a lead that she might be in Durban. That lead allegedly came from someone in the Kenya police who had interviewed a trafficker and got the information in exchange for leniency. Do you know anything about that?'

'Durban? Why would Nathan be in Durban?'

'Nathan?'

'Nathan Jennings, the ranger I was telling you about. Disappeared on the day of the killings along with Timu Obote. She found Timu hiding in Nairobi in less than a day.

Now she's escaped, I'd bet the opportunity to drink again that she's after Nathan.'

'Why?'

'Because Nathan and Timu let them in. They were bribed. Timu told them as much. I got that from Akinyi, who got it from Wawuda, you remember her, ay?' This aside to Mwai's dad along with an expression that suggested Wawuda was worth remembering. 'Wawuda's daughter, Naomi, you know the one who became a vet, married Kennet, Jane's brother. She thinks Nathan knows who killed the rhino. Bet you the opportunity to drink again she's hunting him.'

Mwai sat back.

'Do you know this as you, or do you know this as Kenya police?'

Sergeant Mburu – Andy – looked confused.

'I mean, if someone had a conversation with one of your colleagues and asked them what they knew about Jane Haven, and in an unrelated sentence offered to, say, fund a child of that colleague through university, could that colleague have told that someone what you just told me?'

Sergeant Mburu's face wrinkled in concentration.

'Possible. Not all of it, but some of it. We had Timu Obote in the cells for a bit, then he was released after he testified. He talked. A lot.'

Mwai nodded.

'Thank you, Andy. That helps me. One last question. Do you know where Nathan Jennings is?'

'No idea. He vanished off the face of the earth. They ran a trace on his phone. Last recorded use was inside Bandari on the day of the killings. Then nothing.'

After Sergeant Mburu had left Mwai sat down at the table again.

'It's my bedtime,' his dad said, picking up the empty cup and glasses.

'Of course, Dad. But...'

'Yes?'

'Do you remember Granpa's stories? About when he used to work in Klabu Viziwi up on the plateau?'

'Yes?'

'Tell me them again.'

CHAPTER TWENTY-SIX

THE CLOUDS SCURRIED OVER THEIR HEADS LIKE A FEVER OF stingrays, the wind pushing them through the pale-blue sky northwards along the lake. The cheap motor of the open boat continued its nasal whine right up until the moment the craft beached, and Walker killed it. Makena was first out, hauling it up the sand as far as he could. He reached in for the bags. Walker picked up two more. Jane rough-handled Nathan onto the shore.

'Seven kilometres to the landing strip. Are you sure he will still be there?' Jane said.

'Of course, he is—' Makena began.

'I know, he's your cousin. Let's go. Get up,' Jane snapped the instruction to Nathan who had fallen to his knees on climbing out of the boat.

'You can't take me back,' he said. 'These people are—'

'Less of a threat to you than I am,' Jane said.

'They will kill my family,' Nathan said. 'You won't.'

Jane stopped. She looked him straight in the eyes.

'You need to tell me who "they" are, don't you?'

He looked away.

She grabbed him by his good arm and dragged him to his feet. The other, the one with the wrist Jane had broken, was bound in a rough field splint held in a tight sling against his chest.

'Let's go,' she repeated.

The four settled the heavy bags on their backs, Makena's the lightest. Jane and Walker carried fifty kilos each. In Walker's case, that was like carrying herself on her back. They had experimented with Makena and worked out he could just manage twenty, and that was a struggle. They loaded Nathan up with something in between.

They set off at a rapid pace, after Walker had scuttled the boat and pushed it back out into the lake to drown.

The land rose almost immediately, and Makena was soon sweating. Vegetation crowded them, forcing them to single file, Walker out front, Makena behind her, Nathan with Jane breathing down his neck in the rear.

On even ground and city streets, seven kilometres an hour is a good walking pace. In this terrain, and with Makena struggling, it was nearer two. But they reached the landing strip without seeing life beyond plants and insects.

'I told you my cousin would—'

'You did,' Jane said, nodding. Makena impressed her. As fit as a football fan, but he did what he said. She remembered their first encounter, that shiny suit she'd parcelled up and dismissed. Appearances.

The plane was still where they'd left it. Beneath one wing was a neat camp and the remains of a fire. The fuel tanks on the Cessna were in the wings. Makena was ok, but the cousin was a moron.

The cousin had spent the time on the ground neatening the natural landing strip he had brought them down on. As they walked to its far end, he hailed them and stood up, picking up a rifle and slinging it over his shoulder.

'Why the gun?' Walker said when they got close enough.

'Mosquito!' Makena's cousin laughed.

They loaded the plane and, as the afternoon was ending, took off into the Tanzanian sky. Makena took his cousin's rifle and sat watching Nathan. Jane watched Makena for a while, and his vigilance seemed good. She looked out of the plane's window at the passing landscape.

'This is not the way we came,' she said at once.

'No. My cousin will take us all the way back to Kenya now. No need for a side-trip to Mwanza this time,' Makena said. 'Less explanations needed.' He nodded in Nathan's direction.

'OK,' Jane said.

Below them the stubby hills held different trees to the plains, sometimes even pines reminding her in a small way of home. Though the sandy earth and wilting grass soon counter-acted that feeling. The Cessna droned on, its shadow bouncing over the earth below them, elongating as the sunset began. The group fell silent, watching, listening, thinking. Jane's main worry was Makena would fall asleep. But she and Walker were behind Nathan, in case.

Eventually the hills gave way to plains, bush, and scrub. Occasional impala and buffalo sauntered through the grass, shadows stretching in the setting sun. The plane flew above a flock of birds heading south. Jane tried to identify them. Storks or cranes. Big wingspan, long legs, gliding effortlessly for minutes between slow, languorous wing beats.

'Look!' Makena's cousin called.

Jane crossed to the other side of the plane to see what he was pointing at.

Below them, on the edge of small stand of short trees, lay an elephant on its side. A large bull, fallen, knocking down at least one of the trees. Even at this distance and in this light, she could see the blood where a tusk had been hacked off.

'Poachers.' Jane said. 'This is as good a place as any. Land the plane.'

'Don't you want to stick with the plan?' Walker said.

'Land,' Jane said. She got out of her seat and grabbed Nathan, pushing him to the window so he could see.

'Remember what we do?' she said.

He looked at the carcass.

'They'll be long gone,' he said, with echoing sadness.

Suddenly the elephant's great head came up. It wasn't dead. Its other tusk was still in place.

Jane held Nathan's face to the glass. His eyes were glistening.

'Find somewhere to land, NOW,' she said to Makena's cousin.

'It's too dark,' he replied. 'We won't be able to see to take off again.'

There was a rapid discussion between Makena and his cousin in a language Jane didn't recognise. It ended with an angry word from the cousin, but he circled the plane back towards where the elephant lay. After a second pass, and in fading light, he brought it down on the best line he could. It bounced in hidden scrapes and lurched violently as he steered hard right to avoid a sweet thorn tree, but they came to a halt a hundred metres from the dying beast.

Jane dragged Nathan out of the plane towards the animal before the wheels stopped moving.

'The Winchester. And the .458s,' Jane shouted back over her shoulder.

Walker joined them a minute later with the largest bore rifle in the small arsenal they'd brought from the stash under Jane's floorboards.

Jane pushed Nathan to the ground close to the elephant, not close enough for any sudden moves to risk injury. It was a very large bull, perhaps five tonnes. He was riddled with bullet holes along his flank and chest, in many places blood almost black had trickled through the crags and crevasses of his thick skin. His head was not hit, but the stump where the missing tusk had been bled onto the sandy earth. His side was dusty over the bullet wounds. The part of the other tusk not covered by his great head had been hacked at but not cut through. The elephant opened its eye which glistened as if with tears. He gave a sigh that sounded almost human.

'Rifle,' Jane said, holding out her hand.

Wordlessly, Walker passed it to her.

'Look at him,' Jane said to Nathan.

Nathan raised his head.

'This is what they did to Douglas,' she said, loading the rifle.

Walker was examining the ground.

'Er, Jane. I know what you're about to do, but whoever did this isn't long gone.'

'Exactly,' Jane said.

A single shot rang out into the Tanzanian evening. Wings whirred and birds called in startled response before a silence that felt so deep it might last forever. The elephant was still.

'They'll have heard that, Nathan. They'll either run away faster or come back. You and I have been a team, many times, hunting men such as these. And yet you became one.'

'They went that way,' Walker said, still looking at the ground.

Jane nodded.

'Get the Remington. Find a position.'

Walker nodded and ran back to the plane.

'Your wife told me you were a good man, Nathan,' Jane said. 'A good man who always said goodnight to his son. Even when he goes to the bars, she said. Why does a good man let this happen?'

She ejected the cartridge from the Winchester rifle and slid in another bullet. Walker ran past them, the Remington rifle, complete with sniper scope and suppressor, in her hands. Makena came with her but stopped by Jane and Nathan. The pilot remained in his seat.

'Makena, get the big torch from the plane, it's in the Bergen. Set it up over there pointing that way,' Jane motioned to the back of the elephant in the direction Walker had said the poachers had gone. 'Don't switch it on till I tell you. When I do tell you, hide.'

Makena ran to the plane.

'It doesn't make sense, Nathan. No one threatened your family. Because if they threatened your family, you would have taken your family with you. Someone threatened you. Tell me what happened.'

Jane swung the huge rifle up and pointed it at Nathan's knee.

'This gun is so powerful it will tear your leg in half,' she said.

There were shouts, voices from the direction Walker had run in.

Makena came back with a huge torch, six thousand candle power.

'The men who did this are coming back, Nathan. You can hear them. I only have one bullet. You're in a uniform. I can melt into the night with Makena and Walker and leave you to them. I can shoot you myself. I have so many options. You have only two. One choice. Tell me what happened or die tonight.'

Nathan stared at her, his face crumbling. He started crying. The shouts of the men grew louder, and there was the sound of a machine gun firing, a wild burst designed to scare them off, then another, they heard the whistle of the bullets this time, far too high. Jane didn't move, held the rifle motionless, her finger on the trigger, one third pressure, the barrel pointed at Nathan's knee.

'Choose,' she said.

'I speak Afrikaans!' he shouted.

There was a moment of silence, of calm. Then another burst of shots and Jane moved.

'Switch it on,' she said, swinging the big rifle to her shoulder. Makena switched on the torch and took cover behind the elephant.

The beam of light picked out four men running, all with guns in their hands. One stopped, raised his weapon.

'*Drep dem!*' Jane shouted.

Thup, thup. Thup, thup. Thup, thup. BOOM.

The four men died. Three falling sideways, shot by Walker, somewhere in the gloom. The other one's chest exploded, and he fell backwards as the .458 bullet passed through him as if he wasn't there.

Makena had his hands over his ears. Nathan was still crying.

'You speak Afrikaans? I'm going to need more than that,' Jane said, ejecting the cartridge and reloading the rifle.

It took Nathan a minute to control himself enough to speak.

'I was kicked out of the army. I went to South Africa, got a job as a ranger. I learned Afrikaans. The big white guy we let in, I heard him say to one of the others, in Afrikaans, "When we're through, kill them." So I ran,' Nathan said, his whole form deflating, as if a great pressure was leaving him.

'Why? What do you know?'

'How they contacted me. Through Riba. Someone I knew in South Africa. He has... connections.'

'And where will I find Riba.'

'Mombasa. He lives in Mombasa.'

'What happened that day, Nathan?'

He swallowed, staring at the ground.

'We told Jomo we had a call from Tony. Left him with the rhinos, went to the gate, let them in.'

'Who did you let in?'

'Three Land Cruisers. At least eight men, four in the first car, two in the front of the other two. Could have been more in the back, I didn't see. Only one got out of the car and spoke to us.'

'What did he look like?'

'He was big, tall. White guy. Dressed in, I don't know, khaki shirt, trousers the same I guess.'

'What did he sound like?'

'South African.'

'And the others in the cars?'

'Only saw the ones in the first car really. They looked serious. I mean none of them were smiling. They were all wearing sunglasses. Same haircuts.'

'Then what?'

'They told us to go. We went. Drove through Bandari, past the ranger station.' He hesitated.

'What did you see?'

'Kennet. We saw Kennet, lying on the ground next to a car. We just kept driving.'

'What car?' Jane said.

Right at that moment, Makena started screaming.

CHAPTER TWENTY-SEVEN

MOMBASA. MWAI HAD LEARNED OF THE CITY WHEN HE WAS young, studying history in school. A place of magic and mystery where the Portuguese trading ships stopped off on their way to the Far East, loading up with ivory and gold and returning with spices and silks. It had remained in his memory ever since, somewhere below the surface. Despite travelling all over Africa, he had not been there before. It was nothing like his imagination had painted it.

One-and-a-half-million people crammed together around the two natural harbours either side of Mombasa island. The approach in Clive Andrew's plane gave Mwai a fantastic view of the habitat of man. The flight path to the airport meant they flew up the coast over the golden beaches and the blue-green reefs. Over Kilindini port from which a transport ship quarter of a kilometre long, carrying hundreds of containers each the size of a lorry, was leaving. Over Mombasa island and its medieval fort. Over the mazes of streets through the jumble of apartment blocks, hotels, warehouses, before banking round and coming in to land over industrial plants and a pipeline terminus.

————

Andrei Petrov had lived in a wealthy district close to the beach, a first-floor apartment overlooking the ocean. Large and expensive. Whatever Andrei did, it paid well. Mwai and Budd went in over the balcony and were through every room in three minutes. Andrei lived alone, and other than a fridge full of beer and a two-metre-wide television didn't seem to have any hobbies. Though he had a laptop.

'We need a password,' Mwai said after switching it on.

Budd shrugged.

'Try "Password",' he said.

'He's Ukrainian,' Mwai said.

'What do they speak in Ukraine?'

'Russian.'

'Try "Password" in Russian.'

'Russian has a different alphabet.'

'Keyboard doesn't.'

Mwai looked. Budd was right. The keyboard was in English. He typed "Password".

The laptop screen shuddered a bit and displayed an access-denied message.

'Good thought,' Mwai said.

He looked around. He got up. He walked through the apartment again, more slowly this time. Budd flicked on the TV. Found a cable channel showing American football. He went to the kitchen and took one of the beers out of the fridge. Tusker. Andrei drank Kenyan beer. Budd opened the bottle by banging the cap on the edge of the countertop, sucked off the foam, and settled down in front of the television.

Mwai paced.

He went to the bedroom, opened the wardrobe again, flicked through the clothes. Nothing out of the ordinary. Nothing to give Andrei Petrov a personality. Nothing to tell Mwai anything about how the man thought.

Two-metre-wide television and a fridge full of beer.

Mwai sat down at the laptop again. Typed "Tusker".

The laptop screen shuddered and displayed the access-denied message.

Mwai thought for a minute. Tried again with "tusker" in case Andrei hadn't been too bothered about punctuation.

The screen didn't display the access-denied message. It let him in.

Mwai used the track pad to open programmes. Email, browser, file store, address book.

The email messages were encrypted, but Andrei had saved the key, and they opened as if they weren't.

There were hundreds from a company called "Health and Beauty Vietnam".

Mwai's phone rang.

Not his personal phone. Another one Rus Crewe had given him. For the job. The only people who had the number were Rus, François, and Budd. The phone had been pre-programmed with their numbers. The screen displayed "Crewe".

Mwai answered it.

'Mr Crewe,' he said.

'You didn't drop those phones off,' Rus said.

'Sorry, Mr Crewe, which phones?'

'The ones you took off the men in Durban.'

'Oh!' Mwai slapped his forehead in an unnecessary gesture given Rus couldn't see him. 'I am very sorry. I forgot. They're charging in my hotel room. I'll make sure you get them when we are back.'

'Which hotel? I'll send someone round.'

'Very sorry, Mr Crewe, but I have a policy of keeping where I sleep to myself. I sleep easier that way. I shall not forget again.'

'When?'

'We could be in Mombasa for another few hours, but should be back this evening,' Mwai said.

'See to it.'

The line went dead.

'Another few hours?' Budd said, sitting up from what had become a game-watching sprawl. 'Have you found something?'

'Health and Beauty Vietnam,' Mwai said.

'Two of the guys in Durban were Vietnamese.'

'Quite possibly. And the biggest market in the world for rhino horn is...'

Budd stared at him.

'I have no idea.'

'Vietnam,' Mwai said, with a sigh.

———

Health Sciences Clearing and Forwarding Company Limited had a warehouse on Mombasa island several streets from the waterfront. Mwai drove the van he and Budd had rented at the airport, slowly passed the main roller door, and pulled around the corner.

'Are you sure?' Budd said.

'That's what the internet tells us. Health and Beauty Vietnam is the holding company for, among many others, Health Sciences Clearing and Forwarding Company Limited of Mombasa.'

'Shall we go in?'

'No, we should watch, get a feel. There's only the two of us.'

'What do you think they might have in there? An army?'

'Caution, my friend,' Mwai said. 'We're hunting some fairly serious people.'

'Can't be that serious. The lock's busted.'

Mwai kept the van moving, but turned into the next street, reversed into an alley, and drove back the way he had come. As they passed the Health Sciences warehouse for a second time, he saw it. The lock on the inset door in the big roller door was missing and the place where it had been was surrounded by a tell-tale smoke-grey ring. Someone had blown it open with a charge.

'Good eyes, Budd. You up for a little unarmed investigation?'

'There'll be a tyre iron in the trunk.'

'This is a van, Budd. There's no trunk.'

'I was speaking metaphorically.'

Mwai looked at Budd in surprise, then shrugged.

———

Another warehouse. This time in daylight. The lock had been blown recently. Within the last hour at Mwai's guess, from the residual heat and smell. They stepped inside. This was a much slicker operation than the one they had raided in Durban. It wasn't rows of stacks of crates, it was rows of shelves with parcels and packages, much smaller than the crates from the other warehouse.

'Hello!' Budd called once they were inside the door.

Mwai looked at him.

'When you ain't got a gun best to announce yourself and take the guns from whoever comes answering,' Budd said.

Mwai shrugged again. It was an approach he had used.

But there was no answer.

They walked straight forward down a central aisle leading from the doors. They checked each set of shelves to their left and right as they walked. No one.

They reached the end of the warehouse. There were stairs going up to an office suspended on a platform four metres off the warehouse floor.

Budd shrugged and climbed the stairs. Mwai had a quick look around before following him.

'What're the odds that what you want to find isn't here anymore?' Budd said. He was ahead of Mwai and could see into the office already. Mwai joined him.

The office was a mess. There were three desks, two overturned. A filing cabinet stood with its bottom drawer open, many files and piles of paper lay scattered around it. One wall had windows looking out over the warehouse. Another had a door with a bar. The door was marked "Fire Exit." In the middle of the floor, lying face down with one arm outstretched towards a water cooler, was a dead man. The water cooler had exploded, and the wall behind it had a big chip out of the plaster.

He had two bullet holes in his back, about three centimetres apart.

'Double-tap,' Budd said.

'You're not wrong,' Mwai said.

Mwai turned the body over. The bullets were pass-throughs, which explained the destroyed water cooler. The man was unremarkable. Average size, youngish, perhaps thirty. Mwai patted him down. His pockets were empty but for an enormous ironed handkerchief and a wad of Kenyan shillings.

'Wonder what they were after,' Budd said.

'Wonder what he was reaching for,' Mwai said, looking where the body's outstretched arm was pointing. He kneeled, then got his face on the floor. 'What's...'

Mwai stood up, walked to the ruined water cooler, and picked it up. Underneath it was a phone.

'Guess it was this,' he said, picking it up.

'I heard something,' Budd said, head on one side. 'Out there.'

Mwai listened. He didn't hear anything.

'I heard something,' Budd said, quietly and seriously.

Mwai looked around. The only way out was the fire exit. He motioned with his head. Budd nodded. Mwai went over, pushed down the bar.

An alarm went off.

CHAPTER TWENTY-EIGHT

JANE RAN TO MAKENA. HE WAS LYING ON THE GROUND, thrashing, holding his leg.

'What happened?' She tried to grab his hands to see if there was damage.

'Felt like I was hit in the leg by a hammer,' Makena said, his face twisted in agony.

Jane got his hands off his leg and saw two puncture wounds through the fabric of his trousers, blood soaking through.

'Snake bite,' she said, leaping to her feet. 'We have to find the snake!'

'Why?' Walker said.

'To know what type of poison it is. If we don't find the snake, he could be dead in minutes.'

Jane ran to the torch, picked it up, ran back, sweeping the beam in an arc, holding the rifle by the barrel and the stock close to the ground. Walker got the idea and used the torch on her phone to mirror Jane's movements in a different arc moving out from where Makena lay against the elephant. She held the barrel of the Remington with her cap to avoid burning her hand.

'Nathan, help me!' Jane shouted. He got to his feet, came with her, watching the grass on the edges of the torchlight.

Makena's cousin, the pilot, burst from the plane.

'What?' he said.

'Makena's been bitten by a snake. We need to find the snake. He needs a tourniquet on his leg. Then we're going to have to get him to a hospital as quickly as possible, so get ready to take off.'

'It's too dark.'

'Find a way.'

'OK.' He disappeared back into the plane.

'There! I saw something,' Walker called.

'Are you sure?' Jane didn't break off searching, just in case Walker was wrong.

'I can see it, it's quick. Come on. It's about a metre and a half long, and bright green.'

'Trap it's head against the ground with the stock of the rifle, understand? Make sure it's jaws can't get anywhere near you.'

'Got it,' Walker said.

Jane ran to her. Looked at the snake.

'What devil is it?' Walker said.

'I don't know,' Jane said.

'Green mamba,' Nathan said, quietly.

'*Faen ta deg*,' Jane said.

'What? How bad is it?'

'He's got about thirty minutes. We need to get him antivenom in thirty minutes. Let it go.'

'What?' Walker said. 'You don't want me to kill it?'

'No, it wasn't doing anything. When the elephant fell it

must have knocked down the tree it was sleeping in. Makena probably sat on him by mistake. Not the snake's fault.'

Walker shrugged, stepped back as far as she could without having to loosen her grip the rifle, then released the pressure on the back of the snake's head. She flicked it away into the dark with the rifle's stock.

'Get him up and into the plane. Nathan, help me!'

Nathan and Jane manhandled Makena back to the plane.

'Do you have any anti-venom?' she said to Makena's cousin.

'For what venom?'

'Green mamba.'

'All the gods,' he said, shaking his head.

'Get us in the air. Nearest hospital that will have some. Now.'

'I need light,' he said, 'There are no lights. We'll hit a tree.'

'Where?' Walker said.

'What?'

'Where do you need the lights?'

'That way, at least four hundred and fifty metres in that direction.'

Makena tried to say something, but it came out as a grunt. He was sweating heavily, his face contorted.

Walker nodded, ran back to where Jane had left the big torch, and then ran as far in front of the plane as there was grass, and set the torch down twenty metres from a clutch of trees. She ran back.

'Only four hundred metres to the trees,' she said. 'Torch is twenty metres in front of them.'

'Go,' Jane said, through clenched teeth.

'There's only one light! We'll crash into the trees!'

'What's your name?' Jane said to the pilot.

'Godknows!'

'It's not a time to be funny!'

'That's his name. His name is Godknows,' Makena said, his eyes rolling, his head lolling.

'Godknows, get us off the ground and find the biggest hospital within thirty minutes, or he is going to die.'

Godknows stared at Jane, then at his cousin. He blinked, then nodded.

'How tall?' Godknows said. Walker didn't understand. 'The trees, how tall are the nearest trees.'

'Oh, less than ten metres.'

'OK. Should be ok, just. And where shall we go?'

'How fast can you fly?'

'Maximum speed a two-hundred-and-fifty kilometres an hour. But at low altitude, take off, and landing, one-ninety, tops. Call it one-sixty.'

'Then we need the biggest hospital within fifty kilometres at the outside.' But Makena didn't seem to hear. 'Doesn't matter. Anything that's likely to have good stocks of anti-venom.'

'There aren't any!'

'How do we find out?' Walker said to Jane.

'Iringa.' It was Nathan. 'Iringa Regional. They'll have anti-venom.'

'That's too far. A hundred-and-sixty-kilometres from here,' Godknows said.

'It's not too far,' Nathan said. 'It will be longer than thirty minutes. You read that in a book, thirty minutes. That would be the worst possible case, and that was a young male. Less venom than the females.'

'How long?'

'An hour at least, possibly two.'

'Can you find it?' Walker said to Godknows.

'Yes, but where will we land?'

'In the carpark! On a field! There'll be somewhere, just get us there! Take off! Now!'

Walker shut the door behind her, and the plane started to move towards the beam of the torch ahead of them.

Jane put a tourniquet around Makena's leg above the bite and bandaged the wound as best she could.

Nathan was crying.

———

Makena was sweating so much it was as if he were melting. Walker held a rag to his brow, tried to keep his eyes clear. Jane looked at Makena's face, the increasing number of involuntary movements of his legs, arms, and head, as delirium took hold.

She crouched along the cabin to sit behind Godknows who was holding the steering column so tightly he seemed to have fused to it. His eyes were moving, scanning the night through the cockpit windows.

'How far?' Jane said.

'I have no idea where we are,' he said.

'You know where we were and the direction we're heading in. Work it out.'

'I can't calculate, I need to concentrate.'

Jane took out a notebook and pen, used her phone torch to see.

'Airspeed, direction, wind direction,' she said. Godknows told her.

She drew a triangle, calculated. Checked the time,

minutes in the air. Took the charts Godknows used to plot his courses, found Tanzania, worked out where they had started inside the border next to the lake, how far they'd flown before they landed, where they were now.

'We should be over a road,' she said. 'A104. Leads straight to Iringa.'

Godknows peered into the night.

'Can't see a road from here, even if there is something on it,' he said. He leant forward. The plane dived.

When Godknows levelled up again Jane looked out of the window in the plane's door. She could see nothing below her but blackness. She crossed to the other side of the plane. Again nothing.

No.

Wait...

'Over there,' she said. 'Thirty degrees to starboard.'

Godknows looked.

'I don't— Wait. I see it. Headlights.'

'Follow them,' Jane said.

Godknows leaned and the plane banked. Five hundred feet below them a yellow cone of light sliced through the night.

'It's too slow, we can't follow it, we'd stall,' Godknows said.

'The road is almost straight, heads almost exactly north-east. Follow its direction.'

Godknows nodded, banked, straightened, kept altitude.

After the longest twenty minutes Jane could remember she saw a glow on the horizon. The lights of a large town. She checked the charts.

'That's it,' she said. 'The hospital is five hundred metres back from this road after it doglegs through the town centre. It's a dual carriage way and it's largely empty.'

Godknows didn't react for a moment then slowly turned his head to look at her.

'You want me to land on the road?'

'Got a better idea?'

Godknows held her gaze, quite steadily, for ten seconds, fifteen. Then he nodded.

'Talk me through it,' he said. 'The dogleg. Where's the hospital?'

Jane showed him the chart.

'Can you get signal? Get me a satellite image?' Godknows said.

Jane pulled out her phone, looked at the signal strength.

'Just, but it's very weak.'

Godknows nodded and pushed forward on the steering column, sending the plane into a shallow dive.

'That's better,' Jane said. 'Hang on... There.' She handed the phone, its screen showing a satellite image of the hospital and the A104 road, to Godknows. He looked at it carefully, checked the airspeed, the altitude, the heading. He looked out of the window and watched the trees.

'I'll come in from the north, land with the traffic. If I don't hit anything I should be able to turn into the road that leads to the hospital and get as close as we can before we have to carry him.'

Jane nodded.

Godknows increased the plane's speed. Below and to the left Jane could see the hospital building, identifiable because an ambulance, lights flashing red, was pulling up behind another ambulance in a well-lit unloading bay.

Godknows was banking the plane, angling it right – north of north-east – to swing round in a large arc that would leave them facing south-west on the line of the road.

Iringa lit up the night like a dusty jewel. It was a city of more than a million, an urban sprawl at the heart of a vastness of mountains, forests, and savannah. Jane hadn't expected it to be so big, for there to be so many houses, for there to be so many cars on the road at night.

'This is a really bad idea,' Godknows said, easing the plane lower towards the dual carriageway. It was dotted with cars. Not just the occasional truck doing fifty kilometres an hour, but many cars doing a hundred, changing lanes, overtaking.

'They'll get out of the way when we touch down,' Jane said.

Godknows gave her a look, then turned to the front.

They were lower. Lower. Cars were going faster and slower than them as Godknows eased them down. He was heading for an empty patch of road, between two groups of vehicles moving at constant speed.

'Watch the back,' Godknows said.

'Check,' Walker said, leaving the rag on Makena's brow and moving to a rear window.

Godknows pushed the column forward. The plane sank lower. They were moving ahead of the rear of the two groups of vehicles, aiming for that clear patch between them. The plane was four metres above the ground.

'Boy racer inbound,' Walker said. 'Doing at least a hundred and fifty.'

Jane watched Godknows' face. Saw him calculating. At that speed, the car would be past them before it was a problem. He pushed forward on the column. The plane lowered. Two metres.

A car, a BMW, shot underneath them in the outside lane barely thirty centimetres from the wheels. The driver seemed oblivious, kept going straight, disappeared around the bend ahead.

'The road's not straight,' Godknows said.

'I told you, it doglegs.'

'Shit,' Godknows said, and touched them down with a thump.

Everyone was thrown forward. Walker dived from the seat she'd moved to in an effort to protect Makena, but he banged into the metal legs of the seat he lay next to. Jane gripped the edges of her seat and remained firm. Nathan slammed into the seat back in front of him.

The squeal of tyres on rubber filled the cabin. Some of the noise was from the plane's wheels as Godknows fought to keep it under control. But a lot of it was from the group of vehicles behind them as a number of the drivers slammed on their brakes. Three, however, didn't, which only became obvious as they screeched past the plane, one slamming into the central reservation and bouncing back onto the road, the other two skidding off onto the verge. The plane bounced and shook and then smoothed.

Jane looked up. Godknows was still steering, sweat running down his face, hands fused to the steering column, but he was in control. He turned left abruptly, causing a blast of horns behind them. As he turned the plane Jane saw what had caused him to turn. A large sign, pointing to Iringa Regional Hospital.

Godknows drove the plane as close to the turning into the hospital as he could then stopped.

'There are going to be police,' he said.

'It doesn't matter,' Jane said.

Makena's clothing was soaked with sweat and he hadn't said a coherent word for a long time. It had been forty-five minutes since he had been bitten. He had almost lost control of his limbs.

Jane and Walker pushed him out of the plane and half-walked, half-dragged him to the hospital entrance. Walker saw an empty wheelchair and grabbed it, pushing Makena into the seat.

They burst through the doors, causing everyone inside to look up. There were patients, receptionists, and at least one nurse.

'Green mamba bite,' Jane said. 'Forty minutes.'

The nurse dropped her clipboard and ran.

———

Jane expected to get back to where they'd left the plane and for it to be gone. And if it wasn't gone it would be crawling with police and Nathan would be gone.

There was a Tanzanian police force car parked where they'd left the plane, but the plane was still there. And so was Nathan.

Two policemen were chatting with Godknows, not laughing, exactly, but the body language wasn't threatening. Jane approached with caution. Nathan was sitting in the plane, still, but there was a nurse next to him, binding his wrist.

'How is he?' Godknows said, seeing Jane approach.

'We were in time. Your bravery saved his life,' she said.

One of the policemen slapped Godknows on the back and shook him by the hand at the same time.

'You are a hero, my friend,' he said. 'You are all heroes, to save a man this way. Though I should, of course, arrest you.'

He left his words hanging, for a moment. Then laughed.

'But I will not. I will lead you to a field, a kilometre ahead.

You can pull the plane in and take off from there in the morning.'

'What sort of field? How big is it?' Godknows said.

'Playing fields of a school. Athletics track then two football fields. It is long enough to take off for a small plane, I have seen it done.'

'I am forever in your debt, officer,' Godknows said.

'No, I am in yours,' the policeman said. 'This is the most entertaining story in the whole year. Life is stories, and they all seem to have been told too often. This is a new one, it will last.'

He patted Godknows on the back again and motioned to his colleague to get back in the car.

The lights on the police car roof flashed, and the police drove slowly down the road with Godknows' plane behind them, then turned and drove off the road. Godknows followed, stopping the plane in the athletics field.

'I am not taking off in the dark,' Godknows said quietly.

Jane nodded and went back to the hospital to tell Walker.

———

Once on the ground in Mombasa they taxied to a hangar beyond the main terminal building. When the plane stopped, Godknows climbed down the steps and greeted two uniformed men whilst the engine was still cooling. Money changed hands, and the men gave him a piece of paper and walked away.

'How much do I owe you?' Jane said when he returned.

'You owe me nothing,' Godknows said. 'Makena is my cousin.'

Makena joined her by the plane door, leaning heavily on

his good leg. The trouser on the other was torn and bandages were visible through it.

'Do you think you can find a man called Riba in Mombasa?' Jane said.

'My niece will find a man called Riba,' Makena said, his voice still weak.

They packed the bags whilst Makena made a call. Jane sat under the shade of one of the wings leaning against her Bergen, watching Nathan who she'd made to sit three metres away. Walker put a little effort into teasing Makena, whilst he was trying to concentrate on the call. Once it was finished, they both sat in the plane doorway and chatted to Godknows.

An hour or so later, a battered van that had once been black pulled into view round the side of the hangar. A woman drove it. She climbed out and waved to Makena.

'Uncle Denis, how are you?' she gushed, and ran to give him a hug, then stopped when she saw his face clearly. 'You look awful.'

Makena smiled, weakly.

'Just a snake bite. I was taken care of. This is my sister's daughter, Marceline.' He introduced her to each of them. 'She is a journalist, because she likes being abused online.' He laughed again, though Marceline scowled. 'Nice van,' he added.

Marceline's smile returned as quickly as it had gone.

'Borrowed it from a neighbour. You wouldn't all fit in my little car. It's a bit temperamental.'

'Let's go,' Makena said, leaning on his good leg. Marceline put her arm round him and helped him stand.

Walker and Jane loaded the bags into the back of the van. Makena and Godknows embraced.

'Goodbye, cousin,' Godknows said.

'Thank you, cousin.'

Jane led Nathan to the back of the van, pushed him in, and climbed in after him. Walker joined them. Makena and Marceline sat in the front, Makena taking advantage of the bench seat to stretch out his injured leg as best he could after the cramped plane. Marceline turned the ignition. The engine tried to turn over.

'It takes a few tries,' Marceline said, a little defensively.

'Let me have a look,' Jane said. She did not want to rely on a vehicle that didn't start first time.

Marceline released the hood and Jane set to work. She made a list of parts that needed replacing. Cleaned the spark plugs. Brushed off some rust. Someone needed to look after this relic.

———

Marceline lived in an apartment on the edge of the Kongowea district. One window looked inland, over a jumble of older buildings packed together like badly stacked boxes in an abandoned warehouse. The view from the balcony on the other side of the apartment facing the coast was of a different city, of villas and embassies with high walls and swimming pools. Mombasa Island, and beyond that the cranes of the port, were clearly visible.

The five of them filled the small living area. They almost seemed bigger than the room. The first thing they did was plug in all the devices that needed charging. Then they got down to business.

'Riba?'

'Yes, Riba.'

'That's all you have. Someone in Mombasa called Riba?'

'There can't be that many,' Makena said, cheerfully. 'Everyone in Mombasa is Russian. Or Ukrainian. Or Kazakhstani, or Belarussian. You're probably the only native Kenyan in the city.'

'You have nothing else other than his name is "Riba"? Marceline said.

Jane looked at Nathan.

'Where's my phone?' he said.

Jane stared at him.

'You have his number?' she said.

Nathan nodded.

'Then call him.'

CHAPTER TWENTY-NINE

Mwai stopped running. Budd caught him up. They stepped into the shadows at the mouth of an alley and waited, controlling their breathing, listening.

Five minutes. Ten.

If anyone had followed them, they were either slow, patient, or lost.

The warehouse alarm was still ringing in the distance. Suddenly it stopped, leaving a hole in the sounds of the city. They waited another five minutes. Another ten. No sirens.

'Risk it?' Mwai said.

'Going back for the van?'

Mwai nodded.

'Nothing in it we need. Booked under a false name. No paper trail. We should leave it.'

Mwai nodded again.

'Let's walk somewhere busy and get a cab,' he said.

It was Budd's turn to nod.

They continued down the alley, which opened into another of the streets in the docks. Mwai had seen a map of the port area on his phone for long enough to think taking a right was the best thing to do. The number of vehicles and pedestrians increased, and the warehouses gave way to offices, and then shops.

Mwai felt a movement near his hip. He put his hand there. A phone was vibrating in his pocket.

He was carrying four now. One Crewe had given him on the first day, two from the dead men in Durban, and the one he'd just picked up from under the water cooler, the one out of the reach of a dead man.

That was the one that was ringing.

He took it out.

Caller ID showed: NATHAN JENNINGS. A name he'd heard for the first time only last night. Interesting.

Mwai answered it.

'Hello,' he said, neutrally.

'Riba?' said a voice.

'Who is this?'

'It's Nathan. Look, we need to meet.'

'Why?'

'I'm in trouble, man, I need your help.'

Mwai couldn't remember the last time anyone had called him "man". He had assumed it had gone out of fashion.

'Can't help you, man. I'm busy.'

'I can make it worth your while, you know I can,' the voice said.

'Keep talking.'

'Meet me. Are you in Nanyuki?'

'No. But I can be.'

'Tomorrow evening. Same place as last time.'

Mwai thought fast. How would he know where the same place as last time was?

'Which last time?' he said.

'Riff's, man. By the airstrip. Nine pm.'

''K,' Mwai said, and hung up.

'Who was that?' Budd said.

'No idea. But whoever it was wants to meet the dead guy in Nanyuki tomorrow night. Might be worth showing up.'

Budd raised his eyebrows. 'Might just be.'

Riff's. What were the chances of that?

———

Mwai was tired when they pulled up in front of the bunkhouse for the second time in two days. The lights were blazing again. He wouldn't be surprised if Klabu Viziwi was visible from space. It seemed better lit up than the whole of Nanyuki. The bunkhouse was a shadow beside it.

Mwai and Budd climbed out of the Range Rover. Mwai took the bag with Andrei Petrov's laptop from the footwell and they went inside. The hall was starting to have a certain familiarity. Crewe was in the same place, in what looked like the same clothes, but they were clean and crisp. Perhaps he always dressed the same for work. The need to be in a uniform hardwired in his brain.

'You bring the phones?' Crewe said.

'Yes, Mr Crewe.' Mwai handed over the phones he'd taken from the bodies in Durban. Crewe glanced at them and put them in a drawer in his desk.

'What did you find?'

'Andrei's laptop,' Mwai held it up. 'The password is "tusker". All lower case. Load of emails to and from a company called Health and Beauty Vietnam. We paid them a visit. We weren't their first callers of the day.'

'Oh?' Crewe seemed disinterested.

'Someone had blown the locks an hour before we got there. Killed a guy, ransacked the office.'

'Anything?'

'Nothing.'

'Who was the guy?'

'No idea. He was cleaned out.'

'You learned nothing.' It wasn't a question.

'Don't think so. I've some things to work through, but they're most likely nothing. Do you have anything? On the fingerprints?'

'Not yet. Our guy in South Africa said to give him forty-eight hours. Our guy in Kenya didn't answer. He will, but he's not exactly an employee.'

Mwai nodded.

'What about Jane Haven? Has she shown up anywhere?' Mwai said.

'What do you mean?'

'Obvious channels. Ports, airports, phones, watch on her place. I assume you're doing all those things.'

'The ports and the airports won't give anything, as I am sure you know. Only an idiot would use them. Refugees from Syria can get across Europe without passports armed only with a need to survive. She has training, and borders in Africa are long and mostly unguarded. She's not going to hand in her passport anywhere.'

'But she has a phone?'

'Had. Last recorded use was the night she was captured near where she was captured. It wasn't on her then.'

'And a watch on her place?'

Crewe looked up.

'Maybe.'

'Maybe?'

'There's been a watch. From a car a little way down the street. Three shifts, changing every eight hours. Four days ago, one of the shift changes was compromised when the outgoing team found their fuel and brake lines had been cut in the night whilst they were sitting in the car. Both men are adamant they were awake all night.'

'Were they, Mr Crewe?'

'I don't know. They're not my people. Seems the army has taken an interest in her as well. But the woman protects big, slow animals, Odinga. She's hardly likely to be able to approach a car, isolated on a street, with two vigilant men in it, crawl under the car, cut two lines, then get away without them being asleep, is she?'

'Her service record was redacted,' Mwai said.

'She's a woman. It will be because she slept with someone she shouldn't have,' Crewe said, looking down at the pad in front of him. Which was blank. Mwai got the message. He was dismissed.

Bogey man.

———

Back in the Range Rover Budd waited until they were off Klabu Viziwi land before he spoke.

'You didn't tell him about the other phone, or the phone call.'

'And neither did you, Budd.'

'None of my business.'

'So why have you mentioned it?'

'Just curious. In the warehouse you needed to satisfy your curiosity about my business. I didn't object. Helped me out some. I couldn't have lifted those crates. Thought you'd maybe satisfy mine.'

'What are you curious about, Budd?'

'Did you not tell him about the other phone because everyone else he's known about turned up dead before you spoke to them?'

Mwai looked at Budd. The only electric lights they could see were the headlights of the Range Rover, knifing into the night as the vehicle bounced along a rough track on its way back to the C76. But there were stars, and the moon was close to full, and Mwai could see enough of Budd's face. He read nothing in the expression.

'That's an interesting hypothesis, Budd. You could almost rephrase it as, everyone else who might have been able to help me find the woman Mr Crewe is paying me to find has turned up dead before I even heard of them.'

'That's why you didn't tell him about Nathan Jennings?'

'How'd you know about Nathan Jennings?'

'Saw the caller ID.'

Mwai looked at Budd for a moment. Deliberating.

'Maybe,' he said, eventually. 'But more I didn't tell him about—' Mwai glanced, subconsciously, at the driver, who was staring impassively ahead, '—the meeting because of where it is. This is my town. Someone I went to school with owns the rendez-vous. I don't want two units going through it without knowing who it is they're looking for.'

'Fair enough,' Budd said. 'And, despite it being none of my business, I'm happy to help, if you think I could. Nothing else to do this evening anyway.'

Mwai processed the tone of Budd's voice. He sounded sincere.

'Thank you, Budd,' he said.

The Range Rover dropped him off in the same place as the night before. Mwai followed the same route back to his dad's house, for a way. Then he stopped. He took out the two phones he still had. The one taken from the dead man in Mombasa, and the one Crewe had given him. He thought for a moment. A minute. Five minutes.

He was standing next to the corrugated iron shacks, in sight of the gates to his dad's house. During the day the shacks were fruit stalls. At night they were empty structures. He ran back the way he had come, into the town centre, down streets he had known all his life, and ones that had grown since he had lived here. The town was spreading.

He ran.

Mwai wasn't a natural long-distance runner. He was too big. Over short distances he was incredibly quick. He had good reflexes, could be out of the blocks in a split second. But after three hundred metres it used to be that he'd start to stitch and pull up. In part because he always went off too quickly.

For the last few months in Freetown, though, he'd been training to run more slowly. Really slowly. He would never cover a kilometre in less than three minutes. But he'd disciplined himself to cover two kilometres, and a little more, before having to stop.

The place he was running to was about two kilometres away. On the other side of town. Almost.

The Spice Garden hotel. Very nice. Mwai had never stayed there. He'd never been in. But he knew the new owners.

He stopped running a hundred metres from the hotel

entrance, stopped dead, from a run to standing still, just like that. He let his hearing adjust. Traffic noise, not much. Nanyuki was quiet at night. It was a market town, traffic was a daytime event. Now, in the dark, there was the occasional car, truck, or piki piki. A street away, maybe two, he could hear the sounds of a bar. Nearer, in the grasses and bushes on the edges of the lots and tracks, the insects played their night time tunes, though that noise was quieter than he'd ever known it. Because of the drought, he guessed.

He could see the entrance to the hotel, well lit, its coloured neon spilling onto the road. He breathed. It had been a long time.

He started walking again. A bead of sweat had formed on his brow and trickled down the side of his face. His body was hot. He felt energised. Ready. The other side of the road was a big, empty lot. Nanyuki was full of them. It was a town with space. Perhaps someone owned it and had forgotten. Perhaps someone didn't, and no one else had noticed. Whichever was true, the lot was about two acres. A hundred trees and nothing else. Mwai turned and looked at it, stared into the darkness.

He walked across the street and into the lot. Stood and listened. Towns and cities made him feel tense. He knew it now. Only recently had he worked that out. He was happier out on the plateau, out where the influence of man was less in evidence.

The happiest he had ever been was in Mozambique, half a decade ago, when he'd been part of a patrol that got lost in the mountains. They'd walked for two days through the forest, then reached the tree line and found themselves on a snub mountain peak. Raw and empty, but with a stream and a sheltering bluff, they'd made camp. The next day Mwai had woken when it was still dark and walked to the top of the mountain. He'd sat and watched the sunrise. He'd expected to be alone.

His expectations had been dashed, in the most amazing way. Butterflies, hundreds of them, fluttered, flickered, coupled, and dispersed before the heat of the day. When the patrol had reoriented, set a new direction, a new goal, Mwai had been sad.

He took out the two phones, the one from Crewe and the one from Mombasa. He switched them both off. Then he left the lot, crossed the street, and entered the grounds of the hotel.

He walked up to the front door, opened it, and went in. It was a hotel. He didn't think he needed to knock.

It was, what was the word, "bijou." French for jewel. He would have learned that in Mombasa if he'd been there before today. Instead, he'd learnt it in one of his father's books. Bijou. Small and precious. The hotel had been laid out by someone thinking that way. The colours were Kenyan, but multi-Kenyan. Maasai, Kikuyu, Luhya, yes. The famous and the most populous represented. But the Kisii, the Mijikenda, the Luo, the Kalejin. Whoever had designed the décor of this room had thought of them all. Mwai felt himself break into a huge grin.

'I thought you would come tonight, my brother.'

Mwai turned. Five years, was it? That wasn't the voice of a bitter man.

'Barasa,' Mwai said, turning to face the voice. Mwai had deliberately, after thinking it through as he ran, picked that tone. Not quite apologetic, not quite superior.

'Big brother, I am happy you are here.'

Mwai looked at his brother for the first time in half a decade,

'Big brother,' he said. 'I am happy I am here.'

Barasa stood up. He had been sitting in the hotel's reception area, reading a book that was now spreadeagled open on the table next to the chair.

Mwai was the older, by two years. Barasa called him "big brother" because of his age,

Barasa was bigger, five centimetres taller and thirty kilos heavier. Mwai called him "big brother" for those reasons. Mwai hadn't seen Barasa in five years. Thirty kilos was now a fifty.

They stood three metres apart.

'I am sorry,' Mwai said. 'I am so sorry. I failed you. I failed our family.'

Barasa stood. And he smiled.

'I am sorry. I have done what father taught us, I have researched. I learned the facts. I did not understand. Not then. I think now I do.'

Mwai stood. He realised he was crying. Tears dribbled into his mouth and down his beard.

Barasa broke it. Broke the impasse. He took five steps and wrapped Mwai in the only hug he ever had where he was the smaller participant. Mwai sobbed. Barasa held him for the longest time.

'That should be my job,' Mwai said, rubbing a hand across his eyes and mouth, slapping his brother on the back.

'Where have you been?' Barasa said.

'Everywhere but where I should be,' Mwai said.

They broke apart. Mwai stepped back. Barasa stepped back. At the same time, they both started laughing, like they had when they were in school. In less than a minute they were in another embrace. And then they stepped apart again.

'Dad says you're doing well,' Mwai said.

'Dad says he doesn't know what you're doing,' Barasa said.

Mwai felt his face drop, turn to stone.

'I can't tell Dad,' he said. 'I...'

'You kill poachers, Mwai. Just because we couldn't talk doesn't mean I didn't keep my ear to the ground. You've been to South Africa, Mozambique, Namibia, Chad, even Angola for a time that must have been hell, and Gambia, and most recently, Sierra Leone. You're still trying to find the men who killed that elephant. I know that. I have watched. I have asked questions. Have you found, I want to say "peace" but that's not quite what I mean. Have you found... calm?'

Mwai put his arms around his brother again and held him.

'Not yet,' he said. 'But I came, and you welcome me, so.'

He smiled and stepped back, let go of his brother's arms.

'Barasa,' he said.

'Yes, my brother.'

'I'd just like to watch out of the window at the lot across the road for a few minutes.'

'Why?'

'Do you still own Riff's Bar?'

CHAPTER THIRTY

'I DIDN'T EXPECT TO SEE YOU AGAIN SO SOON,' GODKNOWS said, climbing out of his plane to greet Makena on the tarmac of Mombasa airport. 'You are looking well for a man bitten by a snake not twenty hours ago. How are you feeling, my friend?'

In truth Makena looked awful and was walking with the aid of a stick Walker had cut from a sapling by the side of the road. His bandaged leg was heavily swollen.

'A little dizzy now and then, nothing to worry about. The trip on the boat was worse,' Makena said. Walker snorted at that. 'I need another favour, cousin.'

'Where can I take you this time? Barbados? The Maldives? Cicely, Alaska?'

'Nanyuki,' Makena said.

'I have already been to Nanyuki today. I went straight away after leaving you here. I am pleased to report it is still there and awaiting your return with eagerness and anticipation.'

'What have you been smoking?' Walker said.

'I am very pleased to know my favourite cousin is going to be alright. When would you like to leave?'

'Now,' Jane said.

'Now? Now is not possible, my friends, because I have been in the air for twelve hours today. Landed on a road. Took off in the dark once, and from a field once. And I need to stretch my legs, drink some coffee, eat something nutritious, and go to the bathroom. And not necessarily in that order.'

'Please, cousin,' Makena said. 'It is important.'

Godknows appraised him for a moment.

'Alright, cousin, since you have had a brush with death, I shall make this sacrifice for you. I shall stretch my legs whilst walking to the bathroom if you supply me with some coffee, and something nutritious to eat.'

Makena smiled.

'I'll get the food and coffee,' Walker said. 'Where is it?'

'I'll show you,' Godknows said. They walked off towards the terminal building.

'Get the bags,' Jane said to Nathan.

They loaded the plane. Makena stood leaning on his staff, his eyes closed.

'Get in,' Jane said.

Nathan climbed in and took the same seat he'd used on the flight from Iringa. Jane watched him. Then he stood up, stooping under the plane's roof, and walked forward to the cockpit. He picked up a newspaper lying on Godknows' seat and took it back to his own.

Jane looked at Makena. She had no idea what to say. Her ability to console the wounded was limited to "looking forward to having you back on the line, soldier." She could only see the world when it was working as it should. The times when parts of it were out of kilter were confusing to her.

'Like being hit by a hammer,' she said.

Makena opened his eyes.

'Yes, that was what it was like,' he said. 'And that was the highlight.' He smiled. A weary smile but with real warmth. 'We'll find them,' he said. 'We'll find the men who did these terrible things. And then what?'

Jane didn't answer.

'Jane.' It was Nathan, inside the plane. His voice had an edge to it. A wobble. Like that of a small child calling his mother when he'd seen something he didn't like. 'Jane, you need to read this.'

Jane leaned in through the plane door, keeping Nathan in view as she did so. He had the newspaper in his hand. He was holding it out for her.

She took it.

It was today's copy of The Standard, Nanyuki's daily paper.

The headline was about the refurbishment of the railway line between Nanyuki and Nairobi. Why was that interesting? Jane looked at Nathan.

'Bottom right,' he said.

"Young ranger killed in hit and run" was the sub-header in the bottom right.

And, next to it, a picture of Timu Obote. The one from the Bandari website. Jane read.

'They killed him,' Nathan said, his voice rank with fear. 'And they will kill me. Take me back to Malawi. I will disappear from there.'

Jane read. Dusk yesterday, just as they had been landing next to the elephant in Tanzania, police in Nanyuki had responded to a report of an injured man lying on the side of the C76, near what locals refer to as "The Graveyard". He died before the ambulance arrived. Police say he was hit by a car crossing the road.

The article described Timu's schooling, his joining the Bandari rangers, and his involvement in the recent death of the last male northern white rhino. It went on to describe how he had been implicated as an accessory and then exonerated by the conviction of the real culprit, Jane Haven, who had escaped, and was currently the subject of a major manhunt.

'They'll catch and kill you, and then they'll kill me,' Nathan said. 'Let me go.'

Jane climbed into the plane, the newspaper still in her hand. She crouched and walked to the back, brought her face to within centimetres of Nathan's.

'You know me,' Jane said. 'You know who I am. What makes you think that they are more dangerous than me?'

Nathan's face changed. He considered the question seriously.

'All that you've seen me do, Nathan. What makes you think that anyone you have ever met is going to catch me?'

'They caught you. In Bandari. They put you in Lang'ata.'

'That is fair. I made a mistake. I thought I was working with the system to find the men I will find. And that cost me. It cost me time. But that is all. I have corrected for that mistake. I know the system is working against me now.'

'You can't—'

'Can't what? Escape from Lang'ata? No. Never been done before, had it? Can't find you? You were gone. You did well. No one else found you, did they? And yet here we are, having this conversation. How long did it take me?

You're afraid of the wrong people, Nathan.' Jane sat back, breathed out. 'I talked to Saachi. You're a lucky man. She has faith in you. I saw your children. They are beautiful.' Jane paused. She had his attention. 'When you next see Saachi ask her. Ask her what happened to the men who came to your house looking for you. Ask her who stopped them.'

'Men came to my house?' His voice went up an octave, quivering.

'Yes. I broke a bone in your wrist because your tried to pull a gun on me. It's a small price to pay for your mistake. The men who came to your house paid a higher price.'

Nathan stared at his hands.

'Nathan, you're a soldier. You're a ranger. You made a mistake, whatever it was that got you kicked out of the army. That mistake has snowballed, and you've made another mistake. You took money to let people kill Douglas, Jomo, and Kennet. But you're still a ranger. You're still a soldier. This is a war. Whose side are you on?'

Nathan stared at his hands.

'When we meet Riba tomorrow, whose side are you on?'

Nathan stared at his hands, but moved them, turned them over. Then looked up.

'We won't be meeting Riba tomorrow,' he said.

Jane turned her head, just slightly.

'Why?'

'The man who answered the phone wasn't Riba.'

———

Godknows banked the plane, straightened it, brought it onto the approach for the Nanyuki airstrip behind Riff's Bar. He looked tired, but this was falling off a bike for him. He knew this airstrip. Jane could see that.

They touched down. Light was failing. The sunset would drop in minutes. Twenty-six point five hours from now till the meeting with the man who wasn't Riba.

She could plan a lot in that time.

Godknows taxied the plane to a halt in front of a shack. The engine juddered to a halt.

He nodded and turned.

'The balance of favours owed is tending my way, cousin,' he said.

Makena smiled.

'I'll tend it the other way, cousin,' he said.

Godknows said nothing, just opened the pilot's door and got out.

'Right,' Jane said. 'We have a plan. We know the constraints of that plan. We know what to do if those constraints change. Right?'

'I can help,' Makena said, the strength of his voice contradicting him.

'You have helped,' Walker said. 'Now do what you're told and stay away.'

'And I need you to find something out for me,' Jane said.

'What?'

'I need you to find out if any of the Bandari staff other than Nathan have a history with the Kenya Rifles. Served with them, have relatives still in them, anything like that. Could you do that? Do you have cousins who could help?'

'Of course. Why?'

'Just a hunch. Look at majors especially. I was caught by a company, but a major was the ranking officer. Too senior for a company. What's garrisoned at the barracks on the plateau?'

'Two battalions,' Nathan said.

'There's not going to be many majors. Find out. I'll call for answers.'

Makena nodded.

'Take him to his mother's,' Jane said to Godknows.

Godknows and Makena left in a taxi twenty minutes later.

'Thank you,' Jane said, staring Walker in the face as she swung one of the heavier bags over her shoulder.

'Ten years, Marple, and that's the first time you've said that.'

Jane said nothing. Walker smiled.

'Go,' Walker said.

'Come on,' Jane said to Nathan. They picked up the bags they would need for the night.

'See you tomorrow, sister,' Jane heard Walker call, as the sun disappeared, and the darkness swallowed them. 'See you right here.'

Jane turned to look at Riff's Bar. It onto the airstrip, one of its outbuildings touched the boundary fence. Four small aircraft were parked with their tails against the fence in front of the property. On the other side of the fence the business looked closed, no lights on.

'What kind of bar is closed at four thirty in the afternoon?'

'It's not really a bar. It's a restaurant for pilots and passengers. It closes when the airstrip buildings close.'

'So why did you meet Riba here?'

'Because he'd fly in from Mombasa sometimes. We met out the back by the bins after it closed. No one about.'

'Come on, we need to find somewhere to wait.'

CHAPTER THIRTY-ONE

'What does Crewe think you're doing this evening?' Mwai said.

'Nothing,' Budd said. 'It's a down night.'

'You believe that?'

'What does he think you're doing?'

'Down night.'

'We'll see, won't we?'

'We'll see.'

Riff's Bar. One of the most reputable eating establishments in Nanyuki. Best breakfast and lunch in Laikipia County. It closed at four thirty in the afternoon. Every day.

Budd was a shadow in the window at the front, looking onto the A2 road, the automatic he held making his arm look unnaturally long. Mwai was a shadow in the window in the back, looking onto the carpark and the airstrip. The automatic he held was like a child's toy in his hand. They'd been in place since closing.

'This Nathan Jennings we're meeting, who is he?' Budd asked.

'He doesn't exist.'

'How d'you mean?'

'Jane Haven killed the rhino, so the story goes. Jennings and another ranger called Obote let the killers in, and they weren't Jane Haven, so another story goes. The men paying us, they believe the first story. Nathan Jennings doesn't exist, from our employer's perspective.'

Budd kept his vigil, he was alert. Mwai could see his head watching passing traffic each time he glanced at him.

'What do you reckon's going to happen tonight?' Budd said.

Mwai stared out into the dark of the airstrip. Had he seen something? He thought he'd maybe seen something.

'There'll be what the old cowboy movies termed "a reckoning",' he said.

'You reckon?' said Budd.

'Possibly,' Mwai said.

'What makes you think that?' said a voice, right behind Mwai's head, so close it was in his head. A female voice.

Mwai felt the cold steel of a gun barrel pressing into the side of his throat, but from an angle he had no way to reach, not in the time it would take to pull a trigger.

Mwai froze.

He answered. But not quite.

'You OK, Budd?' Mwai said.

'Naw,' Budd said.

'I'll tell you when to talk,' the female voice said.

'You bring your phone, Budd?' Mwai said.

Mwai felt a jab into the soft spot under his ear, behind his jaw, that caused him more physical pain than he could remember. He pulled his hand to the spot instinctively, and felt another pain, like a bullet, in his wrist.

'Budd has his own attendant,' said the voice. 'Don't worry about him. Concentrate. The man who answered Riba's phone wasn't Riba, but he was Kenyan. It wasn't Budd. It was you. Did you kill Douglas?'

'Who's Douglas?' Mwai said.

He felt pain again. He recognised it from training, fifteen years ago, with that British soldier who had thought he was funny. A small, hard, thing. Bit of wood, the size of a pen. Perhaps a bit of metal. What was really important was knowing which bits of a person hurt when you hit them with something like that. The woman behind him knew.

She also cocked the gun. He heard the click.

'We've got off on the wrong foot,' he said. 'My name is Mwai. The guy over there is Budd. We're only regular guys, Jane. If you don't listen to me, the night is going to get really noisy.'

'Did you kill Douglas?' the voice said.

'Let him go,' a different voice said. The one Mwai had been waiting for. His brother.

Mwai felt the pressure of the gun against his neck removed. He turned around.

The woman was small. Everyone was small to him, well, except the man who had a gun to her head. She was five eight, muscled, slender. Her arms were going up as Basara held his barrel, a peashooter in his massive hand, to her temple.

Over in the other window the same thing was happening. A man, presumably Nathan Jennings, who had been holding a gun to Budd's head was lowering it as one of Basara's employees held their own gun to his.

'You are Jane Haven, I assume. Acknowledge that, because I have a speech, I have reserved for no one else,' Mwai said.

The woman nodded. Right then her eyes were the most alive eyes he had ever seen. She had an earpiece in, and night vision goggles raised over her head. Mwai was very aware he needed to do everything very slowly, even with that gun to her skull.

He looked her in the eyes, swallowed, and began.

'When I was a younger man, I was a ranger, like you. No, not like you. I joined the rangers because they gave us guns. I was a boy. Not much more than a boy. My grandfather was a soldier, went to war for the British against the Italians in Abyssinia and Eritrea. I remember him in his uniform. He wore it when he could, when occasion allowed. He looked smart, like the British soldiers, my *bibi* said. This was when I was a child, when the white men were another breed. Before I realised you were just like us, no more, no less. Though perhaps more... angry.

'I wanted a gun and a uniform. I tried the army, but they didn't want me. I was too big, can you believe. So, I became a ranger. They paid almost nothing, but they gave me a gun and a uniform. A Beretta rifle, taken from the Italians all those years ago, a gun older than my father. My grandfather had seen them, had used them. It still fired.

'The poachers who came into the reserves then, they were mostly not like the poachers we have now. Most were just men trying to feed their families. They were after the meat. Sometimes they'd get away, sometimes they wouldn't. For me that was the game. I had a uniform and a gun, like my grandfather, and I chased poachers. The poachers never shot at us then, they ran. I was a young man, I chased. Until this elephant.

'There was a small herd that ranged around where Ol Faraja now is, and to the north. Twelve elephant. And the oldest mother was beautiful. She was clever. She knew what we were. She knew we were protecting them. When there were hunters near, she would lead the herd to our hut for safety.

'She was wild. If we went towards her when they were out in the valley, they were like any other herd. But if there was danger from man, they would come to us. And we protected them.

'We called her Malkia—'

'Queen,' Jane said.

'Yes, queen. She was big. Almost as big as a bull. And she was intelligent. The first time I killed a man,' Mwai said. He suddenly felt he needed a drink. 'The first time I killed a man it was a poacher, come for the elephants. For the ivory, not for the meat. Malkia had led the herd to the ranger station in the night. I was on duty. I heard them coming and got my rifle.

'The poachers – there were four – were following, not knowing where the elephants were going. The first had a gun to shoot the elephant. He came out of the dark. I saw him raise his weapon, so I fired my rifle without aiming. Hit him near the heart. Lucky shot. The other three ran. I went to where he lay. His skin looked blue in the moonlight, like an alien. He died within a minute. I watched him. I didn't know what to do. I felt bad. Then I felt something on my shoulder. It was Malkia's trunk. She let it rest there for a time, a time I can never forget. She lifted it away and led the herd past me back into the night. Me and a dead poacher, amidst these huge, quiet creatures. They followed her. She kept them safe.'

Mwai felt tears fill his eyes. He looked away from Jane. He went on.

'When we found her, it was a Sunday. She was lying in a

gulley a little south of Kirichu. They'd shot her six times.
From the blood soaked into the earth round her head, she
was still alive when they hacked off her tusks. I never found
the men who did it. I wanted to find them. I have been
hunting them ever since.'

He stopped.

'Budd, it's really important that you tell me if you brought
your phone,' Mwai said.

'I brought it.'

'Is it switched on?'

'Yes.'

'Switch it off.'

Across the room Budd took his phone out of his pocket
and switched it off. Mwai did the same with his, with the one
Crewe had given him. He turned back to Jane Haven.

'The reason I am telling you this is because I want to help
you find the men who killed your rhino. What was he called?'

'Douglas,' Jane said.

'They killed your brother, too. And your lover. But you
asked me if I had killed your rhino. I understand. You weren't
paid to protect your brother, or your lover. You were paid to
protect your rhino, and you failed.'

Jane's jaw moved, just a little.

'I've got an idea. I think I know someone who knows who
did it. Some men are on their way here who work for this
person. When they get here, I would like you and I to ask
them together.'

'What men?'

'The men who killed Omariba Butare in a warehouse in
Mombasa yesterday. The man you call Riba.' Mwai saw
Nathan Jennings react. 'The men who killed Andrei Petrov,
amongst others, in a warehouse in Durban a few days ago.'

'Shit,' Budd said.

'How does that make you feel, Budd?' Mwai said.

'I'm a mercenary. I get paid. Don't care too much about who pays me. How do you know they're coming?'

'We switched our phones off. Yesterday I did a little experiment. Switched my phone off. In a lot opposite my brother's hotel. Then we sat and watched. Thirty minutes after switching the phone off the men turned up, dressed for war. They are tracking our phones.'

'Why?' Budd said.

'Because they expect me to find her. She's the next target. They ask you to tell them what I was doing?'

'They did. I haven't. Don't like sneaking.'

'They're coming to kill her, Budd. You going to let them?'

'I ain't gonna stand in their way. But I ain't gonna help them neither.'

'Fair enough. Go. Now. Before they get here.'

'OK,' Budd said, and started walking towards the door.

'Wait. Barasa, go with him, take your man. This isn't your fight.'

Barasa still had his gun to Jane Haven's temple.

'She hasn't said she's going to stand with you yet.'

'Well?' Mwai said to Jane.

She stared at him, her eyes moving imperceptibly, as though processing a thousand problems at the same time.

'Did you get all that?' she said. He wasn't sure who she was asking. 'Three men coming out. Let them go.'

'You have someone watching outside.'

Jane nodded.

'Let's get ready,' she said. 'How many?'

'Four.'

'SpecOps training?'

'Two by two.'

'How will they come?'

'By road. They parked up a kilometre away last night and came in on foot.'

'Nathan, go out the back, same way we came in. Go wait in the plane.'

'I can help,' Nathan said.

'Wait in the plane. Go.'

Budd, Basara, and Basara's man left. Nathan went out through the kitchen. Jane and Mwai were alone. She looked at him with a question in her eyes.

'What?' he said.

'Why?' she said.

'I told you.'

'I accept that gives some... context. But why? You could just walk away.'

'They're killing everyone who knows they were involved. I'd be a loose end.'

'Someone pissed you off, didn't they? One of these guys?'

Mwai said nothing.

'Don't let it get personal,' she said.

'Should I say the same to you?'

'Do you trust that man, Budd?'

'Not in the least.'

She nodded.

'Let's go.'

CHAPTER THIRTY-TWO

JANE WAITED IN THE DARK, THOUGH WITH THE GOGGLES she could see through the gap in the wall and the bush in front of it, down the road.

She was eight hundred metres from Riff's Bar, in the opposite direction to Nanyuki, on the opposite side of the road. If Mwai was right the men would be here in less than five minutes.

'You in position?' she asked.

'Check,' Walker said in her earpiece.

'These goggles are too small,' she heard Mwai's voice in her ear.

'You in position?'

'Check,' he said, with a sigh.

He was dangerous. He'd known how she'd come at him. He must have concealed his brother and the other man in the walk-in fridge, locked from the inside since lunchtime. Smuggled in by the delivery truck that had come then. Smart. But lucky. There could have been four of them, not just her and Nathan. Lucky meant potentially careless.

Headlights approached from the direction of Nanyuki.

'Get ready,' she said.

'Check.'

'It's not them,' Mwai said. 'It's a car. They'll be in a—'

'Land Cruiser,' Jane said.

'I was going to say Range Rover.'

'The vehicles they used in Bandari were Land Cruisers.'

'It's passed me. One woman driving. No passengers.'

A minute later the car passed Jane's hiding place. It was an old Subaru. One woman driving.

But there was another set of headlights in the distance.

'Land Cruiser,' Mwai said. Long seconds passed. 'It's them.'

The headlights kept coming towards her. The vehicle slowed in front of the bar, then speeded up before slowing again as it passed Jane and pulled off the road barely fifty metres from her. She could see figures inside. All doors opened at the same time, including the hatchback. Four men got out, dressed in black, combat uniforms, balaclavas. They wore the headsets Mwai had described, night vision goggles, cameras.

They went quickly to the back and took out guns, checked them.

'Ready to go,' one said, a hand on his ear. Then he waved his hands, and the four men set off at a jog towards the bar, in two pairs, on either side of the road.

'Eyes on,' Walker said.

One of the pairs disappeared round the back of the bar. The other went to the front door. Jane lost sight of both.

'Infiltration,' Walker said.

'Mwai, get in position,' Jane said. She leapt the wall she had been crouching behind and ran to the Land Cruiser.

They both had eight hundred metres to cover from their hiding places to Walker's position. Jane estimated it would take the men three minutes to clear the building, confirm it was empty. She and Mwai needed to be in place by then to avoid being seen. Eight hundred metres in three minutes was easy for her, but he looked too big to be a sprinter. She fixed the small explosive charge in place above the car's front passenger-side wheel. She heard his breathing through the earpiece. Thirty seconds. She turned and ran, counting in her head. One minute. Ninety seconds. Two minutes. A hundred and fifty seconds.

She reached Walker a moment before Mwai did. They crowded into the gateway opposite the entrance to the bar. Walker was motionless, watching the building through the sniperscope of the Remington.

'They're coming out,' Walker said.

Mwai moved, as if he was going to have a look at the men over the wall, but Jane put her hand on his arm. Too risky.

'They're going back to the car,' Walker said, tracking their movements through the gun. 'Still don't want to cross the road while their backs are turned?'

'No,' Jane said.

'You're the boss. Guns going in the trunk, balaclavas coming off, two men in, three. Fourth one seems to be talking to someone, but not on a phone.'

'Which door?'

'Passenger side. Front, I think.'

'What does he look like?' Mwai said.

'He's wearing a balaclava.'

'What colour are his hands?' Mwai said.

'Green through this scope.'

'Black or white?'

'I'd guess white.'

'Then that's François. He's in charge.'

'He's getting in,' Walker reported.

'Passenger side we need alive,' Jane said.

'That's the other side of the car.'

'Whilst it's upright.'

Walker nodded without changing her stance. 'Lights on. Engine on. Turning, waiting. What are they waiting for?'

The sound of an engine behind them answered the question. Another car went past.

'Now they're on the road, coming this way.'

'Get ready,' Jane said. She had the M9 in one hand and the detonator to the charge she had fixed under wheel arch in the other.

As the car drew level with them, she pressed the detonator. There was a loud noise, and the car lurched to the ground as the front left wheel blew off. Mwai and Jane were out of the gateway and round the car, front and back, whilst it was still sliding to a stop. It tilted forward, the rear wheels leaving the ground as all its weight went onto the broken axle, but it wasn't travelling fast enough to tip, and fell back onto the other three wheels. Walker fired four times to shatter the windows. Then twice more to kill the driver and the man in the seat behind him.

'Clear!' she said.

Mwai and Jane moved in on the car. Mwai fired into the back on the passenger side, reached in and opened the door with the handle from the inside, dragging a man out by his neck.

Jane pointed her gun at the remaining man in the front seat from a metre away.

'Hands!' she said.

Slowly he raised his hands. There was a handgun in one.

'Drop it,' she said. 'Outside the car.'

He carefully eased the hand holding the gun forward and let go.

'Get out,' she said after kicking the gun away into the grass.

'Car coming,' Walker's voice said in her ear.

'That him?' Jane said to Mwai, motioning to the man getting out.

'Yes,' he said. 'That's François.'

François looked at Mwai with contempt.

'Status?' Jane said.

'Shot that one in the leg,' Mwai said, waving vaguely at the other survivor on the ground.

'Leave him. Bring this one.'

Mwai grabbed François and dragged him into the dark down the side of Riff's Bar. Jane followed.

The headlights coming towards them were getting brighter, and the car was slowing down.

'Where are we going?' Mwai said.

'To get Nathan. Onto the airstrip.'

'What about Brigit?'

'Right behind you, big guy,' Walker said from exactly there.

'You're quiet,' Mwai said, breathing harder as they ran. 'When we've got Nathan, where then?'

'I have a place in mind,' Jane answered. She pushed through the gap in the fence behind the outbuilding. 'Did you get the headsets?' she said over her shoulder.

'Yes,' Walker said.

———

'What is this place?' Mwai asked.

'Abandoned,' Jane said.

They had parked on the rise overlooking the ranch. Nathan and Walker remained in the van they'd stolen from the airstrip, keeping an eye on François. François was unconscious. He'd tried to run when they were crossing the runway. Jane had hit him quite hard.

'They sent me here when they were killing Douglas,' she said. She was facing away from the ranch, looking back at the road, following the headlights of a car as it passed the entrance to the track below them. It didn't slow or turn, just kept on going.

'How?'

'Phoned in a report of a sighting. Poachers. Someone had been here and lit a fire to make sure there was evidence, something for me to investigate. But that was it. Only things that have been here in years are rats. And a serval.'

'Who owns it?'

'No idea. Come on. Van goes in the barn, then we talk to François.'

To get the van in the barn they had to drag the disintegrating truck out of it. Which took time and rope.

Walker watched François. Mwai carried him from the van into the ranch. He was still out, and they'd tied his hands and feet, but Walker watched anyway, from the other side of the room, with Jane's M9 in her hand.

Jane watched Mwai and Nathan attaching the ropes to the front of the truck. Nathan was grimacing, but kept working, despite the pain he must have been feeling in his broken wrist.

'Axle will have seized up,' she said. 'Just going to have to drag it.' She stared at the truck. 'How heavy do you think that thing is?'

'Two tons, at a guess,' Mwai said, stepping back. 'Maybe two and a half.'

'Two thousand five hundred kilos and we need to move it about twenty metres, call it two-two-fifty for simplicity.' She muttered under her breath, looking at the ground next to the barn where the truck was to be dragged to.

The van was basic, cheap, and no spring chicken itself.

'Find some water. I'll push as well,' Mwai said.

Jane looked up.

'What?'

'You're about to calculate that the engine doesn't have enough horsepower to move it if it's slightly heavier than my guess and the ground offers up too much friction. Lubricate the ground with water – it's so dry nothing's going to get stuck in it, but a couple of centimetres of mud would help. I'll push as well.'

She shrugged. 'Good idea.'

'I haven't seen any water, though.'

'I'll go look,' Nathan said, and disappeared round the back of the house.

'Why haven't you killed him?' Mwai said when Nathan was out of earshot.

'Why do you think I am going to kill him?'

'Are you convinced he didn't kill any of them?'

'Timu said he didn't.'

'Who is Timu?'

'On shift with him that day. Let them in with him, left with him.'

'Where's he?'

'Dead. Hit and run two days ago.'

'You only have a dead man's word that Nathan didn't do any of the killing? Where did he run to?'

'Malawi.'

'Long way to run.'

'Doesn't feel like it either. He's scared of them. And with good reason. Besides,' Jane said. 'They didn't recognise each other.'

'Who, François? That only means François wasn't there.'

'I know.'

Nathan returned.

'There's a well round the back. Dug deep. Not dry.'

'Anything to carry the water in?' Jane said.

'Just this,' Nathan held up a bucket, and turned it on end. The bottom had rusted right through.

'Let's start by pulling,' Mwai said. 'If it doesn't move, we can try something else.'

It didn't move at first. Jane started the van, put it in gear, engaged the clutch. The ropes tying it to the truck stretched and took the strain. Mwai put his shoulder to the back of the truck and pushed. Nothing happened. Jane gave it some gas and the van's wheels started to slip and spin, churning up dust and dirt that billowed out into the dark. Mwai heaved again, Nathan joining him, and this time the truck lurched.

As it lurched its tyres disintegrated. As they did, exposing the metal wheels to the ground, the truck moved more quickly, sliding through the earth on the wheel rims like it was on ice skates.

Nathan and Mwai were sweating buckets. They had water in the van. They drank, as Jane untied the tow ropes.

Once the truck was where they needed it and the van safely in the barn, they joined Walker inside.

'He's still out,' she said, waving the M9 in François's direction.

'Let's set up a perimeter. Bring him round when we're done.'

'No one knows we're here,' Nathan said. 'Why do we need a perimeter?'

'They were tracking his phone,' she pointed at Mwai. 'Who knows what else they're tracking. And we have their headsets, we must assume they can track those. The only way to outthink someone who's paranoid is to be paranoid,' Jane said. She motioned towards François. 'And check him again, just to make sure. Take his clothes off. Bury them.'

Mwai nodded.

'Why did you want their headsets?' Mwai said.

'I want them to be able to hear us talking when I choose to let them.'

Jane led Walker outside, across the yard to the barn.

'We need another vehicle,' Jane said, pulling out a satellite phone from a bag in the van.

'Who are you calling?'

'Reinforcements. Whatever François tells us, we're going to need an army.'

CHAPTER THIRTY-THREE

Mwai returned from burying François' clothes to find him awake and staring at Nathan Jennings with an expression of fury.

François was lying on the floor, naked, his hands tied behind him, his legs tied together. His eye was swollen and bloodshot where Jane had hit him. Mwai had been impressed. When François had tried to run, Jane had moved like lightning, landing blows on the man as if he were already paralysed, and François was no part-timer. Mwai would bet even money François had been trained by the Recces, South Africa's Special Forces. But François hadn't known how to handle Jane. she didn't play by the training manual.

François turned his scowl on Mwai as soon as he heard him in the doorway.

'Hello, François,' Mwai said. There was a chair on its side by the wall. Mwai went to pick it up.

'I tried it, leg's broken,' Nathan said.

Mwai left it where it was. He'd have to improvise his intimidation.

'I have a few questions, François. Your best strategy would be to answer them quickly before the ladies get back. Otherwise, that might put them in a bad mood, and, well.' Mwai moved his hand to his face, pantomimed hitting himself.

François didn't say anything.

'It's a simple choice. You saw them kill two of your men. You'll remember I only wounded the third, so I'm the nice one. They won't hesitate to kill you. On the other hand, I don't think they give a shit about you, so they might be prepared to rough you up some more and leave you in a ditch.' Mwai stopped talking. He thought pacing would be more intimidating, so he started. The floor was covered in rat droppings, each with a tiny elongated shadow in the lamplight.

'This is the point where you're supposed to spit and say something defiant.' Mwai paused talking and pacing and waited. 'No? That's good, not going with stereotypical macho captive as your persona. Very good. Let me hit you with the really interesting bit. You, in charge of two units on a simple building search op, got taken out by a couple of women. It's a story they'll be telling in all the merc bars from here to South America. No one will hire you to raid a kindergarten. Here's your choice. Talk, and I'll keep my mouth shut. Say nothing, and I'll embellish.' Mwai held his hand up as François was about to speak. 'And before you tell me I won't live through the night so no one will ever know, I've already sent the information, by text, to a third party, with instructions where to send it in the event I don't make it through the night. Now, what were you about to say?'

François glared at Mwai with hatred.

'I knew you were going to be trouble,' François said. He grimaced. Talking hurt. Good.

'I'd make the joke about my middle name being trouble, but it's actually Shida.'

Nathan laughed.

François glared at him, then looked back at Mwai. He said nothing for a long time. Then he spoke.

'What do you want to know?'

'When did you get the job?'

'Four days before you did.'

Mwai nodded.

'How did you get it?' Who called you?'

'Crewe.'

'Worked with him before?'

François nodded.

'Served with him?'

François nodded. Must be less painful than talking.

'Where?'

'Praetoria.'

Mwai nodded again. Where the Recces were headquartered.

'What were your orders in Durban?'

'To kill one of those guys, the Ukrainian.'

'Who gave you that order?'

'Crewe.'

'Who else knew about that order?'

'Shaka.'

'Which one is Shaka?'

'The other South African. The one driving.'

Mwai nodded again.

'You're doing well, François. Very well. My story is losing its bells and whistles as we talk. Might even mention the women who took you out have had a bit of training at this rate. What about Mombasa?'

'What about it?'

'What was the mission, who went, what happened?'

François scowled heavily. He hadn't expected Mwai to know about that.

'Me and Shaka. Kill some guy in a warehouse.'

'What was his name?'

'Don't remember.'

'Orders came from?'

'Crewe.'

'Did he tell you why?'

'No.'

'Didn't you ask?'

'Not my business.'

'Don't you need a reason to assassinate someone?'

'I need lots of reasons. They fold.'

'How many guys are there? Four of you tonight, I dealt with Budd, how many others?'

François thought for a moment before answering.

'Four more.'

'Where are they?'

'Down time.'

'Where are they staying?'

'Hotels in town.'

'Not at Klabu Viziwi?'

'Nah.'

'How many are there? In security?'

'No idea.'

'You been there?'

'Once. You letting me go now?'

'Patience, patience. We must wait for the ladies to return. I shall need to negotiate with them. You will need to support my position. They may be angry. The redhead, particularly, she looks like she could get angry easily.'

'The redhead?' Walker said from behind him. Mwai cringed. He turned. He mouthed "play along."

'A term of affection only, I assure you,' he said aloud.

Walker looked at him, the Remington hanging menacingly in the crook of her arm. She shrugged, turned, and left.

Jane came through the door a few moments later. She had the small rod she'd used when punching François, the same thing she'd pressed into Mwai in several places back in the bar. She twirled it through her fingers without looking at it.

'Well?' she said.

'François has shared some information with me and hopes very much that you choose to rough him up a bit more then leave him in a ditch rather than kill him.'

'Anything useful?'

'Nothing. His briefings were as thorough as mine, in that they weren't thorough at all, and, unlike me, he didn't ask questions.'

'Do you believe him?'

'He's said nothing that I know to have been a lie.'

Jane motioned for Mwai to follow her onto the veranda.

The night was brilliant. Cloudless and no natural light other than that from the lantern inside meant the stars were frosted across the sky like diamonds. Insects played their music. The air was still.

'What did he say?' Jane kept her voice low.

'Served in the Recces with Crewe, worked with him since, called in four days before I was, so several days after the killings. Him and another South African name of Shaka, the driver tonight so already dead, killed Andrei and Riba on Crewe's orders. Doesn't know why. There's another four-man squad billeted in Nanyuki, he doesn't know how many are at Klabu Viziwi.'

'You think that's it?'

'That would be my guess. Budd was just the same. Didn't ask questions. Just took the money. Amoral.'

Jane stepped into the dark, walked a little way, walked back.

'What now?' he said.

'Crewe. Klabu Viziwi.'

'It's a fortress. And there's only four of us.'

'Three of us. Can't take Nathan. He has a family.'

'You sure you're a killer?' Mwai said.

'We'll have to get them out. Set fire to it.'

'You know what this means, don't you? A billionaire's head of security is doling out assassination instructions to mercenaries?'

'Yes,' Jane said.

'Billionaires always get away with it. Bigger the crime the easier it is.'

'Why? Why would he kill Douglas?'

'You told me yourself – the real question is why did they not kill the other two white rhinos? Or any of the other hundred black rhinos? If the motive was the horn, they had the perfect opportunity to kill more rhino. This wasn't about the money. Which suggests that the person who did it doesn't need it.'

'But why?'

'What was special about him?'

'Douglas? He was the last male of his species.'

'Perhaps that's it. The billionaire can boast to his billionaire friends how he ended a species. How many people can claim that?'

'We need to be sure.'

Jane thought for a moment.

'Nathan said the man who spoke to him and Timu on the day they let them in was South African. The men he got a look at in one of the cars were not smiling, wearing sunglasses, and had the same haircuts. He didn't see into the back seats of the two following cars. Sounds like a billionaire going for a drive with his bodyguards to me. How many men does he have up there?'

'My guess is a standard Close Protection team. Three shifts of eight. One head of internal security. They sleep in the bunkhouse when they're on duty, so there's always at least twenty-five to hand. Ex-SF. No amateurs.'

'To question Crewe, we're going to have to take the building. We'll have to kill all the others. We're assuming Andrews is responsible before we've confirmed it.'

Jane paced, lost in thought, muttering to herself.

'Land Cruisers. If he's got two more Land Cruisers somewhere.'

'He does. Training facility and storeroom. North of Nanyuki. Saw three there on my first day. They didn't register at the time – all the vehicles they've driven me around in have been Range Rovers.'

Jane looked straight at him. 'You're sure?'

'Yes.'

She was thinking. She paced. 'To question Crewe, we're going to have to take the building. What was in that storeroom?'

'Vehicle coming,' Walker's voice came out of the darkness.

'The barn. I'll cover the ranch,' Jane said, pushing Mwai in the direction of the barn door.

He slipped inside, picking up a gun from inside the open van.

He looked down the track. He couldn't see anything yet. He listened. He heard an engine.

Headlights came into view. They approached the ranch, driving slowly. Someone unfamiliar with the track.

The vehicle was a Bandari conservancy Land Rover. It slowed as it approached the buildings, coming to a complete stop closer to the ranch house than to the barn. The engine stopped. The door opened, and the interior lights came on.

The driver was a woman. A very beautiful woman.

'She's quite a sight, isn't she?' Walker said right next to him, her night vision goggles raised, making her about as tall as his shoulder. He almost jumped.

'You move quietly,' he said.

The woman got out of the car and was greeted by Jane coming out of the ranch. Jane had her satellite phone in her hand and was offering it out to the woman, asking her to make a call.

'I muffle my steps with my red hair,' she said. She looked serious, and then laughed.

'I...' Mwai didn't know what else to say. 'Shall we go say hello?' he came up with.

'You can meet her later. Her name is Naomi and she's in mourning, so keep your thoughts in your trousers. Let's walk the perimeter. You might need to know where it is.'

'No one knows we're here except the people here. And François doesn't even know where here is.'

'Jane's paranoid. And we have their headsets.'

'You're not paranoid?'

'No. But her paranoia has saved my life several times.'

She lowered the goggles and slipped out of the barn

through a hole in the wall far too small for Mwai. He went out the front door.

When he got to the other side of the barn and the hole she had squeezed through, she was gone.

'Where are you?' he said.

She answered with laughter that sounded a hundred metres away. He set off towards it.

'Don't you think we're stuck?' he said in his normal voice, assuming she'd be close enough to hear and was just dicking with him in the dark.

'No. Jane will have a plan,' Walker said. She was two metres behind him, gun loose in her arms, scanning the night through the goggles.

'You heard our conversation?' Mwai said.

'I heard.'

'You don't take out billionaires for breakfast.'

'If that man killed her rhino... I heard what you said. In the bar. About her saying the rhino's name first. Not her brother, or her lover. Impressed you knew that. That's what she does. That's why Nathan's still alive. Not because of Nathan, but because of Nathan's son. She thinks Nathan fled Kenya to protect his son. If she thought Nathan fled to protect Nathan, she'd have shot him already. And I have a few tricks up my sleeve. I broke her out of Lang'ata. No one's ever done that before.'

'How?'

'Set a charge close enough to the gates to blow them down, set a timer, and drove two bulldozers through the back wall whilst everyone was panicking about the gates blowing up.'

'On your own?'

She didn't reply.

They stopped walking. Ahead the land fell away, the starlight was bright enough to show that, then must have risen again, as there was a long dark strip beneath the sky. In the distance there was another light source. Spotlights shone into the night, lighting up regiments of buildings. Mwai remembered them from a long time ago.

'Alright, on our way,' Walker said. It took Mwai a moment to realise she was speaking to someone who wasn't with them. She had her earpiece in. 'We're ready to go. Must get back. What's that?'

'Go where? That's an army barracks. Kenya Rifles. They refused to employ me when I was younger. Didn't make uniforms in my size back then.'

'I recognise a barracks, idiot. What's that?'

Walker pointed. There was a long thin line of light dribbling out of the spot lit rectangle of the barracks. She raised the telescopic sight of the Remington to her eye.

'Trucks,' she said. 'Jane, there's a column of army trucks coming straight for us.' Walker waited for a reply. Then nodded. 'Check,' she said.

She lowered the rifle, slapped Mwai on the shoulder.

'We gotta run like hell.' She started running.

CHAPTER THIRTY-FOUR

'Stay here,' he said. Rus Crewe was not looking forward to the evening briefing.

He took a folder with him. There was nothing relevant in it, but he always thought people carrying folders looked better prepared. He left the light on his desk on and walked out into the reception hall of the bunkhouse. All the other lights inside were off. Outside was lit up like a prison.

He paused for a moment just before the door. Listened. Nothing. No sounds of television or conversation. Everyone would be on duty. After today.

He resumed, walked out through the doors. There was no one in the compound, but two of the motion-sensitive cameras turned to track his progress across the packed earth. Out onto the Laikipia plateau, thirty metres to the main compound.

The gates for the main compound were locked, manned, and hot. Cameras turned towards him. He could smell the ozone caused by the current passing through the metal.

'Hey,' he shouted.

After a moment there was a buzz, and the left gate swung open far enough to let him through. It began to close as soon as he was in. He ignored the two men he knew to be either side of the gate.

He walked purposefully to the main doors, up the marble-tiled steps. The doors slid back automatically as he approached. He went through, kept walking.

Kioni was standing at the entrance to Clive's private offices. Her face was blank. No smile. It had turned into a big day. The two bodyguards who usually sat in armchairs in the visitors' waiting area were on their feet, hands in front of their groins, standing to attention either side of the entrance to the corridor. Everything by the book tonight.

Kioni turned into the corridor without a word and Crewe followed her. The metal detector set up in front of the corridor entrance beeped. It would be her phone. Crewe handed his to one of the bodyguards and stepped into the corridor. No beeping. The bodyguard handed the phone back.

The walk seemed longer tonight. Their feet on the marble, Kioni's heels clipped and precise, his boots heavy and muted. A rhythm. Discordant.

Kioni opened the door at the end of the corridor and opened the next door on the left into Clive's office. Crewe followed. The room was empty. Clive wasn't there.

Kioni didn't stop, crossing the room and exiting through the glass doors onto the veranda around the pool. Crewe followed.

Clive was sitting at the dining table on the veranda. The table was made of glass. No notes could pass hand to hand unseen by people eating at that table. No hidden weapons in laps. No *secrets*.

Clive was reading a newspaper. He didn't look up.

Four more of Clive's bodyguards stood at the four corners of the veranda, not moving, hands folded in front of them, like pillars in a Roman temple. Except two of them were wearing sunglasses at night.

'Mr Crewe, sir,' Kioni said, and left.

Clive didn't move. Crewe waited.

Clive turned the page of the paper.

Crewe waited.

Clive closed the paper and looked at him.

'Any change?' he said.

'We had someone speak to Pieters,' Crewe saw the subtle change in Clive's expression and reacted. 'The man shot in the leg in the attack. He says there was a man and a woman. The woman he didn't recognise, but she sounded "foreign".'

'What did he mean by that?'

'We played him some samples. He acknowledged she could be Norwegian.'

'Go on.'

'The man was Mwai Odinga.'

Clive sat back.

'The man you brought in to catch her is helping her?'

'That could be the case.'

Clive tented his fingers, drummed them against each other. 'What else?'

'He said the shots that killed the other two came from someone else, from across the road. There were at least three of them.'

'And?'

'When they saw another car coming, they dragged François off towards the airstrip. That's all he saw.'

'Is he...?'

'He's taken care of.'

'What else?'

'Nothing yet.'

Clive stared at Crewe with a smile.

'When will you find them?'

Crewe knew from previous experience not to give an explanation of what he was hoping would happen between now and then.

'Tonight,' he said.

'Where?'

'Here.'

Clive sat up.

'Explain.'

Crewe caught himself gulping.

'François can't tell them anything other than what he did for us. For me. That's all he knows. If Haven is as good as she's supposed to be, she'll be looking for one or both of the men François killed. François will tell them he killed them, and that I ordered it. She'll come here. To find me.'

'And how would he know you were here?'

'He came here once.'

'WHAT?' Clive was on his feet, his face puce. There was spittle on his lips and veins throbbed in his neck and temple. The bodyguards that Crewe could see all turned to look. 'You brought one of your...' he struggled for the word, 'ASSETS here? To my HOME?'

Clive turned to one of his bodyguards, the one just outside the door to his study, and motioned with his head. Just a nod. The man was twisting a suppressor onto a handgun within a second.

'Wait,' Crewe said. 'Wait. I have more. I know where they are right now.'

Clive held up his hand. The bodyguard stopped.

'How?'

'One of my men followed them there. He's in my office.'

Clive blinked.

'Kioni!' he said. Kioni was in the doorway in moments.

'Yes, sir?'

'There's a man in Crewe's office, bring him here now.'

'Yes, sir.'

Clive sat.

'Where are they?'

'In an abandoned ranch, a few kilometres from here, south-east.'

'And?'

'I sent the other team.'

'The first one failed.'

'The first one was surprised. The second won't be.'

'When will they be in position?'

'They are. They're just waiting for the order.'

'Why haven't you given it?'

'They reported a column of trucks from the barracks. Kenya Rifles. Passing the ranch. They are waiting for it to be out of earshot.'

'Send them in! She's wanted by the government! This is legitimate!'

Crewe nodded, took his phone out of his pocket, and made a call. It was answered.

'Breach,' he said. And hung up.

'The gentleman is here, sir,' Kioni said from the doorway.

She stepped aside, and Budd stepped into the space she'd vacated.

'Who did you follow? How many of them?'

'Four. The Haven woman, another woman, a ranger, and Odinga.'

'How did you know where they were?'

'I was with Odinga. We pretended to be a guy we found dead in Mombasa when the ranger called his phone.'

'Whose phone?'

'The guy we found dead. Whoever shot him missed it, cos it was under a water cooler. The ranger called it, set up a meeting with the dead guy.'

'What was the plan?'

'I thought Odinga meant to catch her. But he told her some bullshit about an elephant and offered to help her. He offered to let me go. I didn't have control of the situation, so I took the offer. Drove off. Pulled up down the road and went back. Saw them blow up the car and kill the other team. Two of 'em anyway. They took François. Stole a van from the airstrip. I followed, long way back. When they turned off, I kept going. Pulled in as soon as I was out of sight and crept back. They're in a farmhouse not half an hour from here.'

'They're coming here?'

'They're coming for him.' Budd pointed at Crewe.

'Why?'

'He gave the orders to kill the guys she was looking for. They think he's organised a cover up for someone. All she cares about is who killed some rhinoceros.'

No one spoke. Insects and sprinklers were the only sounds.

'Where are they going to look for him?' Clive said.

'Here. Odinga knows where he is.'

Clive stood up, his face gripped with anger. He spoke directly at Crewe.

'Did you invite all of your off-the-books kill squad to MY HOME?'

Crewe looked at the ground. Fear. He saw Clive glance at one of his bodyguards. Crewe had no weapon on him. No Kevlar vest. They weren't allowed in Clive's presence. Only his bodyguards were armed. Crewe was certain he was about to die.

'They'll know he's in the small compound not the main one. When they come to kill him, you will kill them,' Clive said.

CHAPTER THIRTY-FIVE

Nathan looked calm. Calmer than she'd ever seen him.

'What's changed?' she said to him.

He looked at her through his night vision goggles, the AR-15 nestled in his lap.

'Uganda. I was with the Rifles, with the UN. Policing the civil war. In theory. Really, we were just eating, and drinking, and waiting. One night the drinking got out of hand. There were fights, our guys, locals. A woman was raped. I saw it. One of our guys. Drunk, but so what. He was a nasty piece of work. A Captain. Captain John. A bully. I reported him. There was an inquiry. I was interviewed, arrested, kicked out. Shamefully discharged for making the story up. They didn't broadcast it, just did it. I went to South Africa, got a job as a ranger for a couple of years, then worked in Tanzania for a year. Made some money, came home, married Saachi. Known her since I was seven.

'That's the way the world is. That captain was a captain. I was a private. I spoke, and I was gone. When I was asked to let people in to Bandari I guessed why. I guessed they would kill rhino. More than one. What choice did I have? They were like the captain, the ones who get away with it. I was the private, who does what they're told or gets kicked out.'

Jane didn't think he was telling the whole story, not yet. But she nodded.

'What's changed?' she repeated.

'I let them in. They did what they did. To Douglas. To Jomo. To Kennet. And I feel terrible. But you want to bring the man who has done these things to justice. To real justice. It's the first time in my life I believe it can be done. That the one who gets away with it isn't going to get away with it.'

Jane left it a moment before she replied.

'You have a broken wrist, so fire at least a third of a second before you ordinarily would. If they're coming, they'll be here soon, so go now.'

Nathan's face changed. He nodded. He stood up.

'Still got a problem with me being a woman?' she said.

He stared at her.

'You're a soldier,' he said, holding her gaze.

He walked away into the dark.

Jane stood up, slipped off in the other direction.

She walked slowly, using bushes and trees for cover. They would have night vision goggles too, then men who were coming. And they would be in pairs, capable of watching in two directions at once. The only advantage she had were the motion-sensitive infrared cameras she and Walker had placed out there in the night. Her last four. Four cameras didn't give much coverage, but she had guessed the most likely approach, and François had confirmed it. Billeted in Nanyuki. They'd come up the C76, turn up the track, pass the hill where she's stopped to scout the ranch all that time ago, drive eight hundred metres beyond the turning to the ranch, stop, and come back on foot through the bush.

They'd approach the buildings obliquely, using the blind spots. They'd assume the buildings were occupied as Jane had left lights in both. They'd clear the barn first, and then the ranch house. Systematically, by the book.

It was a good plan. A great plan. Couldn't fail. Unless someone knew they were coming.

The night was green through the goggles. Tufts of grass, stretching away. Clumps of bushes. Trees by the streams. She saw the bright flicker of insect wings on the edge of her vision, and another movement a hundred metres away. A serval. The creature was walking confidently, not yet stalking. It was on its way to a known hunting ground. The same cat she'd seen on her first visit, returning to the ranch for more rats.

She reached her chosen cover. A circle of rocks partially hidden by trees and bushes. It had a good view for almost three-sixty degrees across the plain, towards the ranch, and up to the track, but it was inconvenient to get through unless you knew how to get in, and it was slightly off any of their likely routes to the ranch and barn.

She took her phone out, propped the screen up so it was concealed from outside the circle, and settled in for a wait. She was giving them an hour. If they didn't show in that time, she'd have to leave them behind and risk their following.

It didn't take long. After only seven minutes her phone vibrated. She pressed the notification and the feed from the first camera, facing towards the ranch from the hill beside the track, showed a four-wheel drive vehicle, a Land Cruiser, driving slowly north. It passed the turning to the ranch and continued up the track the army trucks had come down not long before. It didn't have its headlights on.

The second camera was triggered.

Her guess had been poorer with that one. She'd set it up pointed towards the ranch part way up a tree eight hundred metres from the gate. But the vehicle drove past the camera. For a second she thought it might be going on to the barracks, but a shortly afterwards she heard the slam of a car door and a sharp tone of admonishment. A minute later the men came into the camera's field of vision.

One pair, weapons up, advancing carefully, was already diverging from the other. The front pair were heading straight for the barn. The other was walking away from them at an angle of about sixty degrees.

Jane switched the phone off and put it in her pocket. She picked up the ranger's AR-15. A Bravo Mod 2 with scope. She took two steps: the first between two rocks, the second to stand in a gap between a bush and a third rock. She raised the rifle and froze, finger on the trigger, two-thirds pressure

The second two men, clad in black, automatic weapons, their own night vision goggles in place, came into view three metres to her right. They were treading cautiously, each covering a one-hundred-and-thirty-five-degree arc to minimise the chances of being taken by surprise. But they didn't see her because the nook she was in was a blind spot concealed by the bush. She shot them both in the back with two three round bursts, hitting the base of the spine where their body armour stopped.

She approached them, slowly, two-thirds pressure all the way in case either of them moved. She shot them again, once each in the head.

She looked up. No other shots yet. The other two hadn't met Nathan. Either way.

She ran south-west, looping round to come at the barn from the opposite direction.

She kept moving, weapon up, watching where the other men must have got to. Still no shots.

Then suddenly: bang bang. Followed by a second bang bang, but from a different gun. Then a return to silence.

She crouched down and scanned the night. Nothing.

She worked her way forward, towards the ranch house, weapon up, all senses flaring.

It felt like hours passed as she edged forward. Nothing moved, no more shots. But anyone still alive could be watching. She didn't speak. Nathan wasn't speaking, so he was either dead, or within earshot of one or both of the other men. The tiny sound of someone speaking in an earpiece would be the difference between life and death in the quiet of this night.

She got to within fifty metres of the buildings. Pivoted. Headed for the barn. Slipped in through a gap in the dying walls. Stood up, stopped, listened. For five minutes. Nothing.

She walked, a step at a time, down the side of the van, until she was by the door of the barn. She looked at the front of the ranch.

There were two bodies lying close to the old truck.

The first was all in black, balaclava, night vision goggles. It wasn't Nathan.

The second was the serval. The cat that she'd seen take the rat the first time she'd come here.

She'd told Nathan to take up position here, in the barn.

Nathan wouldn't have shot the cat. The other one shot the cat. Saw it out of the corner of his eye and fired instinctively, Jane guessed. And Nathan, surprised by the shots, had killed the killer. But the other man had got out of Nathan's line of fire. And hadn't fired back.

What would Nathan have done then?

He wasn't stupid. He'd given away his position, so he would have moved. He'd have gone out through the hole she'd used to get in. The last of the four would be watching here. *Faen*.

Jane eased backwards, a step at a time. Even as she calculated how much danger she was in she was thinking about the cat's kittens, motherless now.

She reached the back of the van and peered round it, checking the rest of the barn.

Empty.

She eased herself to her knees, and looked under the van, gun first, finger at two thirds pressure.

Nothing.

She laid down on the ground and pulled herself under the van, centimetre by centimetre, until she was below its front bumper and could see the ground between the barn and the ranch again.

She waited.

Three people out there. François, still naked and tied up on the floor of the ranch. Nathan, under instructions to engage then move then wait. Wait until he couldn't wait any more, and then wait more. Not being able to wait killed more people than anything. Ninety-nine percent waiting, one percent speed and aggression. The speed and aggression were easy. Most people could do that. Waiting was the skill.

She waited. They did not have much time, to be in position before the alarms went off. Mwai had his job to do. Walker hers. And the army had its part to play, and armies move slowly. But she didn't have much time. She was going to have to take a risk.

She made her way carefully back to the barn. Slipped in through the hole. Checked it was still clear. Under the van. Looked out at the bodies. At the ranch.

She took a stun grenade from her belt. An M84. Seven megacandela, the light of seven million candles. A hundred and seventy decibels, enough to rupture eardrums.

She looked at the ground, found a stone about the same weight as the grenade. She threw the stone as far beyond the dead truck as she could. She heard the dull thunk of it hitting the earth.

'Close your eyes for three seconds,' she whispered into her microphone, as softly as she could. 'Now.'

Then she pulled the pin and threw the grenade after the stone, turned to face the ranch, and closed her own eyes.

The grenade went off on impact with an enormous BANG, and light so bright she could see it through her closed eyes. She ran, straight across the yard, jumping the dead mercenary, not judging it perfectly and catching him with her trailing leg, stumbling but not falling. Up the two steps and in through the ranch house door.

She got her gun in her hands and dropped to the floor.

François was still lying on the floor, blindfolded, gagged, and bound.

Jane listened.

'Did you see him?' she said into her microphone.

The answer was gunfire. Three, six, ten shots, all from the same gun.

'Yes,' said Nathan through her earpiece. 'He's down.'

'Good work, soldier,' she said. François struggled against his bonds. 'We'll take their car.'

CHAPTER THIRTY-SIX

'HOW ARE YOU FEELING?' NAOMI SAID.

'I'm alright. The dizziness is less,' Makena said. 'And the drugs help the pain.'

'You're on drugs, you're getting dizzy, you have a pain in your leg, and you're driving a car I'm in?' Mwai said from the back of the cab. 'Maybe I should drive.'

'I was bitten by a snake. Green mamba.'

Mwai was surprised.

'How long ago?'

'About forty-eight hours.'

'Then you should be in hospital and I should be driving. I insist.'

'Naomi lost her husband. I will play my part.'

'Very noble, but if you pass out and crash the truck your part might be to kill her, and that would be less noble. Pull over.'

Makena seemed to think about it for a few seconds, then relented, and eased the truck to a stop. He and Mwai swapped places.

'Where did you get this wreck?' Mwai said, putting it into gear and finding the stick surprisingly smooth.

'Saw it in a yard. Offered the owner a few things they needed. Got one of my cousins to fix it up for me in exchange for a few things they needed.'

'Reliable?'

'Always, except when something blows. Then it can take weeks to get parts.'

'Great,' Mwai said.

He drove on, passing the Graveyard, right into the heart of Nanyuki. He followed the C76 until it met the A2, then turned onto the larger road heading north.

'Mr Odinga, you are from Nanyuki?' Naomi said.

'Born and raised.'

'Why did you leave?'

'I got restless. I was looking for something here I was never going to find, so I tried to forget about it by going somewhere else.'

'Did you?'

'Did I what?'

'Forget about it?'

'No. At least not for long. Not for long enough.'

'Will you stay, now you're back?'

'I'm not really back. I just came back for a job. Happened to be here. Next job probably won't be. If there is a next job. This one's not going to end the way it was supposed to.'

'How was it supposed to end?'

'Didn't Jane tell you?'

'She just asked me to drive her Land Rover to that ranch, to pick up you and her friend Brigit, leave Brigit in the Land Rover and wait for Makena to pick you and I up. That's all she said. She seemed in a hurry.'

Mwai turned off the A2 onto a track that led up onto the Laikipia Plateau. He kept the speed up.

'My job was to find the convicted rhino-killer and escaped convict, Jane Haven, and make sure that justice was done.'

Mwai sensed rather than saw Naomi's face change.

'It's alright. I am doing exactly that. The problem I have is that my view of what that justice should be has taken a great divergence from the view my employer has of what that justice should be. But I signed a contract, and they signed it too. I expect people to honour their agreements. WOAH!'

Mwai slammed on the brakes and he and Naomi were slung forward, then pulled back by their seatbelts. Makena in the back gave a cry of pain. There were no seatbelts for him, and he crashed into the back of the front seats.

Ten metres ahead, just on the turn of the track so Mwai hadn't been able to see it sooner, was a roadblock. It was a boulder, a wall. The wall moved a little. It was an elephant lying in the road.

Mwai put the truck in reverse and backed up five hundred metres.

'Stay here,' he said.

He got out. He had walked a hundred metres towards the elephant when he heard one of the truck's doors open. He ignored it and kept walking.

They were ten kilometres from any light pollution now, and the sky was clear. The moon and the stars bathed the plateau. The elephant had its front legs under its body, and its head resting on the ground.

Mwai circled it. Female. Juvenile. It wouldn't be alone. He looked into the night.

To the right of the track the land fell away, not too

steeply. He could get the truck past on that slope if he drove slowly.

To the left the land rose. There was a gulley. There they were. At least six other elephants standing, watching.

'She's sick. I need to call for help,' Naomi said. She had followed him, and was standing next to the animal's head, her hand on the trunk, just below the face. She was reaching for her pocket.

'We haven't time,' Mwai said.

'You haven't time. This is what I do, Mr Odinga. You do what you do. You can get past.'

'What do you do?'

'I'm a vet.'

'Ah, yes. My father told me.' Mwai stood in the night and watched her. 'Alright. I'll drive past as quietly as I can. You'll be able to get people out at this time?'

'Of course.' Naomi took a phone from her pocket, pressed some buttons, and put it to her ear.

Mwai ran back to the truck.

'You alright?' he said.

Makena grunted.

'Safer in the front.'

Mwai waited whilst Makena climbed out of the back of the cab and into the seat Naomi had occupied a few minutes before. Mwai put the truck in gear and eased off the track, passing the elephant at five kilometres an hour, staying slow until he was back on the track and five hundred metres away. Then he accelerated.

'How did you end up in this, my friend?' he said, after a while.

'Naomi is my cousin. I help my cousins.' Makena's voice was strained. He was in pain.

'You're not in a good state, my friend. When we get there, stay in the truck, I'll get what we need. I'll just have to drive like the devil on the way back.'

'Why?'

'I'm on a clock. Jane is something of a planner.'

'Are we going to be late?'

'Possibly. I thought there'd be three of us to get the stuff out. And I didn't expect the elephant. And I still need to drop you off on the way back.'

Makena was quiet. Mwai looked at him. His eyes were closed.

'Are you sure you're alright, my friend?'

'Is there a faster way?' Makena said.

'Last time I was here they shipped me out by helicopter. It's two hours by road to where we need to be. By helicopter it's twenty minutes. But if you haven't got any helicopters in your pockets, road it is.'

'I have a cousin,' Makena said, dialling a number from his phone. 'He can fly. Godknows? Yes... I am sorry to wake you. That favour I owe you. I need it to be a bigger one.'

CHAPTER THIRTY-SEVEN

THE ALARMS WERE RAGING.

Crewe ran through the corridors of Klabu Viziwi, stumbling into furniture, sliding on the marble. He could hear Budd's footsteps behind him, keeping pace.

He reached the security suite. The shift-commander and two other bodyguards were already there, talking into lapel mikes, listening to their earpieces.

The shift commander saw Crewe in the doorway and scowled.

'This is my jurisdiction, Crewe,' he said, and turned his back.

The control panels were covered in flashing lights. It looked like every long-range motion-sensor on the estate had gone off. At the front, along the track down to the C76, and at the back of the property. The only side not flashing was the helipad a little to the north.

Most of the cameras were showing part or all of a line of trucks. The cameras pointing south from the pole out front of the main compound showed the full line. There were five.

Big army troop-carriers, like armour-plated angry beetles glowering along the track.

'That'll be a company. A hundred men. Hope you've got some artillery,' Crewe said. The shift commander scowled, and ignored him, barking orders into his lapel mike as if volume improved responsiveness.

Crewe turned, and motioned to Budd to step outside.

'We need some equipment,' he said.

'Mine's in the car.'

'Mine's in the office.'

Crewe led the way, through the reception hall and out into the night.

He could hear the trucks easily, no more than two-hundred and fifty metres away now. He ran to the gates.

'Open them.'

The guard to the right shook his head.

'Mr Kriel gave orders. Gates stay shut.'

'Listen, you idiot. He didn't mean stop people defending Mr Andrews from accessing their weapons. You don't have to open them fully, just enough to let us out.'

The guard hesitated. Crewe took a step forward, trying to use his size to intimidate. The man on guard was smaller but didn't look intimidated. The guard looked at Budd, who raised an eyebrow and shrugged. The guard reached up to a pad on the wall, typed in a code, pressed a switch, holding it down long enough for the gate to open enough for them to slip through.

Crewe ran to the smaller compound. Looking over his shoulder he could see the line of trucks.

'What if they're not coming here?' Budd said.

'There's nowhere else – this is the end of the track.'

'I've driven those troop carriers myself. Used to look after one. They're heavy-duty vehicles. They don't need a track on this plateau, they can just keep going. Might be this track is simply closest to where they are going.'

'That would be a coincidence.'

'Why else would they be coming here?'

'I have no idea.'

They went to the gates to the small compound, passing a Land Rover parked by the fence. The alarms only rang in the main compound, so were less deafening here.

Budd crossed to his car, opened the trunk, pulled out his equipment, jacket, belt, gun, goggles. Crewe waited for him, staring at a Land Rover on the other side of the fence.

'Was that there when you came to the big house?'

Budd looked up.

'Naw, that's not been there long, you can hear the engine cooling.'

Crewe stepped to his left until he could see the side of the vehicle.

'Got a torch?' Crewe said.

'Sure.' Budd reached into a bag in the trunk and took out two torches, walked over and handed one to Crewe.

Crewe switched it on and pointed it at the Land Rover.

It had the Bandari conservancy logo on the door.

'How the hell did that get here?' Budd said.

'We need to go inside,' Crewe said.

Budd nodded, sweeping the compound carefully with the torch.

'Switch 'em off,' he said.

They did, and Budd lowered the night vision goggles over his eyes and raised his gun. He scanned everything carefully again.

'Nothing,' he said.

They went to the reception hall, Crewe's office at the end.
The doors were open.

'Did you close these when you came out?'

'Yes, but anyone in here will have come out in a hurry
when the alarms went off,' Budd said.

'Everyone was already in the main house. Mr Andrews
watched the footage of François and the team going into that
bar thinking you might be in there with Jane Haven. Police
bulletins describing two dead, one wounded, and a car with
its wheel blown off were picked up half an hour later, put
everyone on high alert. Kriel emptied the bunkhouse. Standard procedure. You should have been the only one here.'

'I couldn't swear I closed it.'

'Let's work on the assumption we're not alone,' Crewe
said, catching himself chewing his lip.

'That sounds like a good idea. Moves like a ghost, this
woman.'

'There are four of them, remember.'

'Should we call the other guys?'

'They're storming that ranch right now. We'll bring them
when they're done.'

'If she's here then there's nothing for them to storm.'

'If she's not and we miss an opportunity, I'm a dead man.
We both are.'

The lights came on automatically as they stepped through
the door. Budd raised his goggles so he could see.

'If anyone is in here, they've been in here long enough for
the lights to go out,' Crewe said.

'How long is that?'

'Fifteen minutes. You first.'

'Why me?'

'You're the one carrying an automatic weapon.'

'I don't know the layout.'

'You've been to my office. Straight there. My stuff's there.'

'Alright. I'll cover the front.'

Budd set off, walking as quietly as he could. The floor was carpeted, which helped. Crewe followed him, watching left and right, listening. All he could hear was the chuntering of a fridge creating ice in one of the kitchens away to the left.

They crossed the hall slowly.

The door to Crewe's office was open. Budd took one hand off the gun, raised his finger to his lips, put his hand back, then stepped into the room, sweeping it quickly then turning rapidly to check behind the door.

'Clear,' he said.

Crewe felt himself deflate, the tension releasing.

He took his Kevlar vest and a large automatic pistol, a Desert Eagle 50, out of a filing cabinet.

'You planning on shooting an elephant?' Budd said, seeing the gun.

'I know this gun.'

'What now?'

'We need to get back to the control room, see the footage of the Land Rover, how many were in it, where they went.'

'How did they miss it?'

'They didn't miss it, they just don't think like we do. They've been in Close Protection so long they think of the thing they're protecting too much. They think the compound is a fortress. The Land Rover didn't go in, didn't try to. The trucks might, so they'll focus on the trucks.'

'They must be here by now.'

They both listened. The alarms had stopped. And there was shouting, amplified shouting. Megaphones.

———

Crewe led the way this time. Cautiously they crossed the hall and slipped out the front door. The spotlights of the main compound next door seemed even brighter. They could see the trucks through fence. The trucks had driven to the edge of the pool of light surrounding the main compound. There were a lot of men running around behind the trucks.

'That's a whole company,' Budd said.

As he said it a man walked from the middle truck and approached the main compound gate. Crewe and Budd crossed the yard to crouch behind the Land Rover on the other side of the fence.

After a moment Kioni walked into the light. Crewe holstered his Eagle.

'Stay here,' he said, and walked quickly, hands raised to just below his shoulder, always a good idea when there are a hundred men armed with rifles looking at you. He, Kioni, and the soldier reached the same spot at the same time, fifty metres from the compound's main gate.

'Captain Awino,' the soldier said.

'I am Kioni, Mr Andrews' executive assistant. This is Mr Crewe, his head of security. What can we do for you, Captain? Why do you have five trucks parked outside Mr Andrews' front gate?'

The captain instinctively came to attention at her tone. Crewe suppressed a smile.

'Apologies, ma'am. We received information that a wanted fugitive was hiding in a ranch not far from 42KR barracks. My company was dispatched to investigate. I spotted the fugitive fleeing the ranch in a Land Rover and we gave chase.'

'What is "42KR"?' Kioni asked.

'Forty-two Kenya Rifles,' Crewe answered. 'Thank you, Captain, your arrival couldn't be more welcome. We have just been responding to a security incident caused by an unattended vehicle.' Crewe pointed to the Bandari Land Rover by the fence. 'Is that the vehicle you were following?'

'Yes, sir.'

'The fugitive was in it, and alone?'

'Yes, sir.'

'Would it be possible for you and your men to search the area, to see if you can find the individual? It is unlikely they have got into the main compound, Mr Andrews' security there is very tight. But the rest of the property is less well protected, and the individual could be hiding in a number of places.'

'Thank you for your cooperation, sir.' The captain turned and barked orders to the men behind the trucks. They spread out in a long line and walked forward.

'I'll arrange for the alarms to be switched off so you can search uninterrupted. I'll ask one of my men to stay with you. Send him to the gate if you need anything.'

'Thank you, sir.'

The captain saluted, then lowered his hand as if wondering why.

Crewe motioned to Budd to join them.

'Budd, there's a fugitive nearby. Whoever drove that Land Rover here. This captain has kindly agreed to have his men search the area. Can you stay with him, call us for any assistance he might need?'

'Yes, sir,' Budd said.

The captain was looking at Budd's weapon.

'Mr Andrews is a wealthy man, he has powerful enemies,' Crewe said. 'His security is paramount.'

'Yes, sir,' the captain said, and walked back to the trucks with Budd.

Crewe and Kioni walked back to the main gate.

'What are you doing?' she hissed.

'Getting a free search of the area from the men who caught her last time,' he hissed back.

'Did you call them?'

'No.'

'Then who did?'

CHAPTER THIRTY-EIGHT

'THIS HAD BETTER BE GOOD,' CLIVE SAID. HE WAS SITTING at his desk in his office. The doors to the pool area were still open, the shadows of the men posted there thrown into the room by the outside spotlights. Kriel lurked by the other door like a golem.

'The army are leaving, sir,' Kioni said. 'They've searched a huge area, the outbuildings, north to the helipad, the whole perimeter of the main compound. They found nothing.'

'Did you search the car?'

'Three times, sir. Everything. Underneath, engine, everything. The keys were still in it, so we moved it inside the service compound.'

'THEN WHERE IS SHE?' Clive's anger was a rare thing. Crewe had not seen it before tonight. He'd seen him order the execution of men without any emotion at all. But tonight, the veneer was gone. He was an angry little man. Because he was afraid.

The realisation hit Crewe like a shot of 20-year-old Van Ryn, finest brandy on the planet, whatever the Grand Armagnac groupies claimed. Clive was afraid of the situation. Of the external situation. He couldn't control it, and he couldn't cope with things he couldn't control.

Crewe was afraid, not of the situation, but of Clive's bodyguards. Despite his title "Head of Security" he had no authority over Kriel's men, and they were cold-blooded killers. One word from Clive and Crewe would be dead.

But Clive was afraid of something Crewe wasn't afraid of. And this gave him power.

'It doesn't matter,' Crewe said. 'You said it yourself, sir, we need her to come to us, set bait, wait. She's not that big of a threat...'

'Not that big of a threat? NOT THAT BIG OF A THREAT? SHE'S TAKEN OUT ALL OF YOUR MEN! THEY COST A FORTUNE!'

'Sir, with the greatest respect, she'd not taken out all of my men. When you set me the task, I brought in two teams for basic clean up, and one unit as contingency. The unit is still operational. I brought in Mwai Odinga to find her, knowing he has a reputation for going rogue, because he always gets his man. He's a legend for it. He's more driven than anyone I've encountered in the business.'

'He's helping her!'

'But he's bringing her to us by doing so. And I brought in Budd Anderson and tasked him with befriending Odinga and bringing us information. And Budd Anderson has delivered.'

'How?'

'They have a weakness. The other ranger. Nathan Jennings. The one who let us in to the conservancy then disappeared. He's afraid for his family. Right here in Nanyuki. We go babysit them, then if she gets in here, we let him know.'

'How would we let him know? I saw the footage. The four you sent to the ranch were dead without seeing anything but a cat!'

'She took the comms equipment from the first team.'

'So?'

'She's listening to our channels. All we have to do is talk on the frequency reserved for my teams. He will hear. He will panic. The operation they are about to attempt has zero risk tolerance. If an individual panics they compromise a unit. If a unit is compromised, the team goes down. And they are but one team. I'll send Budd Anderson. He has proved his loyalty.'

Clive exhaled.

'No. You keep your man here. Kriel, you send someone. And evacuate everyone not paid to use a gun. No witnesses.'

Crewe and Kriel nodded in unison.

Kriel left the room.

Clive stood up and walked out from behind the desk. He crossed the room and went out to the pool veranda.

Crewe and Kioni followed him.

Clive walked to the edge of the pool and stared down at it. The water was still. The pool was complex, several pools joined together by small channels, a bar in the middle, two sun loungers floating near it. The pool was surrounded by vegetation, carefully selected for its looks. The whole thing was lit up by the security lights so bright they hurt Crewe's eyes after the dimly lit office.

The only noise was insects. The grounds were sprayed daily for mosquito, but there were many insects not affected by the poison. They were chirping, whistling, and creaking. The only other sound was a helicopter some way off, a slow thump turning to a whine as it took off. But it was far enough away Crewe paid it no mind.

'Alright,' Clive said. 'You know your shit, Mr Crewe. And you know what the best thing is?'

'What's that, sir?'

'They're after you, not me.'

Clive smiled. It was an ugly smile.

'Go sleep in the bunkhouse. I'll send a couple of Kriel's guys to watch over you. Say "hi" when she turns up.'

'Yes, sir.' Crewe said. 'Sir?' Crewe was thinking of suggesting Clive slept in the bunker beneath the complex. But he realised that would undermine Clive's newly revived confidence in him.

'Yes?'

'Sleep well, sir,' Crewe said, and left him staring at the pool.

———

'We the only ones in there tonight?' Budd said as they walked through the main gate and headed back to the bunkhouse.

'Yes.'

'Then we should be leaving.'

'Can't. We're the bait, and the two following us are the executioners. Don't look back.' Budd didn't.

'Then we need to find somewhere real good to hide.'

'I have an idea.'

'Hope it's a real good one.'

They went through the small compound into the building. They walked to his office and spent a few minutes covering the window with buff files from a box. Held them in place with Sellotape.

'So, what's your idea?' Budd said.

Crewe looked up, staring pointedly at the air-conditioning duct above his head.

'Might work. But if the army didn't search it might already be occupied.'

Crewe went cold. Budd was right. He put his finger to his lips and beckoned Budd out into the corridor. He followed the aircon pipes above them out into the reception hall and then mimed for Budd to climb up.

'That's crazy,' Budd said. 'If someone's up there already they'll hear anything touch those pipes. I ain't going up there. You want to clear the pipes, use smoke.'

Crewe thought for a moment, then nodded.

They went through the rooms in the bunkhouse and gathered all the paper they could find.

They came out of different rooms at the same time, arms piled with magazines and books, and found themselves staring at two men.

Crewe relaxed. The men were from Kriel's squad. The ones sent to execute Haven when she took the bait.

'Don't know if the army checked the aircon. We're going to smoke it.'

One of the men nodded.

Budd set three fires in the intake pipes as far from Crewe's office as they could. Crewe switched the aircon to max. The four of them stalked the building, guns out, listening.

All that happened was the building quickly became smoky.

'Guess it's clean,' Crewe said, stifling a cough. 'Put 'em out.'

There was a noise, somewhere near the main compound. A whine and a bang.

'What was that?' one of Kriel's men said.

Crewe knew. Budd said it.

'Mortar. Sixty mil.'

'Shit,' Crewe said.

'Wait,' Budd said.

They all listened.

More whines. More than one this time. Then more bangs. One, two, three. Towards the back of the compound.

'Where in hell's name did they get artillery?' Budd said.

Crewe went cold again. He'd taken Odinga to the Killing House. He'd shown off.

'We need to get back to Mr Andrews,' he said, and ran to the car park of the small compound. The mortar shells kept falling. Budd and the other two followed him, just as the main compound gate exploded.

———

Crewe ran through the gates of the bunkhouse compound out onto the Laikipia plateau. He had his Desert Eagle in his hand, and he knew he wasn't in control of anything.

The gates to the main compound of Klabu Viziwi were thirty metres from where they should be. The gateposts were gone, the walls were ruins, and the men who had been guarding them were dead.

The gates were *inside* the compound.

'This wasn't the mortars!' Crewe shouted. 'This was demolition charges.'

He ran. He could hear footsteps behind him. Budd and Kriel's guys. Good to have them at his back for a change. The mortar shells continued to fall on the other side of the building. He heard bullets fly, though suppressed. Thup thup, thup thup. A final thup as he and Budd burst into the reception area of the main building. He was running too fast and slipped on the marble, falling. Budd didn't quite avoid him, tripped, and fell to Crewe's right. The wall in front of him exploded about a foot above his head. He rolled on his side, looked back. Kriel's two guys were lying motionless just inside the gates. The front entrance was lost.

'GO!' he screamed, and forced himself up, into the corridor that led to Clive's office. He passed two more of Kriel's men, either side of the corridor entrance. They aimed their guns at him but lifted them when they saw who he was. That was going to get them killed. There wasn't time to see who the target was, in a fire fight like this you either fired first or died. Crewe bounced off the far wall onto the near one, leaned, and breathed. Budd did the same and almost ran into him.

'There are only four of them,' Budd said. 'No need to panic.'

'There are four less of us,' Crewe said, and set off down the corridor, his Desert Eagle held in both hands, pointed forward, his arms straight. His aim was award-winning.

The door to Clive's study was open. Crewe checked it before entering. Kioni crouched under the desk. Two of Kriel's men were visible through the doors to the veranda, guns out, hovering. They looked nervous.

Crewe crossed the room, Budd still on his shoulder.

'It's Crewe,' he said. 'Where's Mr Andrews?'

'He went to the bunker,' one of the bodyguards replied.

Crewe joined the bodyguard in the doorway and looked over the veranda and the pool. At least a dozen of Kriel's men were in the garden, their handguns out. Handguns? Against mortars? Crewe looked beyond them. The garden wall was gone. Blown to bits by the mortars. And beyond, in the darkness, were stars.

Except stars were usually in the sky and didn't move so fast. Crewe dived backwards into the office, tripping Budd as he did so. He hit the marble floor just as the moving stars hit Klabu Viziwi, bringing thunder with them.

It was the thunder of an HMG. Heavy Machine Gun. Crewe lay next to Kioni and put his hands over his ears. Not from the noise. That was bad, but it wasn't the noise by volume. It was the noise on aggregate. Everything was disintegrating. Bullets were passing through the walls, the windows were evaporating into showers of glass shards, bullets were ricocheting off anything they didn't simply pass through. The sound was a solid thing. The onslaught went on for what felt like hours, but it was no more than a minute and a half. Just as abruptly as the firing had started, it stopped.

The silence was oppressive.

It lasted.

Crewe raised his head and risked a glance into the garden. It wasn't there. It took him a moment to work out what had happened. The lights. All the spotlights were gone. Shot out. The east side of the building was in darkness.

'Turn the lights out in here, get your goggles on,' Crewe hissed at Budd.

Budd crawled to the doorway, staying as low as he could, and looked up.

'Where's the damn light switch?' he said.

'They're voice activated.' Crewe had forgotten Kioni was hiding under the desk. 'Office lights off!' she said with authority.

The lights went out as Crewe and Budd simultaneously shushed her.

Crewe let his eyes adjust to the dark, but it took a long time.

'What do you see?' Crewe said.

Crewe heard Budd move a little.

'Garden's gone,' he said. 'Everyone I can see is down. One of them is moving but the others are still. Nothing standing. What now?' Crewe could see a little now. Budd raised his head, peering into the darkness. Budd lowered his head again and lay flat on the floor, his machine gun pushed out in front of him.

'The Bunker,' Crewe said. 'Quick.'

'Where's that?'

'Follow me,' Kioni said. She climbed out from under the desk and sprinted for the door. Budd scrambled up and followed. Crewe did the same. They ran.

CHAPTER THIRTY-NINE

IF HE WAS GOING TO KEEP HANGING OUT WITH THIS LOT, they were going to have to buy him some better-fitting night vision goggles. Mwai had gone through all the pairs Jane had, all the ones Walker had taken from François' team, and they all pinched, even on the loosest fitting. Irritating.

But at least he could see through them. He picked up the Heckler and Koch he'd selected from Jane's private, and quite illegal, underfloor arsenal. An MP5. Possibly forty years old. But it had been loved, and it handled like a teenager.

He circled the heavy machine gun. What had the comedian who had trained him called them? Gimps? An attempt at getting an acronym out of General-Purpose Machine Gun, perhaps. He had to circle it. The barrel was so hot it was glowing. Easy target for any sniper. And the pile of spent cartridges was large and reflected light. Clean-up was going to be a pain in the arse.

The air was getting thicker. Humidity increasing. Above him the stars were going out as clouds rolled in. Could rain be on the way?

He set off down the slope at a run, listening to the whispered banter between Jane and Walker through his headset.

'Front's secure, gates are down, lights out, six suited goons down, doors jammed, back-up distraction in place, then I had a bath, read a book, and now I'm thinking of retiring to bed early with the discerning local of my choice,' Walker said.

'Check,' Jane said.

The machine gun position was on the other side of a small valley. To get to Klabu Viziwi from this direction he had to run down the slope and cross the stream that had formed the valley.

'Careful crossing that stream,' Jane said. 'Crocodiles.'

'Check,' Mwai said.

How the hell did she know where he was? As he came closer to the sound of running water he slowed and watched the ground carefully.

'Hey, Thor, bringer of Thunder, what's it like from your side?' Walker said.

Mwai stepped carefully. Crushed grass, water on the earth, distinctive prehistoric footprints. At least one crocodile had been out of the stream here within the last hour or so.

'Rear wall breached in four places. External lights out, some internal still on. Twelve men down, status unconfirmed,' Mwai said.

'Check,' Jane said in his earpiece. 'Confirm.'

'Check,' Mwai said.

Mwai reached the bank of the stream. It was four metres wide, and the light and the goggles didn't give him an idea of how deep, or how crocodile infested, it was.

Before he stepped into the water, he heard a voice, a way

off. He looked up the hill. A light went out in the ruined building.

'Light inside the structure was just switched off. Room on the east, fifty metres from the north end. Heard a voice just before,' he said.

'Check,' Jane said in his earpiece.

'Hell, they just turned off the big lights and lit some candles waiting for me to turn up wearing nothing but my snow boots,' Walker said.

Mwai tried to ignore the image of Walker wearing nothing but snow boots. It wasn't easy. He stepped into the stream, pushing through the water with his feet rather than splashing, making his presence less visible and less appetising. He heard a splash to his right, downstream. He turned, MP5 ready. But there was nothing to see and whatever had caused the splash didn't do it again.

Mwai climbed up the opposite bank and ran for the boundary wall of Klabu Viziwi. Most of which wasn't there anymore. He navigated the craters the mortars had created. He used them as cover, watching the building all the time.

He reached what was left of the boundary wall. He paused, watching. He counted. He'd been right. Twelve men down in the garden. He could see one was moving, hear him groaning.

Mwai took out a knife.

'Count confirmed,' he said into the mouthpiece a moment later.

'Eighteen down, at least seven left, plus Crewe, plus Andrews, plus unknown others. Any additional?' Jane said.

Mwai made his way through the remnants of what had once been a beautiful garden to the open door of the room that had gone dark.

'Domestics left after the army didn't find me,' Walker said. 'I saw Mwai's friend from the bar. Ran into the main building with a big bastard with a South African haircut, if you know what I mean. I had a choice between them or two guys in suits, and I HATE guys in suits.'

Mwai was starting to think Walker was insane. He rather liked it.

'At least ten people still in that building. Let's clear the rooms. Rendez-vous at the entrance to the bunker,' Jane said.

'That was a guess,' Mwai said. 'My grandad's stories. Could be wrong.'

'We'll find out.'

'Check,' Mwai said.

'Cutting power in three, two, one.' Any lights still visible in the house went out. 'Breach,' Jane said.

CHAPTER FORTY

THE BUNKER WAS AN AFFECTATION. IT WASN'T REALLY A bunker. Bunkers were built to provide shelter from falling bombs. What Clive called "the Bunker," Crewe called an extended wine cellar.

Part of it was still used as a wine cellar. It was the oldest part, dating back to the nineteenth century. It had its own entrance, stairs from the kitchens. It was sealed off from the rest of The Bunker – it was the escape route. A reinforced steel door led from the next section into the wine cellar, but it only had a handle and lock on the inside. From the wine cellar side, it was a rack holding ninety-six bottles of W & J Graham's 'Ne Oublie' port in several vintages.

The door that led into the wine cellar was in a newer section, perhaps fifty years old, built for the taxidermist who had stuffed the heads of the hunters' trophies back when it was a hunting lodge. Clive had converted it into the security centre for Crewe's teams. Banks of desks covered in computers and screens, and to one edge the viewing room Clive used when watching the raids. He was like a child when in that room. "It's like a video game with real people," he'd said once through a smile he couldn't hide.

The main entrance to The Bunker was in this section. A set of stairs that came down into the centre of the room. At the top of them was another reinforced steel door.

And the newest section, built within the last three months, was a panic room. Accessed from the security suite, through the viewing room. Crewe had never been inside.

Budd, Kioni, and Crewe were on the wrong side of the steel door at the top of the stairs, and Kriel refused to let them in.

'Mr Andrews security is paramount.' Kriel's voice came from a speaker built into one of the security cameras pointed at the outside of the door. Crewe could hear the sneer in it. 'When you and the others have caught the intruders, I will open the door.'

'What others? Everyone else is dead.'

'You had better get busy then, hadn't you?'

The faint background hiss that accompanied Kriel's voice disappeared. The conversation was over.

'We need eyes,' Budd said.

'Security office. Come on,' Crewe said.

Budd led the way. Crewe followed, walking as quietly as he could, and as quickly as he dared, with Kioni behind him, her hands too often on his waist. The security office wasn't far, along a corridor, left, then left again.

At the first turning Budd and Crewe stopped, and Kioni walked straight into Crewe's back.

'Sorry,' she said.

Crewe silenced her by holding a finger to his lips. She was a liability. They would need to leave her somewhere.

Budd took a quick glance round the corner. Nodded, then turned.

All the lights went out at once.

'Shit,' Budd said.

Crewe heard Budd's arm moved. Lowering his night vision goggles.

'Shi—'

There was a burst of gunfire from down the corridor. Budd did not fire back. Crewe felt a fine spray whip over his face. He heard Budd crash to the floor.

Crewe dropped to his knees. Behind him he heard Kioni screaming and running away into the dark.

Crewe fired twice into the ceiling, to keep whoever it was where they were for a minute. He reached out carefully, blindly feeling the floor where Budd had fallen. He touched the edge of Budd's body armour, got a grip, pulled the body towards him. He needed the night vision goggles or he was dead.

He ran his hand to Budd's face, found the edge of the goggles. They were sticky with blood. They came off too easily. There was no image. A bullet had passed through them on its way to Budd's brain. He was dead, and more importantly, the goggles were broken.

'Throw the gun in front of you, Rus.'

It was the voice of Mwai Odinga.

Crewe did as he was told. He had no choice. He couldn't see. Mwai evidently could. Crewe was kneeling on the floor, one hand on the goggles. He wouldn't be able to raise the Eagle in time, let alone pull the trigger. He placed the gun carefully on the floor, no sudden movements, and pushed it along the marble. It skittered for a second and then was silent.

'Very good, Rus. Take off the Kevlar.'

'You're going to kill me,' Crewe said. He did as he was told, dropped the body armour on the floor.

'That depends, Rus, on what you tell her. Turn around, put your hands behind your back.'

Crewe did as he was told again. Someone bound his hands with cable ties. The someone wasn't Mwai Odinga, who hadn't moved, who was still just a voice in the dark, in front of him, over there.

'Very good, Rus. Now we're going for a little walk. Turn around, step over Budd. Good. Now take this piece of string.'

Crewe felt a piece of string pushed into his hands. Again, not by Mwai. He took it.

'Follow the string, Rus.'

Crewe heard Mwai move, only barely, just the lightest press of a boot on marble. The string tugged, and Crewe followed it, down the corridor he and Budd had been meaning to use to get to the security office. Which turned out to be where Mwai was leading him. It made sense. It was a secure room, strong door, and, if they turned the power back on, would give them access to the camera feeds all over Klabu Viziwi. All the above ground camera feeds, that is.

'Sit down, where you are, on the floor,' Mwai said once they were in the room. 'What is this place? Some sort of security office? That's a lot of monitors.'

Mwai was the one with the string now. Crewe felt the end of it drop. He heard Mwai walk past him at least two metres away. He heard the door close.

'I'm going to relay some questions to you, Rus. I advise you answer them truthfully with attention to detail.' Mwai moved round so that Crewe was between him and the door.

'You were with Clive and his goons when – I can para-phrase if I like. Alright.'

Crewe realised Mwai was talking to someone else, presumably through a headset. The questions were coming via Mwai, not directly from him.

'You were with Clive and his Close Protection staff when they bribed their way into Bandari conservancy. I know that. Clive killed the rhino. I know that. Where is the horn?'

'The what?'

'The rhino's horn. It was cut from him and taken. Where is it?'

Crewe thought. He didn't have to say anything. He'd been trained to withstand torture. And betraying Clive would mean Kriel would kill him, of that he had no doubt. On the other hand, Clive had probably already decided to have Kriel kill him. Kriel and Clive were in the Bunker. It would be sensible to give answers to the questions that directed Mwai and his associates to the Bunker. That might be his only chance to escape.

'In Clive's trophy room,' he said. 'In the Bunker.'

CHAPTER FORTY-ONE

'IN THE BUNKER,' MWAI'S VOICE REPEATED IN JANE'S EAR, but she'd heard Crewe say it clearly enough.

'Who killed Jomo?' she said. She heard Mwai repeat it.

'Who is Jomo?' Crewe's voice said. Mwai repeated that too.

'He was the ranger guarding the rhino.'

Crewe said nothing for a long time. She wondered if he was not going to answer. Then he did.

'Kriel. It was Kriel.'

'Who is Kriel?'

This time the wait was longer.

There was a noise, a shuffling, the sound of a gun being cocked. Then another voice on the comms channel, a voice with a snarl in it. 'I am Kriel. And that man is lying. He shot the ranger. In the back. Twice. He offered him money to look the other way, and the ranger refused to take it. You're a dead man, Crewe. You're all dead, all of you. Your families are dead. Your friends, dead. But I will give you all one chance. One chance to run. We have one of your families already.

Nathan Jennings, we have your wife, your children. If you leave now, they will be spared. I will give you one hour, and then they will be released, and we will come after you. One hour's head start.'

Jane muted the headset, the one Walker had taken from François' team only a few hours before, slipping it down and round her neck. She and Mwai were on that channel. Walker and Nathan were on the other. She put on her own headset to talk to Nathan.

'See anything, yet?'

'Not yet,' Nathan said. 'Wait, yes, five trucks turning into the track, like before. ETA ten minutes.'

'Good. Get going. Use the Land Rover.'

'Check,' Nathan said.

'Are you sure about this?' Walker said.

'We'll know in nine minutes,' Jane said.

Jane switched headsets again.

'Mwai. The army is coming back. Pull out.'

'What do you want me to do with him?'

'Kill him. Rendez-vous at the Land Rover.'

'Check.'

She muted the headset again and threw it away, putting her own back on. She raised the Remington, which she'd swapped with Walker for the Bravo, increased the pressure on the trigger.

She was in the kitchen, under a large table, watching the door to the wine cellar. She'd tried it – locked.

Two shots sounded elsewhere in the building. She heard an engine start, the Land Rover, Nathan, moving away in the opposite direction to the approaching army trucks, deeper onto the plateau. He'd be driving using night vision, no lights.

She'd warned him to drive slowly and to avoid using the brakes so the soldiers wouldn't see him.

She heard Walker's voice in her ear, so soft.

'Contact.'

The handle of the door to the wine cellar was turning. The door started to open.

The first man through it was the textbook image of close protection specialist. Hair crew cut, suit, shiny shoes, Glock 19 in one hand, torch in the other. He swept the kitchen, focusing on the first of two doors out. The one that was open. The one she'd set a tripwire across.

The second man was a photocopy of the first. He went in the other direction to the second door. That door was locked.

The third man was similar to the first two but bigger and angry. He stepped through the doorway and stopped, looked left and right. The first man had put his head through the open doorway and swept in both directions with gun and torch.

'Clear,' he said.

The second man tried the door handle to the other door which didn't turn.

'Clear,' he said.

The third man nodded.

'Clear, Mr Andrews.'

A woman was next up the steps. The assistant. And she was followed by a fourth man. Clive Andrews. Billionaire. He looked like anybody else. Middle-aged, slightly overweight, strange hair, very pissed off. The assistant carried a torch, but Andrews carried nothing.

A non-verbal exchange took place out of Jane's line of sight. She couldn't see their heads from her hiding place but guessed the third man had nodded to the first to lead the way through the door, which he did. He tripped the wire. The doorway exploded.

Elsewhere in the building firing started again. Short bursts. Walker and Mwai killing the last three of Kriel's men as they came out of the main door from the bunker. They were the decoys. The last three in the building.

Jane shot the second and third man as high in the body as she could see, in the thigh and in the groin. She stood, stepped out of the way of the table, and shot them both again in the head. Even suppressed, the shots were loud in the contained space.

There was a groan from the doorway. The grenade hadn't killed the first man. The blast had thrown him against the wall where he lay slumped and bleeding. Jane put two bullets in his chest.

She heard Walker's voice in her ear.

'Three. Clear.'

'Three. Clear.'

'Do you have him?'

'Check.'

The woman, the assistant, was cowering on the ground, whimpering.

'Leave,' Jane said. 'Through that door. The key is in the sink.'

The woman didn't move.

'Do it now.'

The woman stood up, a spluttering sound coming from her mouth. She used her torch to find the key, unlocked the door, and ran through it.

The torches of two of the three dead were still on, pointing at different walls, so there was enough light for Andrews to see her.

She took a step towards him, the Remington raised, two thirds pressure on the trigger. The suppressor made the gun look enormously long. The way an elephant gun might look to an animal it is aimed at.

'You won't get away with this,' Andrews said.

Jane said nothing.

'We have that ranger's family. If they don't hear from us in the next fifty minutes, they die.'

Jane said nothing.

'I can make you very rich. I can pay ten million dollars into any account anywhere in the world, right now.'

Jane said nothing.

She thought of Douglas with Festo, the keeper, enjoying a scratch with a broom. A rhino that suffered from hay fever and eczema, nothing special amongst other northern white rhinos, except there were only three. This man, this billionaire with the power to do so many things, had chosen to raise a gun, just like this one, and had looked through the sight, just like she was, and had pulled the trigger, killing the last male northern white rhino. Killing her charge.

Jane shot Clive Andrews through the right eye.

The bullet passed through his brain and took the back of his skull with it as it ricocheted off the concrete of the stairwell wall. Jane didn't move as Andrews' body slowly toppled backwards down the steps.

'Done?' Walker's voice asked.

'Check.'

'Recovery?'

'Complete. Exfiltrate.'

Jane lowered the Remington and left the kitchen through the destroyed door, stepping over the body of the first man out of the wine cellar.

She joined Walker and Mwai in the ruins of the garden, and the three of them ran down the slope towards the crocodile stream. They were still alert, weapons up, just in case.

Behind them she heard the engines of the army trucks, and then slamming doors, shouts.

They forded the crocodile stream with care. There were no new tracks in the mud. They ran up the slope, passing the mortar and the heavy machine gun. They climbed into the Land Cruiser Jane and Nathan had taken from the men sent to kill them. Mwai drove. Off down the track, passing the barn and the ranch house where François remained bound, blindfold, and gagged.

'Are you going to explain?' Walker said.

'About what?' Jane said.

'Why you didn't ask either Andrews or Crewe who killed your brother?'

Jane said nothing.

'Because the only explanation I can come up with is that you already knew,' Walker said.

Jane said nothing.

'How did you get the army out to that place twice in a day?'

'We have to get to Nathan,' Jane said. 'Then I'll explain.'

CHAPTER FORTY-TWO

M WAI STOPPED OUTSIDE NATHAN'S HOUSE, IN THE SAME spot the three soldiers had parked in when Jane had been watching the house from under the neighbour's porch. That was less than a fortnight ago, but it felt like a hundred years.

Before getting out of the car Jane phoned Nathan.

He answered at once.

'Is it safe?' Jane said.

'Yes,' Nathan said, though his voice was strained to the point of snapping.

Mwai, Walker and Jane crossed the street. For the first time in the longest time Jane was able to simply knock on the front door. Nathan opened it seconds later.

'They're not here,' he said.

'But Kriel's man is,' Jane said.

'How did you know that?'

Jane held up her phone.

'Watch this.'

Nathan took the phone, watched the feed.

'This is video of the attic. Why do you have a camera in my attic?'

'I left the camera here the day you disappeared, in case you came back.'

'The trap door opens, the ladder goes down too quickly, and then no one comes up. This happened half an hour ago.'

'No one comes up.'

Nathan led the way across the kitchen into the small hall under the trap door. The ladder was down, resting on the body of one of Clive's bodyguards.

'The ladder knocked him out. I took his gun and his phone.'

'Tie him up,' Jane said.

'Where is my family?' Nathan said.

'Tell him, Mwai.'

Nathan turned to the big man, who was pushing the ladder back into the loft. Walker pulled out cable ties and yanked the unconscious man's arms behind his back. He groaned.

'They're at Makena's mother's house,' Mwai said. 'Makena picked them up after he left me at the helicopter. Jane told me to get him to do it. Just in case.'

'You knew they'd send a man here?' Nathan said to Jane.

'No, I thought the army would. They did it once, when I was watching from over there.' She motioned towards the house across the street. 'I was wrong. But lucky. Let's get him in the car. Nathan, I need you to make another call.'

———

Naomi was on her veranda when they reached the ranch. There were lamps hanging from the ceiling. The sun was rising behind Mount Kenya, but clouds now covered the sky, jostling with each other like angry waves. Evidence of the sun rising was shrouded.

Naomi was not alone. Tony Kanagi sat next to her, a drink in his hand. He must have been already awake when Nathan phoned him to get here this quickly.

He stood up when the four of them got out of the car. He had only been expecting Nathan.

'They didn't find me, Tony. I left as they got there,' Jane said.

Mwai and Walker went left and right, just in case, casual and slow. Nathan stayed on the other side of the Land Cruiser they'd arrived in. Jane had got out on the side next to Tony's car, the car that the elephants had destroyed a fortnight earlier.

'It took me too long to realise what I'd seen,' Jane said. 'The elephants were telling me they didn't like this car. Your car. I should have guessed. Timu told me he and Nathan drove past Kennet lying on the ground by the ranger station. But it wasn't until we were in Tanzania and Nathan said he'd seen Kennet lying on the ground *next to a car* that I made the connection.

'You killed my brother,' she said. 'You strangled him.'

She watched him.

Naomi stood up, backed away from Tony, horror blooming on her face.

'Your brother is a major in the Rifles,' Jane said. 'He has dirt on a captain. Captain John. Dirt you gave him after Nathan told you why he was kicked out, about what he saw in Uganda. The captain got away with it when a private accused him, but a major is a different matter. Gives your brother his own company whenever he needs it. You knew I'd find you eventually, so you told your brother to send men to find me at Nathan's house *before* you made the call to the KWS framing me. I was caught when I went to meet you at the ranger station. Someone showed them how to use the Super Bats. I thought Clive Andrews bribed the magistrates, but the two who found me guilty were army. You were behind that too.

'It was very useful, knowing I could send a full company to Klabu Viziwi as a distraction by having Nathan phone you and tell you where I was. It's served its usefulness now. Thing I don't yet know, Tony, is why you did it. What did I do to you?'

Tony tensed. A vein throbbed in his neck.

'What are you going to do to me?' he said.

'That depends on you. You killed Kennet.'

'You can't prove anything.'

'Call your brother,' Jane said. 'Ask him what he's found.' Tony looked straight at her. He took out his phone. 'Don't say where you are, who you are with, or anything else. Just ask what he found when he got to Klabu Viziwi.'

Tony stopped moving, for a moment. He nodded. He touched the phone a few times and held it to his ear.

In the stillness they could all hear it ring. It was answered quickly.

'What have you found?' he said. He listened for a minute, two. Then ended the call without a word.

'Check it,' Jane said, looking at Walker.

Walker came in close, took the phone from Tony's unresisting hand, and nodded to confirm the call was ended.

'Why?' Jane said.

Tears filled Tony's eyes and rolled down his cheeks. Tension went out of his shoulders. He seemed defeated.

'I didn't mean to kill him. He wasn't supposed to be there.

He overheard me on the phone to my brother. I knew they were coming. My brother learned from one of his former men, Riba Butare. I knew they were going to shoot the rhino. Kennet heard me tell my brother I was going to frame you for it.'

'Why?'

'You killed my son,' he said, without blinking.

'No, I didn't.' Instinctive. But she felt the words like a blow. She not expected anything like that.

'You killed my son,' he said again. He held her gaze. The tension in his face was turning to anger, but he was still crying.

'How did I kill your son?'

'I don't know.' He was sobbing now, and his voice raised. 'He knew the shift patterns. He stole them from me. He joined some men. They were going after ivory, the herds in Ol Faraja. Thought they'd make a fortune. Someone gave them guns. They went to Somalia to get them. I didn't know.'

Naomi had stepped away from him as far as she could go, her back pressed against one of the veranda pillars. But her expression had changed.

'When did I do this?' Jane asked.

'September last year.'

Jane thought. The five. The five marks on the tree. September. Their trail had been found by dog teams further north, Ol Faraja. She'd gone to investigate, with Nathan. The poachers were clumsy, inexperienced, didn't know how to hide their trail. She'd found them, followed them, caught up with them in the dark, seen how heavily armed they were – there was no choice, no other option, but to kill them. She'd killed them all and buried them where they fell. They had been young. In old fatigues that were too big for them. She remembered their fear, a small thing, as she'd fired. Tap, tap. Tap, tap. One had eyes like Kanagi's. Not the last one to die. But he'd been backing away, raising his weapon, finger on the trigger. The weapon had been empty, it turned out, but she couldn't have known that.

'They knew the shift patterns but didn't know about me?' she said.

'How could they?' Kanagi's voice was hatred and grief.

'You killed Kennet because you were angry with me?'

'You killed my son,' he said again, though it was more of a wail.

He had it coming, she thought. But she couldn't say it. Didn't he?

She had no idea what to do now. Mwai had said, back in the bar, he was helping her because she had hunted those men down. Those boys? Because she'd done what he wished he'd done to the men who had killed his elephant. And because of that she'd found who killed Douglas. But because of that her brother had died. And Tony had known in advance about the plan to kill Douglas, used it to set her up. If she hadn't killed Tony's son would he have told her? Would Douglas still be alive? She had no idea what to do. She couldn't change a thing.

Tony was angry and crying. He looked like a torn man.

They stared at each other for several minutes.

No one else moved. Naomi was crying. Nathan crouched down, his hands hanging, his head bowed.

Jane had come here expecting to take Tony away, drop him at the police station once it was clear that confession was his safest course. Clear her name, send him to prison for killing her brother. She couldn't do that now.

Eventually she found some words.

'A friend of mine,' Jane said, 'told me about African justice. About how we must atone, make things right.'

Tony wiped his nose. His eyes were still hard.

'Come on shift with me,' she said. 'Let's go look after the girls.'

He held her gaze. His eyes were still full of tears.

'You're not on shift,' he said.

———

Tony stopped the Land Rover by the inner conservancy gate. The sky was angry dark now, and the air moist and oppressive. Festo was waiting for them. He unlocked the gates, let for them to drive through, and locked the gates again. Tony parked behind the enclosure that had been Douglas's. Jane looked back, at the place where she'd found Jomo's body. Just a patch of earth. She saw Jomo's face in her memory, his smile, his laugh.

She followed Tony through the enclosure to the paddock. She looked up into the corner of the roof. She could just see it, the female owl, like a carving in the beam.

Mwai and Walker had taken Nathan to Makena's house, and then gone to collect François and deposit him and the other bodyguard at the police station with a note.

Naomi had gone inside the ranch. Jane had seen her sitting in Kennet's rocking chair. She had asked how she was, but Naomi hadn't answered. How she would process what she learned, time would tell.

The first heavy drops started to fall, loud on the logs of the roof, thwacking into the sun-baked earth with the weight of stones. The overture was brief, and within a minute it was a full-on downpour.

Jane walked out into it, rifle under the crook of her arm.

Both the rhinos were together under a tree, sheltering from the rain. Uzuri, the youngest, Douglas's granddaughter, nuzzled Neema's flank, snorting softly. In a few years, no more than thirty, both would be dead, and the northern white rhinoceros would be gone forever, destroyed by mankind. But right now, Jane watched them with a sense of peace. After ten minutes of hearing nothing but the rain she spoke, her voice clear.

'Tony,' she said. 'Tell me about your son.'

Behind her one of the owls flew out of the enclosure and into the night.

ABOUT THE AUTHOR

Antony was born in Bradford and grew up in West Yorkshire, variously in Cleckheaton, Scholes, Moorend and Ilkley. Grim and dour and wild. But also magnificent and open and kind. Landscape, literature and a hint of mayhem rolled together from the start.

Antony started writing at eleven or twelve when he first wrote things down he had made up.

His next period of creativity started when he was living in York. He was studying history and devouring vast numbers of academic texts on all manner of places and times, and this fired his imagination again.

A little later he moved to Stevenage. A town with no small literary association. Edward Bulwer-Lytton ("The pen is mightier than the sword") entertained Dickens at Knebworth House over yonder. E.M. Forster wrote *Howards End* in Rooks Nest, a house in the town. Here he started to write again. Short stories to start with, then novels. He sent off a short story or two to the odd competition, or for consideration for publication in the occasional journal. He won a competition on the CheerReader website (now deceased) with a spoof Private Investigator story. He had a story called 'A Homecoming' published in the gorgeous Australian online journal *Meniscus*, which allowed him to claim to be an internationally published writer whilst keeping a straight face. And he had a few runner-ups and honourable mention, and third place, and long lists and short lists, and other little thrills of excitement (for the writer).

And then he wrote *Hunted*. *Hunted* is his first, of potentially many, novels. He is currently working on a sequel to *Hunted*, *Endangered*, which is due to be published by Hobeck Books later in 2021.

www.antonydunford.com

ACKNOWLEDGMENTS

Hunted was written as the dissertation for my MA in Crime Fiction at the University of East Anglia. The novel was guided by my final year tutors, Henry Sutton and Nathan Ashman, but shaped, honed, and polished by the tireless generosity of the other wonderful students in my cohort: Laura Ashton, Judi Daykin, Lucy Dixon, Jayne Farnworth, Natasha Hutcheson, Louise Mangos, Elizabeth Saccente, Matthew Smith, Karen Taylor, Wendy Turbin, and Bridget Walsh. My thanks to all of them for their time, support, advice, laughter, Prosecco, and Hula Hoops in the past and in the future. Look out for their novels already published and yet to come. My particular thanks to Jayne, Louise, Bridget, Wendy, and Judi who read the final version of *Hunted* at short notice and provided hundreds of comments that tickled, teased, and tweaked it into a better place.

You would not be reading this without the belief of Rebecca and Adrian at Hobeck books. My thanks to them for taking a chance on me, and I hope you enjoyed meeting Jane and her world as much as they have.

Finally, my thanks to my parents for giving me access to books and the joys of reading from since I can remember. And to my brother, who read an early version of the story and has said he doesn't need to buy it when it comes out because of that. Sorry, Mike, this version is considerably different, so get ordering.

Antony

Yorkshire, December 2020

HOBECK BOOKS – THE HOME OF GREAT STORIES

This book is the first in the Jane Haven series, Antony is currently working on the second book. There will be many more to follow after that.

If you've enjoyed this book, please sign up to **www.antonydunford.com** to read about Antony's inspirations, writing life and for news about her forthcoming writing projects.

Also please visit the Hobeck Books website **www.hobeck.net** for free downloads of short stories and novellas by a number of our authors. If you would like to get in touch, we would love to hear from you.

Finally, if you enjoyed this book, please also leave a review on the site you bought it from and spread the word. Reviews are hugely important to writers and they help other readers also.

Lightning Source UK Ltd.
Milton Keynes UK
UKHW021131280422
402200UK00008B/302